THE SPANIARD'S INNOCENT MAIDEN

Greta Gilbert

MILLS & BOON

First published in Great Britain 2017
By Mills & Boon, an imprint of HarperCollins*Publishers*
1 London Bridge Street, London SE1 9GF

Large Print edition 2017

© 2017 Greta Gilbert

ISBN: 978-0-263-06782-8

Our policy is to use papers that are natural, renewable
and recyclable products and made from wood grown
in sustainable forests. The logging and manufacturing
processes conform to the legal environmental regulations
of the country of origin.

Printed and bound in Great Britain
by CPI Antony Rowe, Chippenham, Wiltshire

Benicio's heart hammered. The woman in white was so close to him, yet so completely out of his reach.

The newly elected *alcalde* of Vera Cruz, Alonso de Grado, stood and selected the woman in orange, bending to his knee and bowing, then escorting the young woman back to the table. Others were not so polite. Pilot Diego Cermeño took the girl in green by the elbow. Sailor Gonzalo de Umbria merely gestured to the girl in red. Then it was Benicio's turn.

There was only one thing to be done. Benicio reached into his boot. Then he stood and walked to the head of the table. He placed the diamond and jadestone ring before Cortés.

A curious grin spread across Cortés's face. 'How came you by this magnificent piece?'

'I found it in a stream near the fields of Potonchan,' Benicio lied. 'I have very sharp eyes.'

'I will accept it as compensation for the woman in white,' Cortés said.

Author Note

This is a story of a clash of cultures and also of their fusion. It takes place during one of the cruellest, most astonishing periods in world history: Cortés's conquest of the Aztecs, beginning in 1519.

At the time the Aztecs—or Mexica—ruled Mexico from their capital of Tenochtitlan, one of the largest and most advanced cities in the world. The Mexica were the Romans of Mesoamerica: their ever-expanding empire covered eighty thousand miles, and they exacted tribute from some six million souls— including the Totonacs.

The heroine of this story is a Totonac woman. She participates in the fateful alliance of the Totonacs and Spanish against the Mexica, but slowly realises that the Spanish are becoming her new oppressors. For her, the only hope for freedom lies in the mysterious lands of the Maya.

Often called the Greeks of Mesoamerica, the Maya lived amidst the ruins of their ancient civilisation. Culturally advanced, but geographically isolated, they were never conquered by the Mexica and evaded Spanish rule until 1697. In some respects they evade it still.

Everywhere the descendants of the Conquest live on. I have tried to present this part of their history as knowledgeably and respectfully as possible.

Thank you for reading!

Greta Gilbert's passion for ancient history began with a teenage crush on Indiana Jones. As an adult she landed a dream job at National Geographic Learning, where her colleagues—former archaeologists—helped her learn to keep her facts straight. Now she lives in South Baja, Mexico, where she continues to study the ancients. She is especially intrigued by ancient mysteries, and always keeps a little Indiana Jones inside her heart.

Books by Greta Gilbert

Mills & Boon Historical Romance

Enslaved by the Desert Trader
The Spaniard's Innocent Maiden

Mills & Boon Historical *Undone!* eBook

Mastered by Her Slave

Visit the Author Profile page
at millsandboon.co.uk.

For my mom: friend, editor, counsellor,
muse, cheerleader, champion, sage,
sag wagon, overflowing fountain of love.

Prologue

Carlos dropped to his knee in the crowded market-place, swept off his feathered hat and asked Luisa Valentina Altamirano if she would do him the honour of becoming his wife. A small stray dog, who had reluctantly agreed to play the role of Luisa, whined mournfully.

'Release her,' Carlos told his brother, Benicio. 'She has made me into a fool.'

'Indeed she has,' agreed Benicio, releasing the scruffy canine, who took a direct route to a nearby butcher's stall.

'I need a more intelligent understudy,' Carlos said, stroking his nascent beard, 'one who will appreciate my poetry.' Carlos eyed Benicio steadily.

'Not I,' Benicio protested, holding up his book of formulas. 'I am a man of science. I am unqualified to assess your effusions of love.'

That was not entirely true. Cursed with the double-edged sword of male beauty, Benicio had had a stream of love interests over the years—women attracted by his piercing blue eyes and towering figure, which he had been told he moved with a remarkable grace. There was only one woman, however, whom Benicio had ever loved and she was about to receive a proposal of marriage from his younger brother Carlos.

'If you will not play the role of Luisa, then I will ask Armando to do it,' said Carlos, beckoning to their portly older brother, 'though he is less suited to it.'

Benicio scoffed. 'Armando is perfectly suited,' he said. 'Just look at how he preens before that hatters' mirror.' As Benicio and Carlos laughed mockingly at their older brother, Benicio slid a glance to the avenue that led into Seville's bustling Plaza del Triunfo. Any moment, Luisa's painted carriage would appear and La Belleza herself would disembark in a flutter of skirts and ribbons.

Benicio was already steeling himself against that moment, for he held a secret that even his brothers did not know. Only two months past, he had made his own proposal of marriage to Luisa and had not yet received her answer.

Tranquilo, he told himself, continuing to laugh

rather too gaily. Why was he finding it so hard to control his nerves? He had known Luisa since childhood, after all. For most of their lives, they had been the best of friends. There was no reason for his heart to be racing as it was, or for the sweat to be surging beneath his chemise in a soaking torrent.

She had had the same effect on him the evening of the Feast of the Epiphany, when he had urged her to marry him. But she had only stared at him with those lovely green eyes, pondering something. What had it been?

'I have returned,' said Armando, rejoining them. 'Why do you stare at me so piteously?'

'You have been selected to hear Carlos's proposal,' explained Benicio.

Before Armando could protest, Carlos had dropped to his knee once again and was sputtering some muck about the colour of the rose in the light of dawn after the first rain. Undaunted, Armando embraced his role as Luisa and was soon heaving a false bosom and feigning a maiden's tears. Benicio erupted in riotous laughter.

'Knaves!' shouted Carlos. But his sour expression quickly turned sweet, as his gaze travelled beyond his two brothers to a vision just behind them.

'Dearest friends, what merriment have I missed?' trilled a delicate, familiar voice.

Benicio and Armando turned. It was none other than Luisa. She had sneaked up on them with fox-like stealth. Benicio felt a rush of blood to his cheeks.

'Carlos, what wretched errand do your brothers demand that requires you to kneel before them so deferentially?' She offered her hand to Carlos to kiss, which he did for many long seconds. 'And, Benicio, you are as red as a cock's comb. Are your humours out of balance?'

She slid Benicio a playful grin, and his heart flickered. Had she just teased him? Searching for confirmation, his eyes stumbled upon her lips—two large, luscious impediments to his otherwise rational thoughts.

'Benicio?' Luisa asked again, her voice leaking concern.

She wore her curly hair pinned up, almost the same as when they were children, with two gentle ringlets framing her round face. As she spoke, they seemed to bounce in rhythm with Benicio's racing heartbeats. 'Tell me now,' she demanded. 'What are you three devils about?'

'We were just…practising,' said Carlos.

'Practising?'

Carlos opened his mouth once again, but no sound emerged. Benicio stepped forward. 'It was nothing—a scene from an old book. We had not anticipated its comedic effects. What a lovely summer day, is it not?'

'Which book?' asked Luisa. 'Perhaps I know it.'

'Ah,' Carlos stumbled. 'Ah…'

'Ah… *Amadís de Gaula,*' Benicio finished.

'Amadís de Gaula!' Luisa exclaimed. 'Which scene?'

Now Benicio was in a tangle, for in truth he had laboured most of his life in order to avoid reading the ever-popular *Amadís de Gaula.* 'It was the scene in which Amadís the Brave battles the terrible…' Benicio paused, for he had forgotten the name of the monster.

'The terrible monster Endriago?' said Luisa, her green eyes glinting.

'Indeed!' cried Benicio. 'I was playing Amadís, of course, and Armando was playing…'

'His assistant Gandolin?'

'Yes, yes! And Carlos was playing…'

'The beautiful Oriana?'

'Exactamente!' Benicio exclaimed. 'And that is why we were laughing, for Carlos—I mean, Oriana—was pronouncing her undying love for Amadís with the conviction of a practised thespian.'

Carlos was now smiling at Benicio with something like a monstrous rage beneath his grin.

Luisa smoothed her voluminous dress. 'My dear

Benicio, in all the years we have known each other, you continue to surprise me. I had no idea you were such an avid student of our beloved Castilian literature.'

Her admiring smile had produced two perfect dimples at the edges of her round cheeks, causing Benicio's insides to rollick unbidden. 'Indeed, I am very fond of Amadís,' lied Benicio. 'The chivalric romances have been an integral part of my university studies.'

'Ah, the university,' Luisa said and her dimples disappeared. 'You are still at the university?'

'I am.'

Why had she asked that question? He had told her as much the evening he had presented his suit. He had also explained the professorship he planned to seek and the life he would be able to provide her as an academic—a humble life, but one full of love and wonder.

'Remind me when we part,' she said, 'I have a gift for you.'

'A gift?' Benicio sputtered. If joy were made of water, then he was surely drowning. 'I will most certainly remind you, *mi bella dama*,' he said. He slipped her a devilish grin and watched with satisfaction as she swallowed hard.

Then, with the practised diplomacy of the most

sought-after young lady in all of Seville, Luisa turned her attention back to Benicio's brothers. 'Of course, we will not soon be parting, not if my dearest childhood friends will walk with me a while?'

She nodded at her wary driver, then wove her hands beneath Carlos's and Armando's arms. 'Tell me, when was the last time we were all together?' And with that, the three began to stroll.

'We came to your family's *latifundia* for the Feast of the Epiphany two months past,' noted Armando.

'Ah! I remember! What a wonderful celebration, was it not?'

She stole another glance at Benicio. 'And since then, *caballeros*, what news of your lives?'

Carlos spoke first. 'I have been accepted into the Order of Santiago. I am apprenticed to become a knight.'

Benicio smiled to himself. After the Reconquista of Spain by the Christians, Queen Isabella had fleeced the Orders of their dominion. The world had changed and knighthood was no longer anything to brag about.

Still, Luisa was staring up at Carlos as if he had just hung the moon. 'Is it not very dangerous? To command a horse in battle?' she asked.

'Any equestrian pursuit carries some measure of

danger, my lady. But it is worth it to serve in Christ's army.'

'Though the bloody Crusades are indeed a thing of the past,' Benicio pointed out, feeling a twinge of jealousy. 'Was it not Aristotle who wrote that the best men behave moderately?'

'Easily said by a man who rides atop a wooden desk instead of a horse,' countered Carlos.

Thankfully, Luisa had become distracted by the shimmer of a fine fabric being displayed at a nearby stall.

'What have we here?' she asked. A Moorish man was unfurling a bolt of red silk. Luisa touched the fabric to her cheek. 'My father can no longer indulge me such extravagances. He has lately lost much land to the Ponce de Leon clan in court. Have you not heard of it?'

'A terrible injustice,' said Armando, getting Luisa's attention.

'But do tell me of your life, Armando,' urged Luisa, sauntering on. 'I assume you are training with your father to take over your family's estate?'

'No, I have enlisted in the Tercios Regiment.'

Now Luisa halted her stroll. 'But you are your father's first son. Why would you risk your life in battle?'

'To bring glory to my family and to Spain.'

If Carlos had hung the moon with his news of a future knighthood, then surely Armando had lit the sun. 'You do your country proud,' Luisa said, staring at Armando as if he were Amadís himself.

'Would you look at that strange fruit over there?' Benicio cried suddenly. Across the plaza, a young man was describing a misshapen melon to a crowd of onlookers.

'We must examine it immediately!' Carlos seconded.

Benicio and Carlos hurried Luisa and Armando across the plaza.

'The papaya is not what it appears to be,' the young man was saying.

'How much?' Benicio interrupted, desperate for anything to help him regain Luisa's attention.

'Ah…half a *real.*'

Benicio slapped his half-*real* into the young man's hand, pulled a papaya from the bin and sliced his pocket knife through it to produce a bite-sized cube. 'Sweet fruit for a sweet woman,' he said, holding the cube to Luisa's lips.

Luisa opened her mouth and the four young men watched reverently as she chewed. She gave a lusty swallow, then her review: 'Absolutely delicious. Thank you, *Señor.*'

'I am Rogelio,' the young man said, bowing low.

'Rogelio, it is your job to sell, not to woo young women!' A grizzled old man appeared and, noticing Luisa, he stepped towards her. 'Well, hello, my dear.'

Benicio jumped protectively in front of Luisa and the old man was left to survey Benicio instead. 'You have a commanding stature, young man,' he said with surprise. 'Tall but strong, and with a long reach.'

'And you have an aggressive manner, *Señor*,' Benicio growled.

The man snarled, then cheered. 'But coming from one so well made, I shall take it as a compliment!' He held out his hand. 'I am Vicente Yáñez Pinzón, former captain of the Niña.'

'You sailed with Colón?' asked Benicio incredulously.

'I did, rest his soul.' The old conquistador crossed himself mockingly. He studied Benicio's arms. 'I am in search of strong, able-bodied young men who would like to bring riches to the Kingdom of Spain,' he said. 'You, *Señor*, have the stature and reach of a fine rigger. Why not serve your country and get rich? There is more to be had in the New World than simply fruits.'

'Thank you, Capitan Pinzón, but I serve Spain with the fruits of my mind.' Benicio caught Luisa's hand and they started back across the plaza with Armando and Carlos following behind.

As they walked, Benicio reminded himself that he was happy. Luisa's hand was in his, after all, and she had not yet refused him. Still, a pall seemed to have been cast upon the day—an invisible foreboding that even the bright spring sun seemed unable to defeat.

'It is no small thing,' said Luisa, 'to be invited to the West Indies. I have heard that men pay twelve *ducados* or more for the passage. And you have just been invited to make it at no cost.' She peered up at him curiously, then pulled her hand free of his. 'Well, look at us, gentlemen! We have returned to where we began.'

Indeed they had. There was Luisa's driver waiting beside her carriage. The baker had sold his loaves, the fishmonger his fish and even the nearby butcher's stall was almost empty of its offerings. 'Look at that adorable little dog,' Luisa said, pointing unknowingly at her failed understudy, who was lingering at the butcher's stall. 'She appears to be trying to choose between sausages.'

Benicio gave an ironic chuckle, though his brothers did not appear to understand the joke. Suddenly, the chimes of the noonday bells commenced. Benicio bowed his head, though he could not remember a word of the Sext hour prayer.

As he pretended to pray, he told himself not to be a fool. Women were capricious and nothing could be relied upon but the stars in the sky. Still no matter how many pretty young ladies batted their eyes at him, Benicio could think only of Luisa.

He was so consumed with thoughts of her that he did not even notice the conclusion of the bells. Nor did he perceive the quickening of Carlos's breaths, or how his younger brother fumbled in the pocket of his jerkin. Before Benicio could do anything to stop him, Carlos had dropped to his knees before Luisa, removed his hat to the ground and was holding up a tiny silver ring.

'Dear Luisa,' he began, 'my aromatic rose, every day you grow more…fragrant. The rain, the mist, the abundant dew…'

Overcome by nerves, Carlos shouted his professions, drawing a small crowd. 'The light of dawn, the rosy glow of morning, your eyes, your lips, your beautiful…teeth. My dear…aromatic Luisa… Can I be your husband?'

There were a few giggles among the crowd. Then a terrible silence descended.

A lonely breeze blew past, tousling Luisa's curls. 'Oh, Carlos, do stand,' she cried at last. She reached out her arms and lifted him to his feet.

'I am honoured that you would ask me to be your

wife,' continued Luisa, 'but I cannot accept your proposal.'

'You…what?'

'You are a fine young man, but I cannot become your wife.'

'But our engagement can last as long as necessary,' argued Carlos. 'I am well into my apprenticeship at the Casa de Contratación. My knighthood shall be granted in only four short years.'

Carlos looked around desperately, as if searching for something to cushion the fall of his breaking heart. 'Is it my physical form that does not appeal? I know that I am not handsome like Benicio, nor am I strong like Armando, but I—'

'My dear friend, it is nothing to do with your physical form. I must consider the interests of my family. I am my father's only daughter and you are…'

'A second son,' Carlos finished.

And there it was.

Carlos, like Benicio, had been born into that particular class of Castilian nobles whose names were respected, whose education was complete, but whose wealth, in the end, would have to be earned—*the second sons.*

Luisa placed a single kiss upon Carlos's cheek. 'I shall treasure your friendship always.'

Carlos dusted off his hat and placed it back on his

head. 'And I yours, my lady,' he managed. 'But this is not the end.' He turned towards the cathedral.

Luisa sighed. 'I think it is time to go,' she said.

'I shall accompany you to your carriage,' said Benicio. 'I believe you have something for me in it?'

'Ah, yes—the gift!'

'I believe I will join you,' said Armando.

When they arrived at the carriage, Luisa retrieved a thin leather-covered tome and presented it to Benicio. 'I have been meaning to give this to you for some time.'

Benicio's eyes slid down her creamy neck, catapulted off her glorious bosom and finally settled upon the small book lying in her hands. *'Amadís de Gaula?'*

'Did you not say that you were especially fond of it?'

'I will savour the insights that lie upon each page of this magnificent work,' Benicio said, bowing low.

'Indeed he will,' added Armando, 'for he spends his days amassing knowledge, not glory or fortune.'

Luisa turned to Armando. 'I shall await your swift return from service.' Then she kissed him on the cheek. 'Godspeed, noble warrior of Spain.'

'I shall not return unless I have acquired wealth worthy of a *marquesa*,' Armando proclaimed.

That was when Benicio saw it. There, beneath her

practised expression—the flame of her life's ambition: *marquesa.*

Benicio helped her into the carriage. 'Enjoy the book, Benicio. Every page of it.'

She measured her nods equally between the two brothers as the small painted chariot moved away. Benicio and Armando were left staring into each other's eyes.

The world seemed to press at Benicio's sides. 'I think I shall walk on my own for a while,' Benicio told Armando and, without waiting for an answer, he turned and made long strides back across the plaza.

While he walked, he opened the book, flipped through its pages, and spotted a piece of paper wedged therein. He caught his breath as he beheld the image it contained—a charcoal sketch of a woman so beautiful she could not have been real. Her face was turned away from the artist, revealing her rounded profile, her long, beautiful neck, and a cascade of curls. A lump came into Benicio's throat. It was a sketch of Luisa. He flipped the sketch over to discover a note written in her elegant, looping script:

My Dear Benicio,
I love you, but I must take care to marry well.
Seek a fortune. I will wait for you as long as I can.
Your Luisa

Benicio's heart overflowed. There it was, written in her own hand: her answer to his proposal. She loved him as he loved her. She would wait for him and become his wife. All she required was a bit of wealth, to keep her in the lifestyle she wanted. The lifestyle she deserved.

Benicio looked up and saw the old captain, still there, still waiting at the other end of the plaza. He might have been the Devil himself, considering whether or not to take Benicio's soul.

Benicio began to walk towards him, letting his book of formulas drop upon the ground. Benicio was a man, after all, and the purpose of a man was not to sit at a desk, but to seek a fortune. To make himself worthy of the woman he loved.

Luisa, I promise, he murmured.

He caught the captain's eye. The old man flashed Benicio a knowing grin.

Chapter One

Cempoala City, Totonac Territory,
Mexican Empire—March 1519

Tula was not afraid of the dark. She was not afraid of the spirits that lurked in the shadows, whispering their complaints. The darkness was good; it concealed her. It wrapped around her like a magic cloak, letting her pass unseen to the places where she kept her secrets.

Even now, as she walked softly between the mats of her sleeping family members, she felt no need for the aid of light. The warmth of their breath told her where to place her feet and she could feel the fresh air that seeped through the front doorway, beckoning her.

She pushed open the thin wooden door and closed it gently behind her, stepping out into Cempoala's central plaza. She scanned the sprawling space for movement. Not a single living thing stirred beneath the moonless sky and the darkness of night greeted her like a trusted friend. No, Tula did not fear the dark.

What Tula feared was the colour black. Black was the colour of the Tribute Takers' hair. They wore it pulled back, tight to their skulls, and trapped it in buns at the bases of their necks. They lived in a great floating city high in the mountains, where their leader, Montezuma, whispered to the gods.

Black was the colour of the ink on the scrolls the Takers carried—long lists noting the tribute the Totonac people were required to provide every eighty days: four pots of vanilla, twenty-eight bins of maize, twenty-one bins of smoked fish, two thousand feathers, four thousand cotton cloaks.

Black was the colour of the mushrooms the Takers ate—mushrooms that gave them visions of the end of the world. A menace from the heavens was coming, they told the Totonacs, and it could only be prevented with the blood of sacrifice.

Totonac blood.

Tula walked around her stone house and into the garden behind it. She dug beneath the tomato plants and found her stash of spears and arrows. Digging deeper, she seized her atlatl, which would send those arrows to their marks. She had killed so many creatures in her lifetime—far too many than was good or right. But the Takers demanded meat, more and more of it, and the Takers had to be fed. She ran her finger softly across the sharp, obsidian blades.

They, too, were black.

'Daughter?' whispered her father's voice.

'Father?'

The shadowy figure of her father appeared in the back doorway. 'Why do you rise in the useless hours? Where do you go?'

'I go to catch the fish, Father, and the birds. Coalingas and macaws. Perhaps even a quetzal.'

'Nahuatl. Speak to me in Nahuatl.'

Tula sighed. 'I go to find the…the…swimming creatures…' she faltered '…and the flying creatures.' Of all the languages her father had taught her, Tula liked Nahuatl the least. It was the language of the Mexica, the language of their oppressors, yet her father would not speak to her in any other tongue.

'Why do you not wait for the Sun God to be reborn?' he asked her, pointing at the eastern horizon.

'I do not wait because the swimmers do not wait,' she lied.

'You rush to find fish, but you delay finding a husband.'

'Why seek a husband if he is doomed to die?' She bit her tongue. She had spoken too quickly and too loudly. Her father bent his neck inside the house, listening for her elder sister, Pulhko, who slept lightly and without rest. Satisfied with the unbroken peace, he shook his head. 'Your sister Pulhko will remarry as soon as she is well,' said her father.

But she will never be well, thought Tula, saying nothing.

'And your sister Xanca seeks a husband already.'

'Xanca is young and her head is full of colours. She knows little of the cruelty of the world.'

Her father did not respond and she knew that it was because he agreed. Xanca was not old enough to remember when Pulhko's husband and two boys were taken. Nor had Xanca been instructed in the history of the world, as Tula had been. As a result, Xanca's spirit remained light. Too light, perhaps.

'Your husband is your protection,' her father said finally. 'As long as you are unmarried, you are exposed.'

'We are all exposed. Marriage matters little.'

Now he whispered, 'The Takers have asked our Chief to provide women for the festival of the fifteenth month. They seek noble young women, Tula,' he said significantly. 'Women without carnal knowledge.'

Women like me, Tula thought. 'If they come for me, Father, they will not find me.'

'The Takers are everywhere. They will find you.'

'I am slippery like a fish,' she said in Totonac.

'You must marry.'

'Pulkho was married. Now look at all she has lost. I will not follow a path that leads only to blackness.'

A lump of anguish plugged Tula's throat.

'I cannot protect you always, Daughter. If you do not marry, you will be taken. Then, it will not matter that you speak their language, or that you know the history of the world, or that you are slippery like a fish. You will suffer the flowery—'

'The place of fish is four hours' journey,' Tula interrupted.

Tula's father sighed. 'There are fishing grounds much closer to Cempoala. Why must you travel so far away?'

'Where I go, there are so many fish that you can walk upon their backs!' said Tula, hoping that exaggeration would help conceal the lie she told. 'In a single day, I can obtain our family's entire contribution.'

She knew he could not argue with her. Their family's share of tribute was fixed—there was nothing to do but make and gather it each cycle and be done.

'I will return late tonight with my basket overflowing,' Tula assured him.

'Be safe,' he whispered.

'I will, Father,' she replied. She pointed to where

her atlatl poked out of her basket. 'You taught me how.' She blew him a kiss and set off across the plaza.

Yes, Tula loved the dark, for lying to her father was much easier in it.

Chapter Two

Benicio lay on the scorched maize field, covered in blood. He stared up at the pale blue sky, trying to picture the stars. He had come to the Island of the Yucatan to take part in trade, not war. He had brought glass beads and fine mirrors and the hope that he might still fulfil the promise he had made to Luisa that day two long years ago: to find treasure.

Now a thousand Maya warriors lay all around him, slaughtered. They had not been his enemies. They had merely been defending their lands from men like him—strange, bearded thieves who had floated upriver on their temples of deceit.

That was what the Maya emissaries had called the Spanish brigantines—floating temples. They did not have a word for sailing ships in their language, nor did they have a word for the Spaniards themselves, so they called them bearded gods. If they had only known that Captain Cortés and his men were much more like bearded devils.

Benicio pulled off his helmet and unbuckled his chest plate. It had been so very hot inside his shell of steel, even in the depths of the night. It was a relief to finally be free of it. Above, the first rays of sun stretched into the sky, illuminating the gory scene. Not a single body stirred.

The Maya of the city of Potonchan had politely asked Cortés to leave, but El Capitán would not listen. Instead, he had told the Maya emissaries the same thing he had told Benicio and his five hundred other conscripts as they set out from Cuba: that they were on a mission of trade and discovery.

Benicio should have known better than to believe the bellicose Captain Cortés, who had filled their ships with more gunpowder than goods. Even the small brigantine for which Benicio served as navigator had been fitted with deadly falconets, though Benicio had managed not to notice them.

Nor did he bother to translate the banner that flew atop Cortés's flagship, though he had spent years studying Latin: *Amici, sequamur crucem et, si nos fidem habemus, vere in hoc signo vincemus.* Friends, let us follow the cross and, if we have faith, let us conquer under this banner.

Benicio had ignored all of it. He was willing to

overlook anything, it seemed, for the hope of finding gold. 'Gold is nothing to the *naturales* of Yucatan Island,' Cortés had assured his conscripts. 'They trade it for beads and trinkets. It will be no effort for each of us to obtain a treasure fit for a king.'

Or a *marquesa*, Benicio had thought.

Had hoped.

What Cortés had not mentioned was that when the beads and trinkets failed, the men would have to fight. And kill.

The flies were descending in droves, creating a black frenzy of movement above the once-verdant field of maize. Benicio knew that the remaining Maya soldiers would soon arrive to collect their dead. When they did, they would discover Benicio and kill him. If not, the desiccating heat of the sun eventually would.

It would be a fitting end. The sun, which Benicio had so ardently believed to be the centre of the universe, would finally snuff out his life. He had been so very proud of all his book-learned knowledge, yet so very naive. To think he could simply sail to this new world, extract his treasure, and return to wed the woman he loved. That it would be that easy. That there would be no cost.

He pictured Luisa's face, as he always did when his heart filled with despair. Round cheeks. Dancing curls. Dimples. She remained in his memory exactly as she had been that day in the Plaza del Triunfo, her sparkling green eyes gazing up at him in admiration, as if she beheld some errant knight.

Forgive me, Luisa. I have failed you. He closed his eyes and waited for his death to come.

But instead of death came the sound of rioting birds and a familiar voice tumbling across the field. 'Stop, savage! Give it to me!'

Benicio sat up to behold a vision of feathers and light. The mid-morning sun was shining behind the figure of a giant bird. The bird flapped its massive wings, but it did not fly. Instead, it ran towards Benicio at great speed.

Benicio blinked, realising that he beheld not a bird, but a man covered in feathers. They wrapped around him like a heavy cloak, slowing him as he attempted to escape his pursuer.

'Give me the ring!' the voice shouted behind the man and Benicio lay back, playing dead. Out of the corner of his eye, he saw a large Spaniard throw off his breastplates and overtake the feathered warrior, pinning him to the ground near Benicio.

The Spaniard cursed and spat, unsheathing his hand blade. 'Give it to me!' he commanded. 'Or I will take another finger!' The feathered warrior babbled helplessly in his language, covering his face with bloody hands. The Spaniard threw off his steel helmet in frustration, revealing a shock of red hair and a face so familiar that Benicio gasped.

It was none other than Rogelio—the young man Benicio had met that day in the Plaza del Triunfo. They had crossed the ocean together in the company of Captain Pinzón, but when they had reached the Island of Hispañola, they had parted ways. Benicio had not seen the lithe, handsome papaya pedlar since.

Now Rogelio was no longer lithe, nor in any way handsome. A ghastly red scar traversed his haggard face and Benicio could see that he had grown corpulent and soft beneath the Toledo steel that protected him.

Rogelio held the Maya man's bloody hand upon the ground, threatening to sever another finger. Had Rogelio lost his mind? Benicio crawled closer.

The Maya man was painted from head to toe in thick stripes of ochre and white. There were grey hairs sprouting from beneath his headdress and skin hung loosely from his bones. Benicio guessed he was a religious figure—perhaps some kind of priest. His strange, plaintive speech was incomprehensible, but it was clear he was begging for mercy.

'Where is it?' Rogelio shouted and dealt the old man a blow to the face. The man fell backwards and

Rogelio ripped what appeared to be a golden necklace from his neck. 'Where is the ring?' Rogelio raised his blade squarely over the man's heart.

'Stop!' Benicio cried. He dived at Rogelio from behind and thrust him upon the ground. 'Have mercy, Rogelio. The battle is over.'

Benicio rolled Rogelio on to his back, keeping him pinned. Rogelio smiled at Benicio in a moment of recognition. 'Yes, Brother, and now it is time for plunder,' he said. He thrust his knee upwards, sending a gut-splitting blow through Benicio's loins.

In the meantime, the priest had staggered to his feet and was attempting to run away. Rogelio lunged and caught him, slashing a blade across the priest's chest and wrestling him to the ground.

Recovering his senses, Benicio pulled Rogelio off the injured priest once again. 'Cease!' Benicio commanded and he smashed his head against Rogelio's, knocking him senseless. He thrust Rogelio's heavy body to the side.

The priest was writhing on the ground, trying to sit up. The gash that Rogelio had drawn across the holy man's body had reached the base of his throat, and blood spilled on to his painted chest.

Benicio searched for something to stop the flow of blood, seizing upon a large piece of cloth hanging from Rogelio's belt. Benicio folded the cloth and moved to place it upon the wound, but the priest flinched and tried to move himself away.

'*Ma tu'ub,*' he coughed, pointing to the cloth and shaking his head in warning. '*Ma tu'ub.*'

He seemed strangely concerned with the cloth Benicio had taken, so Benicio set it aside and ripped off his own shirt sleeve. The priest made no protest as Benicio helped him to a sitting position, then stuffed the ripped sleeve into his wound, trying to stop the bleeding. Benicio ripped his other sleeve and tied it around the priest's neck, securing the first cloth in place. Still, the bleeding would not stop.

'Be at peace, Father,' Benicio said soothingly, for he feared the old man did not have long. The priest peered at the ground where the first bloody cloth lay. Benicio shook the cloth clean, then opened it to reveal a strange geometrical design traced in blood.

'*Ma tu'ub,*' the priest repeated, nodding at the cloth. He pointed at the centre dot with the stub of his finger, then cringed with pain and returned the bloody limb to his fist. He nodded coaxingly at Benicio. '*Ma tu'ub.*'

Benicio nodded worriedly, placing the cloth to the side. He arranged the man's headdress beneath him and smoothed its feathers, fanning them outward in a halo of green, red, and white. Then he helped the old man backwards, wedging a clod of grass beneath his head like a pillow. 'Rest now, holy soul,' Benicio whispered.

A look of soft gratitude came over the priest's weathered face. He nodded at Benicio again, then opened his mouth and stuck out his tongue. Upon it Benicio beheld the largest, most beautiful ring he had ever seen.

Benicio stared at the sparkling jewel in amazement—a thick, round jadestone surrounded by many large diamonds.

The holy man plucked the ring from his tongue and held it out to Benicio, urging him to take it. *'Ma tu'ub.'*

Benicio folded his hand over the priest's. Certainly the old man had lost his wits. *'Ma tu'ub,'* the priest muttered a final time, and the life went out of him. The ring tumbled to the ground.

'Ma tu'ub, holy one,' Benicio repeated. *'Ma tu'ub.'*

The morning sun passed behind a cloud and the cacophony of birds ceased. All the world went still and Benicio had the overwhelming sensation that it had just lost an important soul. He placed the priest's arms across his chest and closed his eyelids. For some unknown reason, Benicio was overcome with grief.

Benicio reached for the cloth lying at his feet and studied its strange design: a diamond with circles around each of its four points. In the centre of the diamond was a small dot the size of a man's fingertip. Benicio pictured the priest pressing his bloody finger on that spot, fearing for his life, while Rogelio threatened to take another finger. But why? What important thing did this cluster of shapes represent?

Perhaps it was some kind of map. Some of Cortés's men whispered of a city of gold hidden deep in the jungle. Benicio had always believed the rumours to be nonsense—the wishful thinking of desperate men. Still, the priest had pointed at the map, then urged Benicio to take the golden ring.

The golden ring! Benicio stuffed the cloth into the side of his boot and spotted the shiny object where the priest had dropped it on to the ground.

He grasped the ring and studied it in his palm. No wonder Rogelio had pursued the priest so relentlessly. The figure of a feathered dragon, wrought in gold, overlaid the jadestone's polished façade. The detail of the figure was beyond anything Benicio had ever seen and he wondered if some unknown god had not fashioned it.

But it was not the detail that made Benicio's heart begin to race, it was the dozen large diamonds that lined the ring's perimeter, framing the golden dragon in a glitter of light. The diamonds were larger than any single diamond Benicio had ever seen. He knew that he held a treasure truly fit for a king.

A sneaking joy bubbled within him. He could not believe his good fortune. He swelled inside as he imagined returning to Spain and presenting the prize to King Charles himself.

'How may I compensate you for such a gift?' the King would ask him and Benicio would humbly request a small allotment of land, a place where he might run cattle and plant orchards and keep his noble wife in the way of life she deserved.

And thus it would be done. A dream that he had all but abandoned, suddenly fulfilled.

How strange and unpredictable life was.

Where had he put his breastplates? Ah, there they were, just a few paces away. Steel armour was highly valued among the people of the West Indies and could be traded for essentials like food and transport. And where was his book? Where was *Amadís*? He touched his chest. There it was—right where he always kept it, covering his heart.

He heard a sudden rustle of maize leaves upon the ground. Sensing danger, he popped the ring into his mouth and threaded his tongue through its golden hoop. He turned to behold Rogelio, who remained where he had fallen not three paces away. His eyes sparkled with greed.

He had witnessed everything.

Benicio jumped to his feet and secured his armour. He found the place on the horizon where the sun had risen. He would only need to make his way west, to the coast. There he would find one of the friendly coastal villages. Surely there would be some native man willing to trade his canoe and some supplies for the shiny armour Benicio now wore.

It would be a fast journey across the short stretch of ocean that separated Cuba from this strange island, if an island it was. He would arrive upon Cuba and seek passage to Hispañola, where he would board the next ship returning to Spain. There, he would present his precious ring to King Charles and come what may.

Rogelio was struggling to his feet. He eyed Benicio with a simmering rage, then lunged towards him.

But Benicio would not be caught. His future was in reach. It glittered like diamonds, like Luisa's green eyes in the noonday sun. He stretched out his long legs and broke into a run. All he needed to do now was reach the coast.

'Luisa,' he breathed. 'I'm coming home.'

Chapter Three

When Tula reached the coast, the day was still new. The Sun God glowed white in his victory over the night. She was glad to see that the remote beach remained empty, its quiet cove still untroubled by the wind. She had planned her visit for this day because she knew that Goddess of the Sea would be asleep, her blue waters rolled up like a blanket. The moon charts said it would be so.

Tula retrieved a single spear from her basket. She told herself that she was not lying to her father. Not really. She was simply waiting until the time was right to make her secret known. 'Within each thing exists its opposite,' her father always told her. She knew that all her people would soon know the mystery she held inside her heart.

But for now, it was only hers.

She pulled off her shawl and skirt and stuffed them away inside her basket. She placed her belongings at the edge of the jungle, tightening her loin-cloth as she skipped bare-breasted down the beach.

She felt like a child misbehaving. It gave Tula such a thrill to step out on to her empty beach alone, as if she were the only person in this crowded world. She savoured the moment, knowing that it would not endure.

Her father, who sat upon the Totonac Council of Elders, would be obliged to tell the Totonac Chief of Tula's discovery. When her secret became known, Totonac nobles would be swarming this beach like fire ants. Tula did not pretend to understand the affairs of the men who ruled the Totonac nation, but she knew well enough that she had found something important.

She also knew that if there was treasure to be had, she wanted to find it first.

She stepped into the clear blue water, sending a prayer to God of the Hunt, Mixcoatl, to help her find treasure in the form of gold. The strange yellow metal was so very rare and to Tula's mind held little practical use. But the Mexica Takers would accept it in place of many cloaks, and if she could obtain even just a small amount she knew she could bring great relief to her family.

She gripped her spear and peered into the under-water world. It was more likely that she would find a fish. Over the past few cycles of the sun, she had become an excellent fisher, though she would never let the fault of pride weight her steps. Her people believed that fish had once been human and she entered their blue-green realm with humility and reverence.

'Forgive me, fishes,' she intoned, letting the water of the Endless Sea pool around her knees. She spied the black spots of a mature jaguar fish, a Totonac delicacy.

With a quick downward thrust, she impaled the magnificent swimmer, then finished its life with her blade. 'I am humble,' she whispered to Mixcoatl. With a great heave, she tossed her family's dinner on to the shore.

She journeyed deeper into the water, stepping past a group of boulders and sighting a polished tree trunk protruding from the depths. She sucked in a breath, then slipped beneath the water.

She followed the tree trunk downwards, kicking past where the seafloor made a short drop, until she reached the hulking wooden temple.

This was her secret, her true quarry. She had discovered the submerged structure half a moon ago in search of new fishing grounds. She suspected it belonged to the bearded god Grijalva, who had journeyed through the Totonac waters many cycles past.

He had forged a friendship with the Totonac Chief and the Council of Elders, but he had said nothing about sacrificing a floating temple in this quiet cove.

Though clearly it was a sacrifice—a worthy gift for any god. And today, with the water so clear, she could see the details, including the finely carved rungs of the large calendar wheel, which perched on its central platform.

She envisioned the bearded gods consulting the wheel as they journeyed from their homeland. If temples like this could split the seas, Tula thought, then the world was wider and more varied than ever she could have dreamed.

But she could not allow herself to think of such things now. There was only so much breath inside her and scavenging work to be done. She propelled herself to the main platform and tugged futilely at a thick metal handle she found there. A nearby iron hook proved even less yielding. The last time she had visited the ghostly temple, she had cut a length from one of the thick ropes that floated around the central trunk. Her store of breath quickly decreasing, she decided to simply cut herself another strand.

She propelled herself to the surface to take another breath, then hurried back to cut the rope. As she worked, she gazed down the length of the structure and noticed that something had changed. The last time she had visited, there had been another large tree trunk further down the deck. But that second trunk no longer stood upright: it had fallen on to the sand.

Abandoning her work on the rope, Tula pushed to the surface once again and took another large breath. Her chest full of air, she propelled herself to the site of the collapse.

As she neared, she saw that the falling trunk had ripped the planks that had been fixed beneath it, creating an opening in the central platform. The light of mid-morning was now shining perfectly down into that opening, illuminating the mysterious space below. Her heart beating wildly, Tula followed that shaft of light like a path.

Soon she found herself inside a small chamber. There were large wooden crates piled everywhere, some with blurry symbols painted upon their sides. Several chairs floated against the ceiling, but a small table remained fixed to the floor, its single support thick with barnacles. The room was so littered with debris that it was difficult to discern the purpose of it, but Tula guessed that she was in a place where the bearded gods had prepared their food.

She could not believe her good fortune. She wanted to gather all of its strange objects and rush back to her home, where she would spill them before her father and sisters and watch their faces light up with awe. But already her breath was running low. She reminded herself to stay calm. She had plenty of time to make the many dives needed to gather up this trove of treasure.

She turned to begin her ascent, then spotted the glint of an object beneath a fallen plank—a *metal* object. She bent to lift the plank but couldn't move it. To create resistance, she squeezed her foot inside a small hole in the ceiling of the space. The foothold steadied her and she grasped the object in her hand.

Her chest convulsed. She was dangerously out of breath. With the object now in hand, she tugged her wedged foot, but it would not come free. She gulped, sucking in a breath of water and expelling it with a gagging cough that only caused her to take in more water. She filled with a sudden dread. She wiggled her foot again, feeling the planks pinch her skin.

She was drowning.

Suddenly, an image of the flyers came to her mind. The brave Totonac pole flyers swam like Tula, but in the air. Every sun cycle, they would climb to the top of a tall pole, strap their ankles to long ropes, and face possible death as they twirled to the ground like the Sun God's rays.

Now Tula imagined she was flying through the air like a pole flyer, only she was much higher above the land. She stared down and saw her city like a tiny dot amidst the jungle. To the east was the Endless Sea, that vast, watery realm that led to the first level of the Underworld. To the north was the Great Desolation, where the wandering tribes lived and died. To the west were the Fiery Mountains, and beyond them Tenochtitlan, where the terrible Emperor Montezuma ruled from his throne of gold. Only to the south, where the green jungle stretched into infinity, did people still live free. *In the land of the Maya.*

Tula twirled her body around to look south. Suddenly, her foot came free.

She darted upwards, breaking the surface in a storm of coughs. Water spewed from her chest in a dozen violent spurts and she could hardly move her limbs for the exhaustion she felt. But she was alive, thank the gods. She pulled herself on to the flattest of the nearby boulders, then closed her eyes and lost her awareness.

When she finally regained her senses, she could see that much time had passed. The Sun God's battle with the Women Warrior spirits had already begun and, as they pulled him towards the western horizon, long shadows reached across the beach.

Tula was amazed to discover that she still gripped it in her hand—the object that had almost taken her life. She held it up against the sky, studying it. It was not gold, but silver. Its single shaft was as long as her hand and terminated in a thumb-sized concavity from which extended three equidistant prongs. It appeared to be the specially designed tip of a deadly spear.

Tula compared it against the tip of her own spear and tried to imagine the kind of animal the object might be designed to kill. She pictured a tiny, three-headed beast that scuttled about in some distant jungle. Or perhaps its three prongs were designed to prick a special kind of fish?

She resolved to show the object to her father, whom she was certain would be able to present it to the Mexica Takers in place of many cloaks. 'I am humble,' she whispered to the gods, marvelling at how perfectly the small weapon fit into her hand.

Lost in admiration of her prize, Tula did not notice the sound of the men's voices until they were very close. She slid into the water behind the largest boulder just as the bearded gods exploded on to the sand.

Chapter Four

There were two of them: a fleshy, naked-chested god with hair the colour of flames and a tall, muscular god clad in a sleeveless hide wrap. The red god shouted at the tall god and chased him some distance down the beach.

Tula peeked out from behind her boulder. Had a new army of bearded gods arrived in Totonac territory? But how? The Totonac kept close watch along their coasts. There had been no sign of any bearded gods for many cycles. Besides, the bearded gods came from the sea on floating temples, not staggering half-naked from the depths of the jungle.

Tula snuck out of the water and dashed across the beach, leaving the jaguar fish as an offering to Mixcoatl. She slipped back into her skirt and blouse, placed her weapons inside her basket and stole closer to the two gods, keeping herself hidden amidst the tangle of trees and vines at the edge of the jungle.

She knew it was foolish to approach them, but her curiosity blazed. She had heard tales of the battles between gods—if gods these were. The God of the Morning Star and the God of Earth had fought together long ago, much like these two were doing, producing the Fifth World—the world in which she now lived. In her studies, Tula had learned that the Fifth World was soon to come to an end. Was this contest a harbinger of the new world to come?

The two rolled over and under one another, fighting for supremacy. The red god punched the tall god in the face, then groped at the tall god's mouth. But the tall god, whose muscular arms Tula could see even at this distance, thrust a punch upwards into the red god's stomach.

The red god tumbled on to the sand, coughing. The tall god placed his fingers upon his nose and bent over in agony. It was enough time for the red god to take hold of a silvery dagger and place it against the tall god's neck.

The tall god stood still while the red god shouted menacing words in a strange, rolling tongue. He seemed to be demanding the answer to some question he had posed. The tall god did not respond. Instead, he held his mouth tightly shut.

Enraged, the red god plunged his knife into the

tall god's chest and the tall god fell backwards on to the sand.

Tula shrieked.

She slapped her hand over her own mouth, shocked by the noise that had come out of it.

Meanwhile, the red god had jumped to his feet and was peering into the jungle. Tula cowered behind a rubber tree. Why had she made such a noise? She had revealed herself for certain. She could not see him, but she began to hear his footfalls. He was coming towards her.

Shaking in fear, Tula pulled her atlatl and a single arrow from her basket, though she knew that it was useless to try to kill a god. If he was a god, then her only chance against him was the aid of another god. She braved a quick glance at the tall god, who remained motionless on the beach. She would receive no heavenly help from him, it seemed.

The red god's footfalls grew louder. Closer. If she could create an illusion, perhaps she might confuse the red god enough for him to cease his approach. She gave a high-pitched battle cry, then a low-pitched one, then sent her first arrow flying. The red god swerved behind a tree, but he was not quick enough. The arrow's jagged point grazed past his leg, ripping the tight cloth he wore.

Fuming, he ran towards her, his knife held high.

There was nothing she could do but step out from behind her tree and launch her second arrow.

It was even better aimed than the first. It caught in the sleeve of his wrap, sending him backwards on to the ground. She had not injured him, but she had grounded him well.

Tula scanned the forest floor, finding several fine, fist-sized stones. She threw them at him, one after another, darting among the trees to make it seem as if the stones were coming from many different directions. She needed him to believe that an army lurked amongst the trees, ready to strike.

He shouted angrily, struggling to stand above the cloud of dirt and debris that she was kicking up all around. Just as he was finding his balance, Tula fixed the peg of the atlatl into the notch of an arrow and launched it. It stuck him directly in the thigh.

He howled in agony and his blazing eyes found hers. His blade in hand, he staggered to his feet. She loosed her final stone.

It hit him in the head and sent him to the ground where he remained motionless.

Tula stood in stunned silence. Had she just defeated a god? Impossible. Gods could not be defeated by humans.

At least, that was what her father had taught her. When she had asked him how he knew that Grijalva and his men were gods, he had told her that the bearded ones did not abide by the sacred law.

'Which law?' Tula had asked.

'The law between gods and humans.'

'They do not make sacrifices to the gods and for that reason you believe them to *be* gods?' Tula frowned.

'Either that, my dear Tula, or they are most certainly doomed.'

Tula wondered which was true. Were these bearded ones verily gods? Or were they merely strange, war-like men doomed to die?

The other god was still lying on the beach. If he was truly a god, then he was not dead and it was possible that he could help protect her against the red god, who would be returning to his senses soon.

She rushed from the jungle and on to the beach, trying to think of a way to rouse the tall god. When the god Grijalva had visited, he and his crew had remained inside their floating temples, revealing little but their love of gold and their devotion to the strange, naked spirit they called Cristo.

'Cristo,' Tula said tentatively, hoping the word held some kind of magic. But the tall god did not respond. She stared down at his face. It was so very pale, like the inside of a *chayohtli* fruit. He was like a beast, in truth, his wiry brown hairs growing all around his large face and down past his chin. Crude, thick bushes of it grew over his eyes and tangled around his ears.

Tula took a deep breath. *Within each thing exists its opposite,* she told herself.

She looked closer. Beneath his moustache, his lips were red and plump, and appeared almost soft. The skin of his high cheekbones was clean and smooth, as if it might be pleasurable to touch. She wondered about his eyes. Were they blue like the sea? She hoped not. Many of the god Grijalva's men had such eyes and it meant that their souls had deserted them.

'Cristo,' she said again, but the god did not stir. Perhaps he was dead.

But gods did not die.

Tula bent to her knees and studied his face more closely. His nose was like a coati's—long and strong and prominent. It was bent to the side slightly, and a small trickle of blood flowed out of it.

But gods did not bleed.

She wondered if his mouth held teeth or fangs. She let her finger graze across his lips. They were soft and slightly moist. She gently traced their contours, feeling an unusual thrill.

Man or god, he was fascinating.

She tilted his lower jaw downwards and peered into his mouth. Not fangs—he had teeth. They were the imperfect, slightly yellowed teeth of one who had seen much of life and the set was not even complete. Tula suppressed a smile. If a god, he was quite a besieged one.

The Sun God was nearing his defeat. His last rays shot across the sky, illuminating the man's large pink tongue. She peered deeper into his mouth. For the second time that day, she noticed the glint of metal. It was O-shaped, like a ring. A *gold* ring. The god's tongue squeezed through it like a finger.

Tula knew that the bearded gods hungered for gold, but she had no idea that they actually *consumed* the yellow metal.

Tula looked closer and saw that the ring was the perch for a large gemstone of some kind. Its wide circular base extended across the roof of the god's mouth, stirring her imagination. Maybe it was a moonstone, or even a precious jade. Tula reached for the gem, but his mouth closed suddenly.

Tula jumped backwards. The man's eyes remained shut, but Tula was unnerved. She heard a rustling sound at the edge of the jungle. As she squinted for a better view, she saw that it was just a monkey swinging between tree branches. Still, she knew the red god would be returning to his senses soon.

'Ooa-k-k-k,' the monkey croaked, as if in warning. But now Tula did not want to leave without the ring. To return to her family and community with such a treasure was beyond her wildest hopes. The Mexica Tribute Takers would certainly accept the heavy prize in place of much food and many cloaks' worth of tribute. She remembered what her father had told her about the upcoming festival of the fifteenth month. Perhaps the Takers would accept this jewel in place of Tula herself.

She tried to open his mouth again, but he held it shut. His eyes remained tightly closed and they danced beneath his lids, as if he was living inside some important dream. Clearly he was not dead, just asleep. If only she could somehow enter his dream and coax him into opening his mouth. But how to enter the dream of a god?

On impulse, she placed her lips upon his.

She pressed down softly, hoping that he would imagine some beautiful goddess kissing him and open his mouth just enough for her to retrieve the gem. She moved her lips gently against his and, amazingly, he began to move his lips in response.

Her deception was working—it seemed that he had accepted her into his dream. Softly, she let her tongue slide into his mouth. It touched the hoop of the ring, which remained wrapped around his tongue. She tried to coax it free with her own tongue, but it was so tightly wedged against the roof of his mouth that it would not move. It was several moments before she realised that the tiny hairs upon her arms were standing on end.

She shivered, though it was not cold, and breathed in his musky scent.

This was not her first kiss—if a kiss it was. As a younger woman, she had participated in her share of maize festivals and there had always been plenty of young men eager to join lips with her among the stalks.

That was before the Mexica Tribute Takers had taken her older sister's husband and two boys, when life was still joyous and full of possibility.

After Pulkho's family was taken, the idea of closeness with a man had become terrifying to Tula. Why enter into the sacred union if it could so easily be destroyed? Tula had stopped going to the maize festivals, and had determined never to get close to any man. There was simply too great a danger of losing him.

This was different, of course. This kiss had nothing to do with closeness and everything to do with theft. The excitement she felt was not the excitement a woman felt for a man: It was merely the danger of the situation mixed with the possibility of success.

She lay her tongue atop his, squeezing it into the

ring, such that their tongues twisted together in the small space.

Slowly, steadily, she coaxed the heavy prize into her own mouth.

She felt a rush of triumph as she hovered over him, threading her own tongue through the golden ring. She was so proud of herself that she hardly noticed when his lips reconnected with hers and his tongue began to move inside her mouth.

He was kissing her back. Tula's heart began to pound, and a different kind of shiver ripped through her body. His lips pressed firmly against hers. She tried to pull away, but she couldn't. He wrapped his arm around her back and pulled her against him, keeping her body pinned against his so firmly that she could scarcely breathe. His chest was hard, as if padded with some invisible armour. But his kisses were soft and tender, and his eyes remained closed.

'Luisa,' he whispered.

Chapter Five

Luisa, his dear Luisa. Here she was, at last in his arms. He could feel the warmth of her breath, the softness of her skin. He could even sense her desire—how she drew in the scent of him, how she thrilled and shivered at his touch. She still wanted him, even after two long years. And he wanted her—*Diós*, how he wanted her. She was all that mattered, all that would ever matter. She was the only good thing in his despicable life.

He pulled her against him and heard her sigh, and it was all the permission he needed to shower her with his kisses. He started with her cheeks, which tasted salty and fecund, as if she had swum all the way across the ocean to be with him. He ran his fingers through her damp hair, which she had allowed to grow long and straight. Perhaps she had ceased to cut it the day they parted, just as he had done with his beard.

Keeping his eyes closed, he kissed beneath her jaw, then down her long, elegant neck. '*Mi amor,* how I have missed you,' he said.

Gently, he cradled her breasts, which were swaddled in some soft, vaguely damp textile. How many times had he thought of placing his palms upon the small rises, which were as tender as ripe pears? How perfectly they fitted there now.

Ay, lusty Luisa.

He let his tongue explore her neck's soft chalice, feeling a tingling warmth rising through his body. There had been others before Luisa—silly, fatuous women who had chosen him for what he appeared to be, not who he was. Only Luisa knew who he was. She had known him since he was a boy and he felt certain she could see into his heart.

Now her chest heaved with her emotion and it was all he needed to know that she felt as he did.

'It has been…difficult,' he confessed, keeping his eyes closed. 'I think of you every day.' He kissed her shoulders, which smelled vaguely of the briny air. 'This new world…so much…misery.'

That was all he would say. He would not tell her about the things he had seen, the things he had done. He would not sully her view of him, or shatter her illusions by admitting that there had been many times since they'd parted that he had wished himself dead.

Though perhaps he was dead now. If so, then he thanked *Diós*, for surely he had made it to Heaven. Here it did not matter that he would inherit nothing but his bootstraps. All that mattered was his love, which was truer than the stars, and burned more brightly than the sun.

He plunged his tongue into her mouth. But instead of soft wetness, he felt only a smooth, hard stone.

Then Luisa released a frightful yelp.

Benicio opened his eyes to behold a strange, big-eyed woman staring back at him. He might have believed her a ghost, were it not for the deep honey hue of her skin, the wind of her breath and the large jade and diamond ring resting upon her tongue.

His jade and diamond ring.

'Bruja!' he cried. *Witch!*

The woman jumped backwards in the sand.

'Give it to me!' he shouted. In a blur of motion, he leaned forward and cupped her jaw, forcing open her mouth. Then he plucked the large jewel right off her tongue.

He felt a sudden, piercing ache behind his ribs. He careened backwards in pain, his head swimming. In that instant, it all came back to him—the battle, the priest, the ring, the thrust of Rogelio's blade as it plunged through his chest.

He sat up and peered down at his jerkin, half-expecting to see a spreading bloodstain. But the leather garment was spotless. The only evidence of the stabbing was a coin-sized hole in the pocket that covered his heart.

Benicio struggled to right his thoughts, wondering why he was not dead. Rogelio had chased him relentlessly into the night. By daybreak, Benicio thought he had lost the greedy villain, but Rogelio had burst from the jungle with the first rays of sun.

It was at that moment Benicio had realised the reason for Rogelio's speed: he had abandoned his heavy armour. Wearing nothing but his woollen hose and leather boots, Rogelio had easily caught up to Benicio. When Benicio finally decided to abandon the weight of his own armour, they had already reached the coast.

'Where is the ring?' Rogelio had demanded, pinning Benicio upon the beach.

But Benicio had refused to open his mouth.

'And where is the map?' Rogelio had added, searching the pockets of Benicio's jerkin. Benicio had only blinked mindlessly. 'Do not play a fool,' Rogelio had sneered. 'Where is the map to the Maya treasure?'

And thus Rogelio had given away the secret. It was a treasure map that Benicio carried, just as he suspected.

Benicio looked around now, confused. After such a tireless chase, and after plunging his very knife into Benicio's chest, Rogelio had all but abandoned Benicio, and without taking the ring that he had chased him all night to obtain. Something was amiss, but Benicio could not determine what.

Benicio studied his would-be bandit. Her wet black hair hung in ropes about her breasts, which were covered by a damp yellow shawl that betrayed the shadow of two small nipples.

Benicio felt his desire tighten against his will. If not a witch, then surely she was a siren of the sea, for her lips were pink like coral and her eyes were dark, watery maelstroms. When he finally wrenched his gaze from the pools of her eyes, he took in her whole face. Her cheeks were high, her nose straight and long and her steep, angled eyebrows tilted like twin arrows. She was at once lovely and fearsome, and he felt strangely helpless in the grip of her ancient beauty.

'Leave!' he shouted, but she only stared at him with those unfathomable eyes. Perhaps she was casting a terrible enchantress's spell upon him—some witch's curse that would see his golden prize back inside her mouth once again. And where, oh, where had Rogelio got to? Had she cast her enchantress's spell upon him, as well?

She squared her shoulders to Benicio and he observed that she was quite small, but with all the fascinating dips and curves of a woman. She straightened herself upon her knees, as if to make herself seem larger. But her fearsome posture only served to display her lovely long neck, reminding him that just moments ago, his lips had been upon it. His mouth grew wet with an unsavoury lust. Surely she was an enchantress, for only enchantresses were this beautiful and corrupt.

'Leave me in peace,' he entreated, feeling exhaustion overtake him. Even if she did not understand his language, surely she could understand his tone? 'Now,' he commanded weakly, but the enchantress would not move. Instead, she seemed to grow in stature as she loomed over his prone body.

He gripped the ring tightly in his fist. The sun beat down from above and a menacing chorus of cicadas rose from the jungle. Surely this was part of her enchantment—to paralyze him beneath her sorceress's gaze until he all but begged her to take the ring. Or perhaps her beauty was just a trick of his mind—some sweet illusion to help him cope with his own slow death.

He reached beneath his jerkin, expecting to discover a bloody wound. Instead, he found a stiff, leathery object. He gasped, letting his fingers caress the brick of pages. Ah! It had not been fortune, but irony that had kept him from extinction: It was the pages of *Amadís de Gaula* that had protected him from Rogelio's blow.

He gave a thunderous laugh. Since the day Luisa had given it to him, he had always kept the slim volume close to his heart. Now he saw that the cover had been completely penetrated by Rogelio's blade, as had many of the pages. But the tales of chivalry had not been fully impaled and had literally saved his life.

And now it appeared that the book was also saving him from the enchantress, for she had turned her attention away from him and towards its battered cover.

'You have never seen a book, have you?' Benicio asked, seizing upon a possible advantage. Perhaps if he shared it with her she would reciprocate somehow? If only he could signal to her that he was in need of a sturdy canoe.

He laughed again, for the thought struck him as absurd. Here he was at the far ends of the earth, looking to hire a canoe! Still, he could not give up hope of finding passage back to Spain. And for that, he needed all the friends he could find.

He handed the book to the woman. She paged through the text with familiarity, as if she had handled many books before this one. She placed her finger in the hole that had been created by Rogelio's blade, then shook her head in bemused disbelief. She returned the book to him and, though they had exchanged not a single word, he was left with the uncanny feeling that that they had just had a conversation.

Now the woman fixed her gaze upon his beard. 'This?' he asked, touching the whiskers he had been growing since the day his ship had sailed from Seville. 'You want to touch it?'

She nodded shyly.

If he indulged her this wish, perhaps she could help him with his own? Surely her tribe lived somewhere close. He did not trust her, but that did not mean he could not profit from her knowledge. He nodded and she reached out her hand and stroked his long whiskers.

She laughed softly as she tugged at the hairs, as if trying to ensure they were real. She tugged again and again. She tugged again, a bit too hard, and he caught her by the wrist.

She narrowed her big brown eyes and her smile was full of mischief.

A flood of lust ripped through his body. He wanted to kiss her again, he realised. And that was not all.

Hijo de la... He released her wrist as if it were a burning coal.

No, he would not do that. He might have been a lonely, world-weary wretch, but there were some lines he did not cross. Seducing island women was one of them—whatever island this was. Even if Luisa were not waiting for him back in Spain, he still would not prey upon the innocence of this local woman or any other. It sickened him that many of his compatriots seemed to make careers out of doing just that.

Though as he stared at her lips—still red with the evidence of the kiss they had shared—he found it very difficult to think about anything but how much he wanted to feel them again, this time in full possession of his senses. He watched her gaze slide down to his own parted lips and for a moment it seemed she was seducing him.

He sat deadly still, fighting his desire for her. He reminded himself of Luisa, his one true love, waiting for him back in Spain. He would not betray her. He was responding to the lovely, sensual woman before him as any man would. But it was a response of the body, not of the heart, and it would pass.

As if in apology, she smoothed his beard with her fingers. She scooted closer, her eyes fixing again upon his lips. Would she ask to touch those, too? Part of him prayed for it.

Another part of him demanded that he come to his senses. The first Spaniard to come to these shores—a man by the name of Córdoba—had lost half his crew to a local tribe. And the explorer Grijalva who had come after Córdoba had spoken of highly advanced, warlike peoples living in every corner of this strange land.

And now Cortés had learned that there were not only Maya living in this land, but dozens of other peoples, all with their own languages and customs, all living beneath the heel of some powerful tribe called the Mexica. This sensual enchantress probably had an entire army of strange men behind her, watching from the jungle, waiting to strike.

Gently, she pressed her lips to his. He did not respond. He refused to respond, though *Diós Santo*, her lips were so soft. He stayed perfectly still, concentrating on the rhythmic sound of the waves, trying to remember all of the reasons why he was an honourable man.

His reticence seemed only to spur her. She kissed him with a maddening gentleness, placing small, soft pecks along the length of his bottom lip. She tasted of herbs and strange fruits, and as she placed her whole mouth on his, he found himself wishing to consume her.

He was angry at her for trusting him, for kissing him so brazenly, for flitting about his lips as if she were some bustling bird. Was this some kind of game to her? Some trifling amusement that sirens and witches played? She knew not what she was teasing awake in him.

She probed her tongue deeper into his mouth and he imagined pushing her upon the sand, ripping off her shawl and yanking up her skirt. His need throbbed powerfully beneath his breeches. He should just take her, hard and fast—give her what she so thoughtlessly asked for and show her the error of it.

No. He could not allow himself to think of such things. He was a good man. An honourable man. He would not do what his basest longings demanded. He was so caught up in resisting his desire that he did not even notice her small, stealthy fingers stealing into his pocket.

Chapter Six

She darted among the trees, changing directions to confuse his path. She had not wanted to deceive him, but she had had no choice. Treasure was treasure and a ring that big and beautiful could be presented to the Mexica in place of an entire cycle's worth of her family's tribute.

It was not just a pretty jewel: it was rest for her older sister's hands, twisted from so many hours of weaving. It was relief for her younger sister's shoulders, which had swelled like a man's with so much grinding of maize.

For her father, it represented nothing less than time—time to commit to training the secret army of Totonac warriors, so that when the moment came to throw off their Mexica overlords the Totonacs would be ready.

She gripped the ring more tightly, then realised that she should simply place it on her finger. The heavy gem glided easily on to her thumb and she closed her fingers around it.

Treasure was treasure. She did not like that she'd had to deceive him, just as she did not like to spend her afternoons killing large numbers of birds and fish. It was a necessary evil and something impossible to explain to him. Not now, anyway. Now she could only run as fast as possible out of his reach.

Though that was proving unexpectedly difficult to do. He was surprisingly fast and agile for so large a man. While she leaped over logs and disappeared behind bushes, he followed her steadily, like a jaguar chasing a deer. She wondered if his speed was motivated by something beyond greed. Vengeance, perhaps.

Or perhaps lust. When she had placed her mouth upon his that second time, she'd had to fight to retain her wits. His lips were so large and soft beneath the wiry hairs of his moustache, like doorways to some dangerous, hidden depths. *Go ahead*, he seemed to dare her, *kiss me. See what will happen.* Yet he had refused to kiss her back. It was that icy self-possession that had scared her the most, for she knew that beneath his self-control was a man who cared nothing for her.

Still, her risky diversion had worked. She had repossessed the ring and that was all that mattered.

Yet there he was, still following her. His unruly hair flew behind him in long, unkempt locks. His prominent nose remained slightly bent, as if it had been broken. And while he was the largest, strongest male she had ever beheld, his clothes were ragged and seemed unsuited to his muscular body. He was not divinely beautiful, as a god, but world-worn and imperfect, as a man.

If she had had any doubts about his mortality, they had disappeared when he had revealed the object that had saved his life. A codex! She had read many codices in her studies. They usually contained beautiful, colourful pictures of the gods and elaborate illustrations of the history of the world.

The bearded man's codex contained not a single beautiful picture. Instead, it was full of symbols that looked like the corpses of tiny ants. But while the pages themselves clearly did not contain any useful information, they did perform a life-saving function: They had blocked the sting of the blade that would have punctured his heart.

No, he was not immortal, just fortunate—though the ease with which he followed her was making her reconsider his immortality once again. Even in his battle-weary state, his legs were as strong as a stag's. She splashed across a small stream, then heard not a splatter as he leapt over it entirely, gaining ground.

He was going to overtake her soon. After deceiving him as she had, only the gods knew what he planned to do to her when he caught her.

Then she had an idea. She was nearing the limits of Cempoala. She knew that maize and cotton fields had been planted in this area to help meet her city's tribute requirements to the Mexica. If she remembered correctly, there was a large maize field somewhere after the stream she had just crossed. She ran due east, praying she would find the maize plantation where she supposed it would be.

Then, like a granted wish, there it was—a vast plantation of head-high maize. She slipped into the rows at the corner of the field and held herself still. In seconds, he arrived at the field's edge and let out a great, bellowing laugh. In the heartfelt burst she heard resignation and what she thought was a twinge of respect. She had bested him.

He broke into an angry run. She could hear his heavy footfalls and the loud cracking and bowing of the stalks beneath his feet. What a fool he was! With each angry exertion, he signalled his location.

All she had to do now was listen for his movements and adjust her own location accordingly. Night would fall soon and her friend the darkness would keep her concealed as she slunk out of the field and made her way home.

The same thought must have occurred to the man's mind, however, for in that very instant, he halted his search. She listened closely and thought she heard him march back across the same path he had forged.

Immediately she realised her error. She ran towards the edge of the field, but it was too late. She looked up, and there he was, looking down at her from the rosewood tree that towered over the field. He dropped with puma-like stealth from its high branches and was soon charging towards her.

There was nothing to do but run. His footfalls grew louder behind her and she felt tears come to her eyes as she imagined what he might do to her after he repossessed his ring. When he had grabbed her wrist, she had sensed his capacity for violence and she feared that she had now pushed him over the edge.

But, suddenly, it was she who was falling over the edge. It was as if the very earth had opened up to consume her and her heart leapt into her throat as she accelerated towards a certain, crushing death. Down, down she fell, kicking the air in terror as she careened into a dark chasm.

Then—splash. Not rock, but water broke her fall. Sweet, cool water—a pool without bottom. She held her breath as she plunged through the inky depths, letting her momentum slow. Instinctively, she began kicking.

She kicked and kicked, propelling herself upwards towards the murky light until she burst to the surface. She was exhausted, confused, terrified and never happier to be alive.

She had fallen into a cenote. The sunken, freshwater ponds were rare in Totonac territory and the Totonac priests kept their locations secret. Still, Tula had come across several on her journeys to the ocean and had always stopped to give thanks to the old gods that lurked in their mysterious depths.

'I am humble,' she sputtered now, to any god who would listen. It was her third encounter with death in only a few hours and she could not believe her good fortune. She looked inside her fist. She had even retained her golden prize.

But not for long.

Suddenly, the bearded man surged to the surface next to her, sending a wave of water splashing against the high walls. He had fallen into the cenote beside her and, when he saw her treading the water near him, he swam towards her with cold, terrifying purpose.

She glanced up at the high walls that surrounded them. They were made of smooth rock and were uniformly bare, save for a small cluster of roots that dangled over the edge, totally out of reach.

There was no escape.

He made no loud demands, no violent movements. He simply opened her fist and pulled the ring gently off her thumb. He slipped the golden prize on to his little finger, then narrowed his eyes at her.

She trod water to a dry, rocky area at the edge of the pool, trying not to reveal her fear. Then she lifted herself on to a boulder and pulled her legs up against her chest.

He was like a crocodile in the black water, his large muscular limbs making slow, menacing strokes towards where she sat. He hoisted himself up on to the rock beside her and she readied herself to make another deep dive.

He made no movements towards her, however. Instead, he placed his feet in the water and looked out over the pool. She saw him steal a glance at her legs, aware that the yellow fabric of her skirt clung to them.

She felt a strange thrill travel through her, followed by a withering dread. The light of day was fading fast. In a short time, they would not be able to see anything at all. The distance between the pool and the jungle floor was greater than the height of a house. No man—or woman—could bridge it alone.

But Tula had to try. She could not remain here alone with him. Even if she shouted loudly for help, nobody would be travelling in this part of the jungle at this time of day. If she did not escape now, she would have to pass the night with him.

She stood upon one of the rocks and jumped, uselessly attempting to grasp the cluster of *zapote* roots hanging down from above. She scraped the walls, struggling to find a toehold to sustain her weight. She collapsed back on to the rock in frustration.

They sat together in silence for what seemed an eternity. She knew that at any moment he could simply hold her under the water, or smash her head in anger upon the rocks.

Or worse. Much, much worse.

Surely he considered it. She had humiliated him, after all. She had used her womanliness to distract him so that she could once again steal his ring. It was a shameful thing, what she had done. A dishonourable thing. A Totonac man would be justified in seeking punishment for such an act. Any man would be within his rights to pierce her with cactus spines, or force her to breathe in the smoke of burning chilli, or worse.

Still, something inside her—something she did not understand—went to him.

He was so unusual for a man—so large and pale

compared to the men of her tribe and so gracelessly unadorned. His body was vigorous and immensely strong, yet his eyes were an ethereal, otherworldly blue. It did not seem as though his spirit had deserted him, however. Instead it seemed as if a kind of sky spirit dwelt within him. She wondered if he was some kind of a shaman, though she hoped he could not hear her thoughts. She did not want him to know that despite his uncivilised appearance, she had enjoyed kissing him.

Had enjoyed it very much.

If only she could speak his tongue, she would explain to him about her family and her circumstances and how very sorry she was for stealing his golden prize—twice. Treasure was treasure and surely he could understand that she'd done what she'd had to do to help her family survive?

She stared at the *zapote* roots once again. He was so very tall. If she could just stand upon his shoulders, she might be able to reach them.

He looked into her eyes, as if he was having the same thought. His face was chiselled and balanced, with prominent cheekbones and a heavy brow that he lifted slightly to an unnerving effect. And his nose was…broken.

'Your nose,' she said, pointing at the bent bone.

He lifted his hand and gently traced the length of it, cringing as he travelled past the abrupt bend.

'If you do not bend it back, it will heal that way,' she said in her language, hoping he might glean her meaning.

He shook his head, but she could not tell if it was because he did not understand her, or if he simply did not wish to listen. He stared at the quiet pool.

'*Taak'in,*' he said finally.

She could not believe her ears. 'You speak the Maya tongue?' she asked in that language.

'*Taak'in,*' he repeated, clearly not understanding her question.

'*Taak'in,*' she said and pointed to his little finger. Surely he knew the word he spoke was the Maya name for gold?

'*Taak'in?*' he asked, holding up his finger.

She nodded, studying the enormous diamond-framed jadestone that could have been hers. Upon it was a gilded etching of the Feathered Serpent God, Quetzalcoatl. It was the finest such etching that she had ever seen.

Benicio pointed to the jadestone. '*Taak'in?*' he asked.

She shook her head. *No, no, no.* He turned the ring upside down and pointed to its golden base. '*Taak'in?*' he asked again.

She nodded. *Yes, yes, that is gold.*

He appeared to strike upon an idea. He pulled a cloth out from between his boots and stretched it on the boulder between them. The cloth appeared to be a kind of canvas for a drawing of a large tilted square. Around each of the square's four points was a small circle. A single, finger-sized dot decorated its centre. The man pointed to the dot.

'Taak'in?' he asked.

The man spoke in puzzles. Why did he give the name of gold to a simple dot painted on a piece of cloth? Perhaps the drawing was a form of picture writing—a symbol signifying gold. Like all high-born Totonacs, Tula had learned picture writing as a child, though this shape did not resemble any character that she had ever learned.

He continued to point to the dot, as if that point were somehow more important than the others—a special location of sorts.

She felt a wave of recognition. She was not looking at picture writing. She was looking at a map—and a familiar one at that. She needed to be careful, however. She did not know this man's intentions and the place being depicted was beyond sacred. Still, she needed his help to escape the cenote.

'Tenochtitlan,' she lied.

'Tenoch-it-lan?' he repeated, pronouncing the name incorrectly.

She suppressed a laugh. He could not even say the name of the Mexica capital, the largest and most powerful city in the entire world. She knew that he had come from far away, but surely he had at least a basic knowledge of the world?

'Tenoch-*tit*-lan,' she said again slowly, emphasising the middle of the word.

'Tenoch-it-lan,' he said, incorrectly, and Tula flashed him a smile full of pity.

Returning her attention to the map, she became more certain of what she saw. Her own father had drawn this map for her as part of a history lesson long ago. But if there was gold to be had in the place represented on the cloth, it belonged to the Totonacs, not the bearded ones.

'Tenoch-it-lan?' he repeated. He pointed in all different directions and then made a confused expression, and she understood that he was asking her where Tenochtitlan was.

Tula pointed west. She had never visited the Mexica capital herself, but her father had journeyed there once as a boy. He had explained that the clever Mexica had built their city on an island in the middle of a great freshwater lake high in the western mountains.

Each year the Mexica made their island bigger

by bringing in earth on three long wooden bridges that connected the island to the shore. They piled the earth to create islands, which were separated by canals that led to the heart of the city, a central plaza with so many palaces and temples that one could walk among them, Tula's father had told her, and easily become lost.

At the head of Tenochtitlan's plaza were its most important structures, which had been arranged to correspond with the four sacred directions. To the east was the *tzompantli*, the haunting skull rack. To the north was a set of pyramids dedicated to the gods of agriculture and flowers. To the south, another set of pyramids rose to revere the earth gods and gods of vanquished cities. To the west lay the largest, most imposing temple of them all—the double pyramid dedicated to the Rain God, Tlaloc, and to the Sun God, Huitzilopochtli.

All Totonacs knew of the great double temple, for at its apex was the altar stone where so many of their loved ones had met their deaths. Tula shook her head. It was uncanny how well the map seemed to represent the sacred centre of Tenochtitlan, though she was certain it did not.

'Tenoch-it-lan?' the man repeated and there was so much hope in his voice.

'Tenochtitlan,' she said with certainty, trying to

mask her deception. If she could make him believe that the map depicted the sacred centre of Tenoch-titlan, then she could keep him from where the gold was really hidden.

She glanced at the man's legs. Their thick con-toured muscles suggested a deep well of physical strength. With those mighty legs, he could easily hoist her on his shoulders where she could stand and reach the roots. All he seemed to lack was the will to do it. She needed to motivate him somehow and to make him trust her.

She pointed at his nose. 'I know someone who can help you,' she said in her language, then pointed up at the jungle. *But you have to get me out of this cenote.*

He shook his head sternly and pointed at the map. *Do not tell anyone,* he seemed to be saying. His eyes narrowed and he watched her for a sign of under-standing. She knew he would not help her reach the roots without it.

She nodded. Yes, she would keep his secret—that his treasure map depicted the sacred centre of Tenochtitlan—for his secret was a lie.

What she would not do was explain how her fam-ily had suffered, how they continued to suffer be-neath the heel of the Mexica and how she would do anything for them. And it was not simply her family. With enough treasure, the Totonacs could free themselves of their tribute obligations for a long time—perhaps for ever.

'I will keep your secret,' she said in her language and he seemed satisfied. He removed his codex from beneath his leather vest and placed the folded map between its damp pages. Returning the codex to its place beneath his vest, he pulled his legs beneath him in a squatting position, his palms upon the ground.

He pointed to her legs, then to the back of his neck, then stared downwards, waiting.

She had no reason to trust him, but she did not have a choice. She moved behind him, placing each of her legs upon his shoulders and crouching over his head for balance.

As he stood, she squeezed her legs around his neck and her fingers clung to the hard line of his jaw as he bore her upwards. He gripped her lower legs, steadying her, and she gripped his head without thinking. His hair was surprisingly soft.

He moved closer towards the wall of the cenote, then paused. He asked her a question in his language. Though she did not understand his words, she could guess what he was asking. Would she come back for him?

Yes, yes, of course she would return for him, she

said in her language, trying to sound certain. To-morrow morning. She would bring a rope.

She felt his body stiffen. In an instant, he had pulled her from her perch and was holding her in his arms like a small child. She stared up at him, her back supported by his massive arms, her legs instinctively wrapping around his neck. Terror shot through her as she realised that in any moment, he could simply drop her upon the ground and snuff out her life.

He repeated his question, staring into her eyes with cold intensity.

'Yes, yes, yes,' she said, nodding. 'I will return. I promise.'

He caught her glancing up at the roots just beyond his head. He narrowed his eyes once again. He did not believe her. And why should he? She had betrayed him twice already. Besides, she had no reason to return for him and he knew it.

How could she reassure him that helping her escape was the right thing to do? Another kiss? No, a kiss would merely remind him of her treachery.

She needed to give him something real—something to convince him that she would return. She pulled the silver spear from beneath her cloth belt and offered it to him with both hands, like a gift. He looked at it closely, then laughed.

She felt the heat of anger rising in her cheeks. He found her offering funny? She stuffed the object back beneath her belt, fearing that now he would never let her go. She would spend her last breaths inside this bottomless pit with a man who had every reason to do her harm.

Now he was nodding at her and glancing at her waist. *No. Not that. Please, not that.* She began to sweat, though the air was cool. *Mixcoatl, help me,* she begged in silence. The man stopped nodding and fixed his gaze on the exact place beneath her belt where she had stuffed the shiny spear. Perhaps she had only misunderstood him, for it seemed he wished to see the spear again. She removed the silver spear and, following his brief nod towards the rocks, she dropped it among them.

Seemingly satisfied, he hoisted her back up over his shoulders and edged towards the wall of the cenote, just below the roots. Tula let out a long sigh of relief. She bent her legs and pressed her feet against his chest, scrambling to a standing position. For a moment, his hands rested atop her feet, holding them down. It was as if he wished to remind her of her promise.

Just as quickly, he released them and she clambered up the roots and stood at the cenote's rim.

'I promise,' she repeated in Totonac, though she

knew he doubted her. In truth, she doubted herself. To save this man would mean to take responsibility for him and she did not trust him.

She admitted that she was drawn to him—inexplicably so—and that she had enjoyed the feel of his lips upon hers. But she had always been drawn to unusual things—often to her disadvantage. This man was no history codice or quetzal bird or temple beneath the waves. He was a person, with his own needs and purposes.

Perhaps he had come with an army that meant to harm the Totonacs. Besides, if there was a treasure to be had, then it should be her people, not his, who should benefit from it.

Still, she knew she would return for him. His map was poorly drawn. It was uncertain whether it really led to treasure. The only thing for certain was the ring he wore upon his finger, and she was determined to steal it back. Her heart squeezed, for she knew that she would betray him for a third time, this fascinating savage from across the sea.

Yes, she would return for him. It was a cruel, merciless world and treasure was treasure.

Chapter Seven

Benicio stared up at his sparkling mistress, amazed. Here he was, at the far ends of the earth, stuck in a hole so dark and deep that it might as well have been a grave. Yet the planet Venus had found him. Benicio gave a gentleman's bow to her, flickering above him in her luminous splendour. Surely this was a good omen. It signalled that the beautiful woman he had just sent on her way would return for him.

She would return, would she not? He had her fork, after all—a silver fork that she valued highly enough to conceal beneath her belt. The fork itself was yet another good omen. If the natives of this island had silver forks, it meant that they had silver mines. If they had silver mines, then they had gold mines and if they had gold mines, then surely they had hordes of golden treasure, just waiting to be found.

Benicio studied the fork's elegant surface, amazed that the people of this distant land should fashion cutlery so similar to the cutlery of Spain. He rubbed his hungry belly. If only he had a bit of chorizo to eat with it.

It would be the second day in a row he had gone without food, though at least he had the fresh water of the pool to drink. He crouched on the rock and lifted several handfuls to his lips. It tasted good. Sweet, even. What a strange, remarkable place this was. It was as if a giant had shoved his spade into earth and created a massive well from which to drink at his whim.

Benicio wished he was a giant now, for only a giant could scale the high, sheer walls. Instead he was merely a man relying on the goodness of a woman who had twice betrayed him.

Even now he could not say for sure why he had shown her the map. It had been a foolish decision, though in the moment it was all he could think of to do. When he had sat down beside her, a strange, lusty rage had scorched through his body and the distraction of words and puzzles was the only thing he could think of to extinguish it.

Incredibly, his strategy had worked. She had not only understood the word he spoke—*taak'in*—she had recognised the place depicted on the blood-stained cloth. Tenochtitlan, she had called it, but with a more elegant, staccato trill of tongue. He wondered where the place was, or what it was, and how much gold it might contain. He only prayed that she would return to rescue him, so that he might have the opportunity to seek it for himself.

But why should she return, really? Unless it was to rob him for a third time. Though surely he had earned some small bit of her goodwill. He had not once touched her, not even while she was kissing him with those lovely, soft lips. He had wanted very badly to kiss her back in that moment. Indeed, he had wanted to do more than that.

He was so very glad that he had managed to remain a gentleman. After the two long years he had spent crossing seas and plying through jungles, it was good to know that he retained at least some measure of self-control.

He could not say the same for his countrymen, many of whom ravished the island women at will. And they did not stop at that.

Indeed, when Benicio had arrived on the Island of Hispañola, he had been shocked to discover a land of misery, not prosperity. The Spanish settlers had cleared much of the island for plantations and had enslaved the native Taino people to work in hot fields and dangerous mines. On both Cuba and Hispañola, the Taino were dying in great numbers through hunger and overwork. And now, as the pustules of smallpox had begun to colonise the native people's skins, the Spaniards were simply replacing them with slaves from distant lands.

Cortés's expedition to this new island—the Island of Yucatan it was called—had been Benicio's last hope. The short, exuberant young captain had solicited men for a mission of trade and exploration, or so he had claimed. To Benicio, Cortés had seemed harmless—a typical Spanish *picaro* who lived by his wits, not his blades. And that was well, for Benicio wished only to explore and trade and perhaps find a little gold to bring home to his lady love.

And now, despite everything, Benicio might actually have that chance.

He stared at the ring, remembering the evening he had kissed Luisa and asked for her hand in marriage. Their mothers, who were old friends, had been hosting the Feast of the Epiphany celebration at Luisa's family's estate. It had been just after sundown and their mothers had been busy welcoming their arriving guests. Sensing an opportunity, Benicio had whisked Luisa into his arms and carried her to an upstairs bedroom, where he had swept her out on to a balcony overlooking her family's estate.

'Benicio, you villain!' she had exclaimed, breathless and overcome with laughter. 'It is forbidden for us to be in a bedchamber together.'

'Since when?' asked Benicio playfully.

'Since we were about fifteen,' said Luisa, placing her hands upon her womanly hips.

'But we are not inside a bedchamber, my *bella dama*. We are upon a balcony. We have merely come to admire the view.' Benicio had gestured grandly at the darkening sky.

Luisa pursed her pink lips. 'Have we, now? Well, let us admire it quickly then, for my mother will soon find me missing and she will not stop until she has discovered me.'

'Do not worry,' said Benicio, sliding his hand behind her neck. 'This will not take long.'

He had kissed her then. He had placed his lips upon hers and let a lifetime of yearning pour out of him. All the teasing games they had played as children; all that poking and prodding and pulling; all that restless boyhood lust—he rolled it up into a giant ball and threw it her way.

And to his surprise, she had caught it. She had opened her irresistible lips and met his ardour with her own. They had kissed and caressed each other until the sky had filled with stars and they were breathless once again. Luisa stood to leave.

'Do not go,' Benicio whispered.

'My mother is surely looking for me now.'

'But we have not achieved our purpose.'

Luisa frowned.

'To appreciate the view.'

Benicio had gestured skywards, then turned to marvel at the night sky himself. It was the only thing he loved as much as Luisa. Well, almost as much. When he returned his gaze to Luisa, he had found that she was watching him, not the stars. It was then he realised that he had done it. He had somehow captured the heart of the most beguiling maid in all Seville.

He had taken her hands in his. 'Marry me,' he had said on impulse, before the moment could pass. 'Marry me, Luisa, and make me the happiest man in the universe.'

Luisa had stared at him with eyes as big as planets.

Then the chamber door had swung open. 'Luisa, are you in here?'

She pulled her hands from his. 'Here, Mother!' she said and rushed into the chamber. 'I was just on the balcony. Benicio was showing me the wonders of the night sky.'

And the rest, as the bards always said, was history.

Now Benicio wondered if she waited for him still. He tried to imagine her suitors—men of means and station who could offer Luisa the kind of life she expected and deserved. Benicio was nothing compared to such men and yet she had promised Benicio that she would wait for him as long as she could.

It had been over two years since they had parted and he had received only a single letter from her. He pulled it from the pages of his book now, though he had long ago committed it to memory.

Dear Benicio,
It has been a year since you departed and I think about you every day. Are you succeeding in your endeavour?

It is more important than ever that I marry well. The courts have ruled against my father and our latifundia *is greatly diminished. We have had to sell many of our horses and our servants are reduced to twenty. Needless to say, my dowry is a pittance and the wealthiest of my suitors are withdrawing their suits. All the while I have waited for you to return.*

I cannot wait much longer. I lose my maid's bloom. I must marry soon.

Benicio, make haste.
With all my love,
Luisa
March, 1518

Benicio's pulse quickened, as it always did when he read those words of yearning. He had sent her several letters in response, assuring her that he would fulfil his promise, professing his undying love. But letters from the West Indies often perished on their journeys and he feared his words of love had long since sunk to the bottom of the sea.

He stared up at the sky once again, searching for Venus, as if that distant planet might provide him with some news, or, if not news, then solace for his restless heart.

But already the planet was out of view—disappeared below the horizon, much like his enchantress thief. Benicio smiled wryly. Where did she go, that tiny goddess of beauty and treachery? What did she do with herself in the small hours, when all the world slept?

According to the ancient astronomer Ptolemy, Venus spun in its own orbit, which, in turn, spun around the Earth. But a Polish man by the name of Copernicus had lately begun to question that notion. He had circulated secret papers suggesting that Venus spun not around the Earth, but around the Sun. Venus was not a child of Earth, Copernicus argued, but one of her sisters.

The idea was astounding, especially when considered from the depths of a cenote on the far side of the world. To think that the Earth was not the centre of the universe, but just another planet, small and forgettable in vastness of space.

He thought of the woman's eyes and his stomach briefly clenched. They were so dark and deep—like two patches of night sky. Beautiful and impossible to know.

Would she return for him? He had only the hope inside his heart and the strange notion that their fates were intertwined, as two planets revolving around the same sun.

Chapter Eight

A familiar voice whispered into Tula's ear. 'If you don't wake up soon, I will be forced to drink this delicious chocolate beverage myself.'

Tula heard a long, loud slurp. She opened her eyes.

'Aha! I knew that would wake you,' said Tula's younger sister Xanca, smiling wickedly. She held the cup of chocolate out to Tula, then pulled it away. 'It is the final cup.'

Tula looked towards the kitchen. The light of midmorning was shining through the open window and a pot stained with honey and filled with spent vanilla pods sat empty in the hearth. Tula thought of the bearded man and felt her heartbeat quicken. He had probably already begun to shout for aid. She had to get back to him. Soon.

'Are you not going to try to stop me?' Xanca asked, tilting the cup of chocolate to her lips.

'Indeed I am,' cried Tula, jumping to her feet, 'for I

am your elder and am required to drink before you.'
She plucked the cup from Xanca's hands.

'It is not the eldest who must drink the chocolate
first, but the wisest,' reasoned Xanca, 'and that, of
course, is me.'

'If you are wise, then I am an overripe *guayaba*,'
said Tula, laughing. She drank a long, delicious
draught. 'Though I admit that you do make delicious chocolate.'

'You have been asleep all morning.' Xanca pouted.
'Why did you return so late last night? And where
is your basket? Did you catch any fish?'

'So many questions!' exclaimed Tula. She glanced
at her older sister Pulhko. As always, she sat in the
corner of the room, strapped into her loom, weaving in a kind of trance.

'Do you want a sip of chocolate, Pulhko?' Tula
called.

She did not expect an answer. Still, her older sister's silence made Tula's heart ache. 'Where is Father?' Tula asked Xanca.

'He spoke of an urgent meeting among the Council
of Elders—something about a battle at Potonchan.'

'Potonchan? That is in the south, is it not? A Maya
town?'

Xanca removed the cup from Tula's hands. 'I have
been too busy doing your weaving to think about it.'

Tula thought about the bearded men—how they had burst without warning from the depths of the jungle. They had come from the south.

'Well?' asked Xanca, sighing heavily.

'Well, clearly I must repay you for all of your help,' said Tula, 'so I shall tell you about my adventure.' Tula dived into her tale of danger and discovery, describing the talismanic jaguar fish, the great temple of treasure beneath the sea and the vision of the pole flyers that had saved her life.

'You are raving. You must be struck with the dreaming sickness…or the sickness of love.'

'Love of treasure!' exclaimed Tula. 'Of course, you must not tell anyone about this.'

'Of course not,' said Xanca, though Tula could see by the tilt of her younger sister's frown that she was practically bursting with the news. Xanca excused herself into the next room and after a short time emerged dressed in a red embroidered skirt and matching shawl.

'Where are you going in such finery?'

'Nowhere. To the *tlachtli* court. I am to meet Xanata there. The teams are practising for the Festival of Tlaloc. Xanata's husband is the Tlachtli Master now, you know,' Xanca said. 'Her brother, Anan, is one of the best defenders.'

Tula eyed Xanca. 'Why the sudden interest in ball sport?'

Xanca's cheeks took on a colour remarkably similar to that of her skirt. 'I've always enjoyed the game,' she said. 'Where is the fish?' Xanca asked Tula, cleverly changing the subject.

'What fish?'

'The fine jaguar fish that you said you caught yesterday. I can prepare it for our dinner.'

'Ah! *That* fish!' Tula exclaimed a little too loudly. 'I left it in a…small cenote outside of Cempoala.' Tula consoled herself that in essence she spoke truth. Still, she needed to change the subject.

'Why do you wear Mother's labret?' Tula asked suddenly, studying Xanca's lower lip. It was as if the house had suddenly become a *tlachtli* ball court and they were deep in a volley.

Xanca fondled the small jade lip ornament. 'No reason,' said Xanca. 'It looks well with my red skirt.'

'Who is the one struck with the sickness of love, I wonder?'

Xanca's eyes sparkled with the delight of a secret. 'I am simply going to spend a few hours with my friends. I will be home before Father and probably before you, too. Your fish sounds monstrous.'

Before Tula could respond, Xanca had exited

through the thatched doorway in a whoosh of youth and red cotton.

A suffocating silence settled upon the room in her absence. Surely Pulhko had heard everything, but as usual she said not a word. 'She will have to present the young man to us,' Tula reflected. 'No marriage can take place without the approval of kin—both his and hers.' Tula watched as Pulhko looped her shuttle with a dull brown thread, her ears unhearing, her sunken eyes bereft of life.

'I am going to fetch my fish now,' Tula announced. She peered out of the front window. The Sun God was at the height of his triumph and would provide her with plenty of light to find the cenote, rescue the man and steal his treasure. With the gods on her side, she would return home in time for the evening meal.

'Until later, Pulhko,' she muttered, and stepped out on to the porch. Cempoala's central plaza spread before her like a mural. Women in colourful dresses flitted about the open space like birds, trading goods and gossip with the merchants, whose baskets overflowed with the offerings of the jungle and the fields.

It seemed so eternal and unchanging—as if she might always be able to rely on this radiant scene. Above it all loomed the Great Temple, its slanted walls gleaming white, its flat shaded apex swarming with priests. The venerable old men did their own kind of trading, burning copal incense and making the sacrifices necessary to keep Cempoala's debt to the gods paid.

As a Council Elder, their father was also tasked with Cempoala's safekeeping, though not from the wrath of the gods. He had been granted one of the dozens of stone homes around the plaza so that he, like the other elders and priests, could keep close watch over their city. When he wasn't hunting birds or training soldiers, Tula's father was sitting here, on the porch of their home, ever vigilant.

Tula and Xanca would often join him here, for there was nothing more pleasurable than to watch the daily parade of Cempoala's tens of thousands of vibrant souls.

Pulhko was the only one who never came to the porch. Since her family had been taken, she had not allowed the Sun God to caress her face. Now, as Tula gazed upon the well-worn wooden bench where she, Xanca and her father always sat, it occurred to her what a short distance there was between joy and sorrow. Sometimes only a few paces.

'Tamales,' called a passing woman, carrying a tray full of the delicious corn cakes. Tula hailed the woman with a fistful of cacao beans and soon held a warm tamale inside her pocket.

She was far too nervous to be hungry herself, but Tula guessed that the man would be famished. It was a silly notion, now that she thought about it—to rescue him from the cenote and then hand him a tamale. But perhaps it would endear her to him in some way and he would let her kiss him again. Then she could surely sneak her finger back into his pocket.

Of course, the correct thing to do would be to present the matter to her father. The bearded man was a stranger who had invaded Totonac territory and by law he should be brought before the Council Elders and the Chief. Like any high-born prisoner taken in battle, he could then explain to the Totonac leaders why they should not make him a slave.

But Tula had not taken him in battle. Unless their chase through the jungle had been a battle, in which case she had certainly lost.

Tula arrived at the large maize field where he had outwitted her. The thought of seeing him again gave her energy and she found that she had broken into a trot. Soon, she was peering over the rim of the same cenote into which she'd fallen just a dozen hours before.

'Cristo!' she called, her heart beating with excitement. There was no answer, nor any movement in the water below. She waited for several moments, then said the word again. Nothing. She sat down beside the well, overcome with disappointment.

Finally, a voice echoed softly from below. 'Tenochit-lan,' it whispered.

Chapter Nine

He felt his heart begin to thrum as he saw her peer over the cenote's edge. 'Tenoch-tit-lan,' she corrected, and her chiding voice echoed in the chasm like music.

She demonstrated the long rope she carried, then disappeared from view. He could hardly believe she was real. He wanted to jump and shout with joy. He wanted to burst out of the infernal pit and kiss her, his little saviour, though he reminded himself that he was not saved yet. There could be an army of painted warriors behind her, just waiting to take his map and steal his golden ring and finish Benicio for ever.

Somehow he doubted it. She did not seem like the kind of woman who liked to share. Then he laughed to himself. Of course she had returned for him—it was suddenly so clear. She wished to take the ring for herself once again. Benicio shook his head. How had he not seen it? He had spent the entire night worried that she would never return for him, forgetting that he held something she found valuable enough to risk her life to obtain.

In minutes she returned and tossed the rope over the edge. It was thick and fibrous and resembled the ropes used for rigging Spanish ships. Benicio gripped the familiar rope in his hands and gave several test tugs. He was preparing to begin his ascent when he heard a sudden rustling in the trees. A colourful bird had jumped down and perched itself at the edge of the cenote across from the woman. The bird had a brilliant red chest, which he dipped and bobbed, as if heralding her somehow.

At length, the bird turned towards the jungle and its two long, thin tail feathers descended into the cenote. As long as Benicio's legs, the two feathers twisted loosely around each other in a dance of vivid green and blue. Benicio could not help but marvel at their beauty and he remembered that the Maya priest had worn such feathers in his headdress.

The bird was probably sacred and he imagined quite valuable. He did not blame the woman for her obvious enchantment with it. She signalled for Benicio to wait, then approached the bird. It fluttered its wings just enough to propel itself somewhere beyond the edge of the cenote.

The woman stepped out of view. Sensing an opportunity, Benicio began to climb up the rope. If she was far enough away when he reached the top, he could easily sneak away from her. Then he would have a decision to make: to return to Spain with his diamond prize, or to seek her help in learning the location of the enigmatic Tenochtitlan.

He was not a quarter of the way up the rope when he heard the voices.

Chapter Ten

The quetzal bird fluttered out of Tula's reach. She did not wish to harm it—only to pluck its long tail feathers, which were worth a small fortune. They would grow back soon enough and the creature would be not be harmed.

But this quetzal knew how not to be caught. It shuttled from tree to tree, staying just ahead of her, as if it wished for her to follow. She stepped carefully through the dense underbrush, marvelling at the bird's fearlessness, until it fluttered to a high branch and abruptly ceased to move. Tula stopped, as well.

Something was wrong. There was something unnatural in the breeze—a vaguely foul scent that wafted into Tula's nose like a warning. Instinctively, she dropped to the ground, concealing herself behind a fallen trunk.

There was a man standing at the cenote's rim—

not the bearded man she was trying to rescue, but a man wearing a black cape that stretched the length of his body. Tula could smell his matted locks of hair, even from her hiding place, and she knew that they were caked with blood. She beheld a Mexica priest.

Another man joined the priest at the edge of the cenote. He wore a colourful, embroidered cape that hung in long strips against his gilded loincloth. The man held a yellow flower to his nose to indicate his nobility, though it was not the flower that caught Tula's attention. It was the colour of the man's slick, tightly bound hair. Black.

The man was a Mexica Tribute Taker.

Tula felt her body begin to tremble. A Taker and a Mexica priest, travelling together. What bloody mission were they on? She prayed that the bearded man had been clever enough to conceal himself on the shadowy side of the pool. If he had not, then he was surely doomed.

The Taker studied the rope that Tula had dropped into the cenote. He appeared fascinated by its thickly woven fibres and peered curiously into the depths where it led. Meanwhile, several dozen Mexica warriors surrounded the cenote, their thick, obsidian clubs glinting menacingly in the dappled light.

Tula could not stop trembling. A dead leaf cracked

beneath her foot and she watched the fern in front of her flutter against her heavy breaths. She needed to stay calm. She could not allow herself to be discovered.

She heard the victim's soft whimpers before he came into view. He was a young Totonac man who could not have seen more than four and ten years. He struggled with his four warrior escorts, writhing and twisting in vain against their merciless grips.

A slave lit a brazier and placed it in the priest's hands. The priest held the copper pan above his head. Its coals made eerie ribbons of smoke that wove slowly towards the sky. 'Like a painting we will be erased,' the priest intoned. 'Like a flower, we will dry up. Like the plumed vestments of the precious bird, that precious bird with the agile neck, we will come to an end. We give you this gift, Great Huitzilopochtli, God of the Sun and War, Guardian of Tenochtitlan, that you may keep this world another day.'

The warriors brought the young man to the edge of the cenote and laid him down on his back, his neck stretched out beyond the rim. The priest placed the brazier upon the ground and pulled a long obsidian knife from beneath his robe. He held it out over the young man's neck, chanting incomprehensibly.

Sacrifice was necessary, Tula understood that.

There had been Four Worlds before this one—all destroyed by dissatisfied gods. To keep this world—the Fifth World—alive, the gods needed to be fed and kept satisfied. That was the purpose of war, after all—to take prisoners who could be used to feed the gods. Tula doubted that this young man was a prisoner of war, however. He appeared to be a simple farmer. And he was far too young to die.

Now the young man screamed as the priest raised his knife to his throat. 'We give you this sustenance, God of the Sun and War, protector of the floating city,' the priest said.

Suddenly, a deep, bellowing voice emerged from the depths. 'No!'

The priest dropped his knife in terror. It fell into the cenote without a splash. The throng of mighty warriors jumped back from the edge of the chasm.

'Stop!' boomed the voice from below.

The men gaped in fear. Several dropped to their knees and kissed the ground, clearly believing they had just been addressed by a god. An angry one.

Moments later, Tula watched in amazement as the bearded man climbed out of the cenote, his large arm muscles flexing as he deftly ascended the rope she had secured for him. The warriors gasped in horror as the towering spirit stepped before them, the priest's fallen blade clenched between his teeth.

To Tula, he was magnificent. His pants clung to the muscles of his legs, which seemed to flex unbidden, and his massive chest heaved with his breaths, threatening to break his animal-hide vest. He surveyed the company without any sign of fear, then plucked the blade from the grip of his jaws and held it in his hand.

The Tribute Taker stepped forward. 'Bearded god,' he began in Nahuatl. 'I know that you travel with Captain Cortés. I have visited your captain and brought him gifts from my city, Tenochtitlan.'

'Captain Cortés?' asked the man in confusion. 'Tenoch-it-lan?'

'I am an emissary of Montezuma, the ruler of the Mexica,' said the Taker more slowly. 'We have welcomed your captain and bestowed upon him many gifts. Now we ask that you take your floating temples and go home.'

The bearded man stood silent, his long beard concealing his expression. At length, the Taker spoke again. 'Allow us to escort you back to your brethren.'

Tula could see that the bearded man understood none of what had been said. Surely the Taker could see it, too, though he did not seem to care. It was as if he were reading some obligatory passage from a scroll. Still, beneath the Taker's placid gaze Tula read a clear command. *Leave this land.*

The Taker turned to the four warriors who had restrained the boy and bade them rise. 'The gods have decided to spare this fortunate young man,' he said. He released the young man, who gave a confused yelp and darted off into the forest. 'Accompany the bearded one to the camp of the bearded ones. Tell Captain Cortés that he is yet another gift from the Great Montezuma, who urges him to return home.'

The warriors eyed the bearded one warily, as they might watch a capture jaguar. The Taker motioned for four additional warriors to join them. Soon eight Mexica warriors had surrounded the bearded man and the group started southward.

Tula crouched low as they walked past her, holding her breath. 'Tenoch-it-lan,' the bearded man uttered as they passed, and she knew it was a message meant only for her ears. 'Tenoch-it-lan.'

Tula stayed behind the log until long after the deadly entourage had departed. She stared out into the shady jungle in a kind of stupor. If the quetzal bird had not come when it did, if it had not led her away from the cenote, she would have surely been caught by the Tribute Takers and become a gift to the Sun God herself.

She touched her skirt and was surprised to discover the small bulge of the tamale she had purchased, still inside her pocket. She placed it atop the log, a meagre offering to the beautiful bird that had saved her life.

She thought of the bearded man who had distracted the Taker and frightened the warriors. If he had not emerged from the cenote when he did, one of the warriors might still have spied her. She touched her shaking fingers on the ground and then placed them on her lips. 'I am humble,' she murmured in gratitude, and she noticed that even her voice was trembling.

It was already dark when she arrived home. A small fire burned in the brazier on the floor of her house. Its low light cast grim shadows on the walls and for the first time in her three and twenty years, Tula found herself wishing there were more light.

'Thank the gods!' Tula's father shouted as she collapsed upon her mat. 'What delayed you?'

'A Tribute Taker.'

Her father gasped. 'What?'

'He was travelling with a Mexica priest and many warriors. They visited a cenote not far from the largest maize field.'

'To make a sacrifice?'

'Yes,' Tula said. *Almost.*

Her father shook his head in anger. 'They took two Totonac children only a moon ago.' Pulhko stopped her weaving and stared blankly at her strings. 'How many warriors did you count?' her father asked.

'Two dozen or more. I hid from them behind a log. Where is Xanca?'

'In which direction did they travel?' urged her father.

'They marched north-west, towards the maize and cotton fields,' Tula answered. 'Where is Xanca?'

'What lies between Cempoala and the cotton fields heading north-west?' asked her father, ignoring her question.

'I do not know. The aqueduct. The practice *tlachtli* court.' The words caught in Tula's mouth. *Tlachtli* court. She felt the world begin to spin. 'Where is Xanca?'

'She is not yet returned,' said her father. 'I thought she was with you.'

'No, no, no,' said Tula, feeling sick.

For the first time in many years, Pulhko turned to face her family. Her eyes were swimming in a sea of tears.

'What is it, Pulkho?' asked her father, his voice rising in panic. 'What is the matter?'

Pulkho was shaking her head. She buried her face in her hands. 'What is it, Tula? What is wrong?'

Tula could hardly speak. 'Xanca is there tonight, Father,' she whispered. 'Xanca is at the *tlachtli* court!'

Chapter Eleven

Poisoned darts. Tula slipped into the garden and dug up her stash of them, which she had reserved for an emergency such as this. She placed them in a basket along with her spitting straw, wishing she had not abandoned her atlatl and arrows at the beach.

No matter. She could use her father's atlatl and arrows. Even better, she could fashion new weapons on the road, but she needed to get going. She pushed back the deer-hide drape and peered out the front window.

She and her father had rushed to the *tlachtli* court in the darkness of the previous night. It had taken them a very long time, for there had been no moon to light their way, and by the time they had reached the oblong stone ring there was not a soul within it. Tula noticed a long pathway of dirt loosened by footprints—evidence of the Taker's line of captives.

As the news spread of the mass abduction that

morning, many people had gathered in the plaza, including mothers and fathers of the taken. The grieving parents had prostrated themselves before the Great Temple, praying to the God of Destiny for aid. Praying for justice.

Tula did not have time to pray. She knew now that the Taker, the priest, and the troupe of warriors she had witnessed at the cenote had continued on to the *tlachtli* court. They had barred the exits of the wall-encircled field and enslaved all the young men and women present within it, including Xanca. Their quarry in hand, the evil company had simply lit their torches and slipped away into the night.

Tula did not have to ask her father the direction in which they travelled. She already knew. They journeyed west, towards Tenochtitlan.

Towards their deaths.

In only five cycles of the moon, Xanca and the dozens of other young souls who had been taken would be standing in a line atop the sacred double temple of Tenochtitlan, while thousands upon thousands of Mexica citizens watched from the plaza below. Soon, Xanca's turn would come and her fattened body would be stretched out across the sacred table and held in place by priests wearing golden masks. A priest would step forward and lift the black-stone blade high above her sister's heart.

Tula's stomach twisted into a knot. She would not allow that to happen. If she had to sacrifice her own life to do it, she would spare her sister that terrible fate. She did not care how hungry the gods were, or how soon the Fifth World would end. She would not allow the Mexica to take another drop of her family's blood.

Flint arrows. Tula would need many of those as well. They were better than obsidian arrows—less likely to break and quicker to penetrate the flesh. She plunged her hand into the dishful that her father kept on the table beside the door.

Tula tucked her warmest wool wrap into her basket. Even the priests had to rest some time, and she knew, if she ran fast, she would overtake the caravan of captives soon enough. But she had to leave now. She rushed towards the door. Her father caught her by the arm.

'Stop, Tula, you know not what you do.'

'I have never in my life known it better, Father,' Tula said. She would not sit idly by while her father and the other Council members allowed this to happen. And she would not end up like Pulkho, lifeless and ruined by loss.

No, Tula would fight.

'The Takers travel with Montezuma's Guard,' her father said, taking her arm. 'They would kill you before you could even get close. To attempt to rescue Xanca alone is beyond foolish.'

'It is the only thing I can do,' Tula said, feeling tears of helplessness gather in her eyes. 'Please Father, let me go.'

'I will not lose another daughter!' he shouted. He unhanded Tula's arm and calmed himself. 'We shall save Xanca,' he explained, 'but with thoughtful action, not suicide.'

'But how?' asked Tula.

Her father took a deep breath. 'Five hundred bearded gods have arrived on the coast. They have already received emissaries of Montezuma.'

Tula did her best to seem surprised. 'Bearded gods?'

Her father nodded gravely. 'Montezuma wishes to win their alliance, I fear.'

'Does he succeed? Have the bearded ones allied with Montezuma?'

'Not yet and I believe we can prevent it,' explained her father. 'One of our Totonac spies avowed that they do not love the Mexica. Nor do they love the Maya. They defeated a force of over ten thousand Maya at Potonchan.'

Tula nodded, trying to appear surprised. She had been right. The bearded men she had discovered on the beach had indeed come from Maya territory to the south. The two men were not random explorers, but part of a much larger foreign army.

'The Totonac Council of Elders seek to win the bearded ones' alliance,' her father continued. 'Early this morning, Cempoala and the other Totonac cities sent representatives to greet them and deliver turkeys and maize cakes.'

Tula felt the needle of guilt prick at her mind. 'Father, I have to tell you something, I—'

'It is our only chance, Tula. We must ally with the bearded ones if we have any hope of saving Cempoala's sons and daughters from the Mexica. I shall not argue with you further.'

'I do not wish to argue, Father. I wish to tell you that I—'

Before Tula could finish, a rumbling sound split the air, like the sound of thunder preceding a downpour of rain. Her father jumped to his feet. 'Stay here, both of you,' he commanded, grabbing his dagger and shield. 'Tula, ready your arrows,' he added. He disappeared out the door.

'But I do not have my arrows, Father,' Tula murmured to the closed door. 'I left them at the beach… where I kissed the bearded god and stole his golden ring.'

Slowly, Pulhko turned to Tula, her eyes as big as plates. It was the first time Pulhko had looked at Tula directly in over seven years. 'Pulhko?' Tula whispered, her heart filling with hope. Then—boom!

Tula rushed outside to behold an army of warriors marching into the central plaza of Cempoala. They were like no warriors Tula had ever seen. They were covered from head to toe in clanking iron shells and carried long, shining swords and metal sticks that spit fire.

At the head of the army, the men did not walk. They rode atop giant, hoofed beasts that resembled deer. 'Look at the centaurs!' cried one of Tula's neighbours, believing man and beast to be one. 'They have come from the Underworld!'

The terrifying animals bucked and reared, emitting high-pitched squeals that echoed across the plaza and into the minds of the awestruck Totonacs, many of whom cowered before them in fright.

But not all of the people cowered. Some Totonacs appeared delighted to see the soldiers. They jumped and cheered, welcoming the strange army, which came to a unified stop at the base of the Great Temple. Tula burst out of her back door and climbed up the stone foothold to the cement roof of her house. Standing before the giant deer, at the base of the Great Temple, was the Chief of Cempoala, along with all the members of the Council of Elders, including her own father.

The crowd of Cempoalans that had gathered around the plaza went quiet. The cicadas sang their ancient song and deep in the jungle Tula heard the agitated squawk of parrots. She searched the throng of warriors for an especially tall, muscular man with a crooked nose and eyes the colour of the sea. But the men's iron masks covered them completely and they all appeared alike.

One of them—whom Tula assumed to be their chief—jumped down from atop his beast and bowed before the group of Elders. The Totonac Chief was brought forward. He lay atop a giant litter, his body too abundant for him to walk on his own. His assistants lowered his litter and helped him stand and one of his servants placed a flower in his hand to indicate his noble status.

The strange iron-clad chief stepped forward to address the Totonac Chief. The stranger took off his helmet to reveal his cocoa-amber hair and matching beard. He made a very loud, grand statement in his language and held his hand out to the Chief.

Tula did not know what to make of the gesture. Did the bearded man wish for the Chief to place something inside his hand? Or was the Chief expected to hold out his own open hand in return?

The Chief did neither. He stared down at the iron chief's open hand for a long while, confused.

Appearing to strike upon some clever idea, the Totonac Chief lifted his massive arm and held out his flower to the iron chief. Tula waited on the roof-top, watching closely.

'Please,' she murmured. 'Take it.'

Chapter Twelve

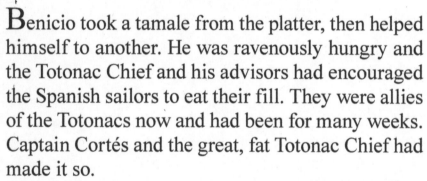

Benicio took a tamale from the platter, then helped himself to another. He was ravenously hungry and the Totonac Chief and his advisors had encouraged the Spanish sailors to eat their fill. They were allies of the Totonacs now and had been for many weeks. Captain Cortés and the great, fat Totonac Chief had made it so.

Benicio peered down the length of the wooden table at the other Spaniards who had been invited to the banquet—eight work-weary men spearing the guava and *zapote* fruits, reaching hungrily for the roasted turkey and tortoise meat, and swilling the exotic *cacao* beverage as if it were the finest wine.

At least he was not alone in his hunger. He reached for a papaya spear and let its sweetness fill his senses, remembering the day he had watched Luisa do the same. Since then, he could not seem to get enough of the delicious fruit. And after a long day labouring to construct the first building of their new colonial settlement, Villa Rica de la Vera Cruz, the papaya tasted especially sweet.

'Soon we will have a proper church,' Cortés was saying from the head of the table. 'A place to start converting these pagan heathens.' The Captain smiled politely across the table at the fat Chief, as if he had just paid him some gentle compliment.

If only the Chief knew the extent of Cortés's treachery. Just a few days before, Cortés had convinced the Totonacs to take five Mexica Tribute Takers prisoner. The Totonacs had protested at first, knowing that such an abduction would be perceived by Montezuma and the Mexica as an act of war. 'We shall triumph against the Mexica together,' Cortés had argued and finally persuaded them to do his bidding. The Totonacs had seized the Takers and imprisoned them.

The next night, under cover of darkness, Cortés freed the captured Takers and gave them a message for Emperor Montezuma: *Captain Cortés has freed us from the Totonac traitors. Cortés is still our friend.*

It was a brilliant ploy, for Cortés had demonstrated his commitment to the Totonac rebellion while remaining in the good graces of Montezuma. Benicio could only hope that Cortés had engineered such a betrayal in order to avoid sending the Spanish sailors to war.

He bit into another papaya spear, but it had lost its sweetness. What on earth was he doing here? He had his diamond prize. Why did he not simply abandon this company of devils?

Benicio watched several young women walk up and down the length of the banquet table, refilling the men's water goblets, replenishing foods, and clearing plates. Unlike many of his compatriots, Benicio took care not to leer at the comely young Totonac maidens. Still, he found himself searching their faces, hoping to find his thief among them.

She was why he stayed—or rather, the knowledge she carried. She was one of two other people in the world—himself and Rogelio—who had seen the treasure map. But she was more fortunate than both Rogelio and Benicio combined, because she recognised the configuration that had been depicted on that thin swatch of cloth. 'Tenochtitlan,' she had said.

She knew where the treasure was hidden.

Demonios. She was probably already camped outside the Mexica capital city with her husband or lover, making some daring plan to extract the treasure. He might have believed any other woman incapable of such boldness, but this woman was different. She was the kind of woman who would steal the gold right out of a man's mouth.

He had been a fool to show her the map. Why, then, had he done it? Perhaps he sensed in her some deep curiosity—the kind required to solve puzzles. It had certainly taken her little time to solve his.

Tenochtitlan. Her big eyes had flashed as the difficult name flitted off her tongue. She had slanted him a knowing grin, as if she also knew exactly which parts of the Mexica capital city were being depicted. He had managed to take back his ring from her, yes, but he had given her something infinitely more valuable: his secret.

'Would you pass the *octli*, friend?' asked Rogelio, his voice syrupy sweet. He had taken the seat beside Benicio and little wonder. After Benicio had rejoined Cortés's company, Rogelio had become like a fly Benicio could not manage to swat away. He hovered near Benicio always, studying him, as if any moment Benicio might reveal where he had hidden the priest's precious ring. Benicio placed the pitcher of *octli* squarely before Rogelio, but did not offer to pour. Rogelio made a scolding sound, then poured most of the alcoholic liquid into his cup. He swilled it down in a single draught and let out a long, satisfied belch. A young Totonac woman ambled over to refill the pitcher, but before she could complete her task, Rogelio had pulled her on to his lap.

The woman smiled tightly, trying to appear friendly, while he groped clumsily at her breasts. Encouraged by several of the other men, Rogelio held the pitcher to the young woman's mouth and forced her to swallow a long draught of the milky beverage.

Benicio cringed. The men knew that the ceremonial drink was reserved for Totonac elders, priests and honoured guests. Women were only allowed to consume *octli* on feast days and on special occasions like weddings. The young woman's forced draught was followed by a fit of coughs. Before she could catch her breath, Rogelio kissed her violently.

'Stop it, *idiota*!' snarled Benicio. 'You harm her.'
' Rogelio grinned crookedly, continuing to grope, then released her to a cacophony of cheers.

The Totonac Chief had asked Cortés to invite his eight 'most deserving' men to this banquet. Instead of his highest-ranking officers, however, Cortés had chosen this motley crew, which included Rogelio and several other ruffians who tended to cause chaos in the ranks. Cortés had also invited a few men like Benicio, who were well respected but known to disagree with Cortés's methods.

That was Cortés's genius, thought Benicio. He had

invited the biggest troublemakers and the likeliest mutineers to be placated by the hospitality of others.

Now Cortés stood to address his host. 'I would like to thank Chief Tlacochcalcatl of the mighty nation of the Totonacs for his generous hospitality,' began Cortés.

On his left, a Spanish priest by the name of Aguilar jumped to his feet. Aguilar and a man named Guerrero had been shipwrecked in Maya territory long ago. When he had heard of Cortés's arrival on the coast, Aguilar had sought him. Guerrero, however, would not come. Amazingly, he had found a Maya wife and an adoptive tribe and was making a family somewhere deep in the jungle.

Now Aguilar translated Cortés's words into Maya, then nodded to a beautiful native woman called Malinali, who translated his Maya words into Nahuatl.

The chain of translation complete, the Totonac Chief nodded in understanding.

It was a slow tedious process, and the Totonac councilmen seated near Cortés passed a tobacco pipe between them. A small dog hovered in the doorway, its eager tail thumping the ground. Outside, Benicio heard the shrieks of monkeys accompanied by a symphony of birds. He smelled flowers on the warm breeze. For a suspended moment, he entertained an unfamiliar feeling of contentment. He imagined that he was Guerrero and that this rich, colourful new world had everything he needed.

Cortés continued, 'As you know, venerable Chief, my men and I suffer from a peculiar disease of the heart.'

As the translated words reached the Chief's ears, he lifted his chin in interest.

'It is a disease,' Cortés continued, 'that can only be cured with gold.'

The Chief sighed. 'We are aware of the Spaniards' interest in that rare metal,' the Chief responded gruffly, for he had been conspicuously unable to supply the Spanish with much of it.

'We have received many gifts of gold from your overlord Montezuma,' said Cortés, 'and have heard of the wealth of the Mexica capital. We are aggrieved, however, that Montezuma and the Mexica keep our friends the Totonacs as vassals. Therefore, we shall rest ourselves until such time as we have recovered our strength for a march with the Totonacs on Tenochtitlan.'

Benicio sat up. Had he heard correctly? Cortés meant to march on Tenochtitlan? Benicio's heart began to beat, though he told himself that it could be another bluff. Montezuma's emissaries had paid Cortés handsomely to return to Cuba. Did Cortés really mean to march into the heart of the Mexican Empire?

'The Totonacs are grateful for the friendship of the Spaniards,' said the Totonac Chief. 'And we welcome their aid in overcoming our Mexica oppressors. But we urge Captain Cortés to act more quickly. The Mexica have taken forty of our young nobles to Tenochtitlan for sacrifice. We entreat the Spaniards to join with us now on a mission to get them back.'

Cortés smiled even before the Chief's words had been completely translated. It was as if he had planted his own intentions inside the fat chief's mind.

Benicio did not know how to feel. It seemed that his fondest wish had just come true. The Spanish company would march to Tenochtitlan, where the map showed his golden treasure was buried. But Cortés's intentions remained unclear. Did he plan to demand justice for the Totonacs, or did he have some other end in mind?

'Are there others who will join us against the Mexica?' Cortés asked.

'The Tlaxcalans of the high mountains will surely join us,' said the Chief. 'They have never succumbed to the Mexica, though they live only a two days' journey from the capital.'

'The Tlaxcalans, eh?' said Cortés. 'Can you guarantee their support?'

The Chief hesitated. 'I cannot. But we the Totonacs shall support you in any way we can. And to encourage your quick action, I wish to bestow upon you the most precious gifts that the Totonacs have to give. Let them be a symbol of the alliance between our peoples. Let them inspire you to our cause.'

Chapter Thirteen

Tula's father took Tula's hand and kissed it. 'It is the only way,' he said.

They were standing behind a wall in the Chief's banquet hall and had been told to keep their voices low. On the other side of the wall, Chief Tlacochcalcatl and many members of the Chief's council were taking food with Captain Cortés and a selection of his men—the Totonacs' new allies.

'But I am made to hunt and to fight, not to lie in a stranger's bed,' Tula whispered, still believing she might convince her father to let her go. 'There are other ways to save Xanca,' she reasoned. 'Why do we not try to rescue her ourselves?'

Tula felt as if she were stuck in the bottom of a cenote once again. This time, there was no way out.

'Every Chief, former Chief and Council Elder was asked to contribute, without exception. You and these seven other women represent the best we have to give.'

'But you are my father! Why do you ask this of me?' It was an unfair question. Tula knew that her father did not have a choice. Still, tears of bitterness streamed down her face. After so many years of resisting her father's urgings to find a mate, she had finally got her wish. Now Tula would never be anyone's wife, for she was about to become a very particular kind of slave.

'Try to obey him,' her father choked. He had not raised Tula to serve any master, yet he was sending her to live with a man who would likely treat her like a servant. 'These bearded men are our partners now. With their help, we shall finally rise from beneath the heel of the Mexica.'

'I will do my duty,' Tula whispered, 'but only until I reach Tenochtitlan. Then I will rescue Xanca and bring her home, or die trying.'

Tula looked around the crowded anteroom. Dozens of high-born mothers and fathers were speaking to their daughters in hushed voices, saying much the same things. Over the past few weeks, the Totonacs had forged an alliance with the bearded strangers— Spaniards, they called themselves. The Totonacs had given the Spaniards slaves and food and even land north of the city. In exchange, their leader, Captain

Cortés, had agreed to join forces with the Totonacs to recapture their sons and daughters, and be free of the Mexica Takers for good.

It was a risk, but it was the Totonacs' only hope. They would give the Spaniards everything they could to help them overcome the Mexica, including hundreds of porters to aid in their trek to Tenochtitlan and an army of Totonac warriors that had been training in secret.

In addition, the Council Elders had resolved to give the bearded strangers their remaining highborn daughters.

Tula overheard the chief of a nearby village talking to his daughter urgently. 'You must attempt to get with child. It is the only way the alliance will stay strong,' he explained to her. The young woman's lip trembled as she stared at the ground, nodding.

Tula's own father knew better than to give her such advice. 'Keep your ears and eyes open in the floating city,' he said. 'Trust nobody. You will be glad for your knowledge of Nahuatl now.' Then he bent and whispered in her ear. 'I do not care how you accomplish it. Just bring Xanca back.'

One of the Elders clapped his hands together softly. 'It is time,' he said. 'Say your goodbyes.' There was a collective gasp as the young women fell into their loved ones' arms. 'Please order yourselves as instructed, beginning with red,' he commanded. 'Quickly now.'

Earlier that morning, the young women had been bathed in flower water and given their costumes, traditional long skirts and undershirts overlain by the fashionable triangular shawl worn throughout the land.

Each costume was a single, bold colour, one of the seven colours of the rainbow, and the Elders had distributed them based on which colour would look best on which young woman. The eighth costume was white and had been chosen for Tula. 'My dear, you are so radiant that you do not require any colour,' an Elder had whispered to her.

It was the first time in her life that Tula had ever been told such a thing. Flattery was discouraged in the Totonac world, for it served to distinguish people based on the unimportant standard of physical beauty. Still, his words filled Tula with gratitude, for she had worried that her new Spanish master might find her disagreeable and punish her for it.

Tula had stared into an obsidian mirror and puzzled over her face, which had always seemed plain to her when she saw it reflected so. Today it was unrecognizable. On the advice of the translator Malinali, Tula and the other young women had been painted to look like children's dolls. Tula's eyes had been lined with charcoal and then powdered white to match her dress. Her lips shone with a thick pollen dye the colour of a ripe tomato.

'It is how the bearded men prefer their women,' Malinali had explained and she had instructed all the women to remove their labrets.

Tula thought of Xanca and tried to stay strong. Still, she feared these hulking men from across the sea. Their Chief said that they came in peace, but they carried long swords and animals of war and strange iron ovens that belched fire. They numbered only a few hundred men, yet they swaggered about Cempoala as if the great city already belonged to them. If they did defeat the Mexica, Tula wondered, what then? Would they not simply become the Totonacs' new Tribute Takers?

Tula took a deep breath. All that mattered now was her sister. If she did not save Xanca, Pulhko would never recover, nor would her father. The alliance with the Spaniards was the only hope the Totonacs had to enter Tenochtitlan. Tula kissed her father and whispered in his ear, 'I will bring her back. I promise.' Then she placed herself at the end of the line and the eight young women were escorted through the door and towards their uncertain fates.

Chapter Fourteen

As the Totonac Chief concluded his speech, a door was opened and eight dazzlingly beautiful young women walked into the banquet hall, each dressed in a different colour of the rainbow. Several men gasped. The women had been painted in the Spanish style, with reddened lips and eyes coloured to match the hues of their dresses. As they found their positions before the table of Spaniards, the room seemed to light up with their presence.

But that was not the reason Benicio's heart skipped. Standing there, at the end of the line, was the woman from the beach. She was dressed all in white, beginning with her floor-length white skirt and blouse, and ending with a triangular-shaped shawl, through which he could trace her shape. Like the other women, she was bedecked in simple jewellery, including a lovely blue shell necklace that hung around her neck like drops from the sea. Her face had been painted to emphasise her almond eyes and generous, luxuriant lips.

When her gaze met Benicio's there was a flicker of recognition, but she quickly returned to her placid stare. Still, it seemed to Benicio that he did not look upon a young woman, but upon some timeless queen.

The Chief spoke grandly. 'By way of solidifying our bond, we give to you and your officers these high-born maidens that you may be fruitful.'

The men stared in rapt surprise. One man's copper goblet went clanking to the floor. They were being given these noble young women? As gifts?

Captain Leon leapt to his feet. He crossed to the closest maiden and took her by the hand. 'This one is mine,' he pronounced gruffly. A handful of other men moved to do the same, but Cortés stood and stopped them.

'You act like animals of the jungle,' Cortés hissed. He made a perfunctory smile at the Totonac Chief, then spoke firmly. 'These are high-born women and they will be treated with respect…at least, in this present company,' he muttered. 'We shall choose in order of rank.'

Diego de Ordaz stood next. A friend of the Governor of Cuba, Ordaz had openly criticised Cortés's ambition. Now Ordaz walked to the end of the line of women, took the woman in white by the hand and escorted her back to the banquet table, where he motioned for her to sit. A satisfied grin spread across the old man's face.

Benicio could not control his breaths. What terrible trick had the Devil just played? His mind raced, trying to think of how he might win the woman in white for his own.

'Rogelio,' called Cortés. 'You are next.' Rogelio had served as second in command on the finest of Cortés's galleons and his selection as the next to choose was beyond reproach.

Rogelio stood, but he was not surveying the remaining maidens. Instead, he was glaring at the woman by Ordaz's side, as if he recognised her. He walked to where Cortés was seated at the head of the table, dipped his hand deep inside the pocket of his jerkin and emerged with a shimmering golden necklace. Benicio recognised the sparkling piece of jewellery. It had hung around the neck of the shaman that Rogelio had killed.

Rogelio placed the necklace before Cortés and, without a word, walked to the place where the woman in white was sitting beside Ordaz. Cortés gave a brief nod, and Rogelio took the woman's arm and guided her to a seat between himself and Benicio on the bench.

Benicio's skin stood on end. The woman was seated right next to him. He could smell her flowery scent, could feel the tiny hairs of her arms graze his. His heart hammered. She was so close to him, yet so completely out of his reach.

The newly elected *alcalde* of Vera Cruz, Alonso de Grado, was next. He stood and selected the orange woman, bending to his knee and bowing, then escorted the young woman back to the table. Others were not so polite. Pilot Diego Cermeño took the girl in green by the elbow. Sailor Gonzalo de Umbria merely gestured to the girl in red. Then it was Benicio's turn.

There was only one thing to be done. Benicio reached into his boot. Then he stood and walked to the head of the table. He placed the diamond-and-jadestone ring before Cortés.

El Capitán did not conceal his surprise. He took the gem in his hands and examined it, enthralled. He nodded several times, then held the gem up for Malinali's inspection. She studied the tiny etching closely, returning the ring to Cortés and whispering something in his ear.

A curious grin spread across Cortés' face. 'How came you by this magnificent piece?'

'I found it in a stream near the fields of Potonchan,' Benicio lied. 'I have very sharp eyes.'

'I will accept it as compensation for the woman in white,' Cortés said. He placed the ring upon his finger. 'Rogelio, take your necklace back and choose again. That is an order.'

Rogelio's lips trembled in anger. He leapt up and snarled at Benicio, shaking his head and muttering bitterly. He grabbed another woman by the arm, returning to his seat with a harrumph. And so it went. By the time all the women were divided among them, the eight Spaniards had grown impatient, eager to take their beautiful prizes to bed.

'We accept your generous gifts with humility and gratitude,' said Cortés. 'And we shall join you in a march to Tenochtitlan, departing as soon as possible.'

The Chief's mouth stretched into a smile and the Council Elders nodded in satisfaction. It was the proclamation they had been waiting for. Their presentation of the high-born women had served its purpose. They would send their warriors with the Spanish to conquer Tenochtitlan, and, with the favour of the gods, return with their young men and women who were taken so many weeks ago.

But Cortés was not done speaking. 'There is one thing, however, that we require before we march with you to Tenochtitlan.'

'We will give you anything within our power,' the Chief said.

'You must cease the practice of human sacrifice. You must smash your idols and accept Cristo as your saviour.'

'I do not understand,' said the Chief.

'Renounce your evil idols, for they corrupt your hearts,' Cortés said, fingering his ring. 'And stop offering the blood of humans to the gods.'

The Chief shook his head. 'If we do that, then the world will end,' he explained. 'We have no choice but to feed the gods. It is the debt we pay to maintain life.'

'You must trust me that your world will not end,' said Cortés. 'In two days, we will meet you at the plaza. You will destroy your idols. Then we shall march on Tenochtitlan together.'

Benicio did not hear the threat hidden amongst Cortés's words. He only heard the vocalisation of Benicio's greatest wish: they were going to Tenochtitlan, just as he had hoped. He was overcome with joy. With the map in his pocket and this woman by his side, he would be able to find the treasure. He bent to Tula's ear. 'Tenoch-it-lan,' he whispered.

Chapter Fifteen

On their way to the Spanish settlement, he took her by the hand. It had become dark and she knew that he was only trying to guide her to his hut. Still, she allowed herself to imagine that he wished to keep her safe.

It was not such an unlikely dream. He had given up his most prized possession to make her his, after all. Perhaps he had come to care about her.

Wake up, Tula, she told herself. It was a foolish idea. She knew very well that he had not traded his precious gem for her, but for her knowledge. Either that or he hated her so much that he had given up his treasure for the opportunity to punish her.

She hoped it was the first explanation, because the idea of the second was making her sweat, which would hinder her in defending herself against him.

The trail they followed flattened and he released her hand. No, he did not care for her. She only hoped he did not harbour some hidden malice towards her. Clearly the red-headed man did. What had Cortés called him? *Rogelio.*

She had seen the anger in Rogelio's eyes: he had recognised her from the beach. After he had seated her next to him, he had run her hand over the bump of his wounded thigh, as if to remind her of what she had done to him. If the tall man had not intervened, she knew that Rogelio would have made her pay for her actions.

She wished that she could speak the tall man's tongue. If she could, she would thank him for saving her from that terrible fate.

She would also ask him whether Chief Cortés meant to destroy the Totonac gods. The Spaniards were the Totonacs' friends, were they not? Why would they wish to destroy the Totonac gods? The Totonacs had welcomed the Spaniards' god with open arms. Indeed, there was always room for a new god. The universe was full of them.

She looked up at them now. The moon had not yet risen and there they all were—the mysterious ones. The gods of the northern and southern stars. They were so very beautiful on nights like this. So numerous that they appeared to form clouds against the black sky. *'Teotli,'* she said, pointing upwards, but he did not respond.

They arrived at a cluster of huts overlooking the Spanish settlement. The Totonacs had helped the strangers build the huts many weeks ago, as a way to solidify their alliance. As he ushered her into the structure, Tula was surrounded by the familiar trappings of greenwood branches and palm leaves.

She placed her basket against the far wall of the hut. She could see very little, but her ears told her that the man was striking flint, surely to light a fire. Tula caught sight of tiny sparks flying in the air beneath a copper brazier. Soon, the brazier was lit and the tent was awash in its blazing light.

The man lit a stick and held it over the top of a small, round pillar. Tula watched in amazement as a small thread at the top of the pillar ignited and, amazingly, stayed ignited, even as the fire in the brazier floundered.

Tula walked towards the small flame and the man backed away, as if she were some dangerous spirit. She paused, watching him retreat to his bed mat. But he gestured to the candle and nodded, urging her to continue her investigation.

She touched the pillar, which was made of a smooth but slightly sticky substance she could not identify. She passed her finger over the flame at the top of the object, marvelling at it.

'Candle,' he said from the shadows.

'Candle,' she repeated. She had never seen such a thing.

'Bees,' he said. He made a buzzing noise, then pointed to his arm and pinched it. 'Ow!' he said.

She smiled, having no idea what he was trying to tell her. He continued to make the buzzing sound, coupled with a twisting of his finger in the air. 'Bees.'

Ah! He was talking about the *pipiyolin*—the insects that made honey. She touched the candle and realised that it was composed of the substance they used to make their homes.

'Pipiyolin,' she said in Nahuatl. She made the buzzing sound again and soon they were buzzing together until they both broke into laughter.

Their merriment quickly faded as they heard the tortured cry of a woman in a nearby hut. The woman was enduring pain and there was nothing Tula could do to help her. Slowly, the cry diminished and Tula found that her own eyes had filled with tears.

There were other noises, too. Grunts and moans and sighs—the sounds of carnal love. Already it had begun. Tula had never known the pleasures of the flesh, though Pulhko had described the act of love to her long ago. Surely the man—her new master—was expecting to enjoy Tula in that way tonight. That was what all the bearded men were doing with their new concubines, all around them.

Whatever he planned for her, Tula would have no choice but to endure it. Like the other seven women, there would be no wedding night kisses, no husband's tender embrace. Instead of greeting their life mates atop their wedding mats, Tula and the other women were greeting strangers and doing their duty for their people. Tula found a seat on the far side of the hut. She scowled at him, then pulled her knees to her chest and put her head down.

She had always hated doing her duty.

When finally she looked up, he had removed his leather wrap and the candlelight was dancing upon his large, bare chest. But he was not looking at Tula. He appeared to be staring at a picture. She could not see it from where she sat and wondered if it was an image of a special god or goddess whom he revered.

'Stars?' she ventured, for that was his word for gods.

He gave a confused laugh. 'No, no, no,' he said, holding up the image. 'Luisa.'

The name was familiar somehow, and Tula craned to study the image in the candlelight. It was a female face, turned to the side, but it did not appear to be that of a goddess. On the contrary, the face was soft and fine, like the face of a woman.

Then Tula realised that it was a woman. *His* woman—the same woman whose name he had uttered when he was inside his dream. Her hair was a cascade of curls that tumbled down her long neck and grazed her fine rounded jaw. Even at such an angle, she appeared ethereally beautiful. In that way she *was* like a goddess, thought Tula.

Tula felt oddly wounded, but flashed the tall man a tight smile. 'Luisa?' she asked, pointing from the picture back to the man.

The man nodded. He took the picture and placed it against his heart. 'Luisa.'

Suddenly it was all so clear. The man was in love with the woman in the picture. She was probably his betrothed. That was why he had said her name when they had kissed the first time. He had been dreaming that Tula was Luisa. That was why he had been so reluctant to return the second kiss they shared. That was why he had helped her escape the cenote, despite the way he had looked at her, despite that strange, magical pull of her body towards his. He did not wish to betray Luisa.

Tula knew she should be relieved. She would not have to lie with this stranger or bear his child. He was a good man, an honourable man, a man who stayed true to the woman he loved. For a fleeting moment, Tula imagined that woman was herself.

'Benicio,' he said, pointing to himself.

'Tula,' she said, pointing to herself. She bowed her head. 'I am humble,' she said in her language, though she knew he could not understand.

He retrieved a cloth from his tall leather shoe. It took her a moment to realise that he was holding the same cloth map he had shown her in the cenote—the tilted square with the four circled corners. 'Tenoch-it-lan,' he said with enthusiasm. He pointed to the map, then to Tula, then to the map.

It was as she suspected, then. He had purchased her for the promise of the riches she could show him, nothing more. He would not touch her—thank the gods—only expect her to show him where the gold was hidden, once they reached Tenochtitlan. She was his means to an end. That was all. She meant nothing to him.

He crossed to his blanket and curled himself up in it, then quickly blew out the candle.

'Goodnight, Tula,' he whispered in the dark.

'Goodnight, Benicio,' she whispered back, mimicking his speech. She heard him laugh lightly. Soon, there was a regular rhythm to his breaths. He had gone to sleep.

And there was her friend the darkness again.

Chapter Sixteen

Benicio had never been much of a gambling man, yet he had just staked his future on a woman he trusted less than a hungry cat. He had given up a very real, very valuable gem under the outrageous supposition that a woman who had robbed him twice would lead him to a cache of a hundred such gems. It was a tremendous risk, not to mention the height of avarice, but he knew that if he succeeded he might return to Seville with both dignity and wealth. He could march into the Plaza del Triunfo and sweep Luisa right off her feet.

It was a chance he'd had to take.

Benicio groped inside his basket of belongings until he found the silver fork. He gave the object a quick shine and placed it beside the woman's bed mat. It was the perfect opportunity to return it to her, for when she woke, she would be reminded of his goodwill towards her. She would also see that he was a man who kept his promises.

He kept his footfalls light as he exited the hut. It was after dawn, but the woman still slumbered. It occurred to Benicio that she was probably only feigning sleep. It seemed she had a rare talent for deception, this beautiful young woman who now, by some bizarre twist of fate, belonged to him.

He smiled to himself. As if she could ever belong to anyone, the little thief. But if she was waiting for him to leave so that she could plunder his belongings, she would be sorely disappointed. Now, thanks to her, he had nothing left to steal.

Securing the reed door behind him, he looked down at the burgeoning settlement of Vera Cruz. It now had as many buildings in its central plaza as ships in its harbour and already a team of Spaniards was at work on the small church, joining its stone blocks together with the concrete paste that a group of Totonac masons mixed nearby.

There were other stone structures, as well, each at a different stage of completion, including a small Casa de Contratación and a thatch-roofed dining tent, whose large stone chimney gave the flimsy structure a hint of the permanence to come.

Radiating outward was the blue halo of the settlement's splendid harbour, crowded with the Spanish galleons and brigantines that Benicio and the other men had sailed across the Yucatan Channel from Cuba so many months ago.

Lately, some of the men, including a few captains, had begun to express their desire to return to Cuba. They argued that the Mexica ruler Montezuma had supplied Cortés with enough treasure to pay for their expedition many times over. *Why not return to Cuba and divide the spoils?* they wondered aloud, arguing that there would be plenty of time and resources to mount a new expedition when the season of heat and hurricanes had passed.

Cortés did not respond to their petitions, however. He had given no specific response to the dissenters, but Benicio knew what was in the Capitan's heart: There would be no going back. They were readying themselves to depart for Tenochtitlan, not Cuba, and this was not an expedition, it was an invasion.

Now Benicio scanned the harbour and sensed something had changed. There were thirteen ships floating there now, not twelve. He looked closer and beheld an unfamiliar white galleon. Its energetic crew was loading its wares on to a dozen shore boats.

Benicio quickened his pace down the hill. A large crowd had gathered on the beach to receive the galleon's captain, who leaped over the crashing waves and crossed to the cheering crowd of men. He might have believed they were heralding his fine disembarkation, but Benicio knew that they were really cheering for the crates of Spanish wine that were being unloaded upon the shore.

Captain Francisco de Saucedo, the lost thirteenth member of Cortés's 'holy company' was soon standing before Cortés, embracing him like a brother. They spoke at length, then Saucedo produced a small leather pouch, which he untied to reveal a stack of envelopes.

Letters. Saucedo had brought letters—news and missives from Cuba and Jamaica and Hispañola and perhaps even from Spain. The men gathered closer, jostling for position as Cortés began to prattle off the names of the lucky recipients.

'Pablo Federico Olas y Brisas,' he began, and a man lurched forward, plucking the letter from Cortés's hands and cradling as if it were the finest plate of porcelain.

Benicio broke into a trot.

'Ramón Lucero de las Casas,' Cortés called, and several of the men sighed as the fortunate recipient revealed himself.

'Benicio Bartolomé Villafuerte,' Cortés said. Benicio was running now, as fast as his legs could take him.

'Benicio Bartolomé Villafuerte,' Cortés pronounced again, searching the crowd.

'Here!' Benicio cried, charging on to the beach. In seconds he had plucked the letter from the Captain's hand and was walking—or perhaps floating—towards a palm tree's patch of shade.

Benicio stared at the letter for a long time before opening it. He studied the unmistakable looping script—the large o's and long, luxuriant f that plunged below the line in a violation of all the rules of orthography. Benicio's heart hummed. *Island of Hispañola*, said the address, *Spanish Empire, Governor Diego Velázquez de Cuéllar, mariner/conscript Benicio Bartolomé Villafuerte*.

The letter had probably languished inside the Hispañola Casa de Contratación for many months. Still, the Spaniards in the West Indies were a lonely lot and someone had surely recognised the nature of the letter and ferried it along.

Still, Benicio could not believe it had found him. In an act of absurdity, he lifted the envelope to his nose, as if he might smell her lingering perfume. For a moment, he thought he did smell it, right there at the place where the flap met the trifold, like the scent of an angel. He was not sure how long he sat there marvelling at the textured paper, imagining her hands upon it.

My Dearest Benicio,

It is with a heavy heart that I place my quill upon this page, for I write to inform you of my engagement. I have waited, as I said I would, for your return. For a year I have pined, holding myself aloof at balls, declining invitations, searching the faces of the seafarers in the Plaza del Triunfo. Alas, God has not seen fit to bear you home.

Meanwhile, your brother Armando has returned from the conquered territory of Navarre, triumphant. He was granted lordship of several pear orchards there and ranch lands that foster cattle and sheep. He travels much between his newly won lands and your father's estate, for as the firstborn he is now charged with its administration.

I tell you this, Benicio, because it is Armando to whom I am engaged. He has already won enough treasure to keep me in the life to which I am accustomed and he says that he will not stop fighting until he has made me a marquesa.

Armando has re-enlisted in the Tercios and might not be back for a year or more. Then we must plan the wedding. I do not know if you will receive this letter. If you do, you will surely wish to move on with your life.

But, may God forgive me, I wait for you still.
I love you still.
Luisa
Seville, Spain
March 3rd, 1518

Benicio read the letter several times in disbelief. She was engaged...to Armando? She had written the letter just over a year ago, which meant that she had only recently begun to plan the wedding. That meant that there was still time to stop it. He reread the last line until he could close his eyes and see it before him: *I wait for you still.*

She waited for him still. She loved him still, even as she planned to wed his own brother. How could she do such a thing?

The shade of the palm had shifted and the heat of the day was beginning to squeeze him. Benicio carefully folded the letter and placed it inside the book he kept against his heart. He needed to think and decided to go for a walk. He absently made his way to the porters' camp, where hundreds of Taino men from Cuba were busy packing their sacks with blankets, bed mats and other supplies.

A short man who called himself Big Tree waved at Benicio. He had come over on the same ship as Benicio and the two had learned to communicate in gestures. There was no mistaking the soldierly steps he performed for Benicio now. They would begin their march to the Mexica capital—to Tenochtitlan—at daybreak.

Benicio flipped Big Tree his last *ducado* and thanked him, though he could not remember what he said, for a haze of confusion had settled like a fog over his mind. Armando? But Luisa did not love Armando. Even as children, Luisa had always favoured Benicio. The two had often made mischief together, frequently at Armando's expense. Indeed, Armando had always found Luisa annoying—like a bothersome pet he was none the less charged with keeping safe.

Armando?

Benicio loved his older brother with all his heart, though ever since he had joined the Spanish army, he had held himself above Benicio and Carlos. His self-importance had seemed to grow in tandem with his waistline and Benicio and Luisa had often made sport of teasing him. What on Earth did Luisa see in Armando?

But Benicio already knew the answer to that question and it maddened him. Armando was a wealthy man.

The sun was low in the sky when Benicio arrived at the armoury tent. Inside, the Quartermaster was explaining the benefits of native cotton armour over heavy Spanish steel to a crowd. Benicio listened as the grizzled old man described the conditions they were likely to face on their journey to Tenochtitlan.

Even with the aid of hundreds of Totonac and Taino porters, the Quartermaster explained, theirs would be a gruelling month-long march into the heart of the Mexican Empire, a road that rose slowly out of the sweltering jungle into vast forests, dry, empty plateaus and towering mountains that played host to unpredictable storms.

The crowd groused as the Quartermaster described the enemies they were likely to face, not only an endless stream of Mexica vassal city-states, but also the Mexica's most formidable enemy, the fearsome Tlaxcalans, whose co-operation was anything but guaranteed.

And when the Quartermaster announced that Cortés intended to send all of the gold they had obtained so far back to Spain, an eruption of dissent ensued.

'It is not just!' someone shouted. 'We are owed our fair share!'

'Cause for mutiny!' another barked.

'Hold your tongues, wretched hounds,' interrupted the Quartermaster, 'and dare to dream bigger. Would you rather rob the banker or the bank itself?'

The crowd burst into a spate of discussion, but the

Quartermaster's voice rose above it. 'There will be no mercy for mutineers,' he clarified. 'Cortés has ordered it.' The crowd hushed. 'Deserters will be found and slain. No exceptions.'

Benicio touched his heart and the ragged book that protected it. He had no choice, it seemed, but to continue. And continue he would. He would not give up now, so close to his goal. Besides, he loved her, and he would win her hand in marriage. Curse Armando and his inherited lands and battle-born wealth. All that was nothing in the face of true love.

'Ready your weapons and fill your bellies,' pronounced the Quartermaster. 'It is a long journey to Tenochtitlan.'

Benicio realized suddenly that for him, the journey to Tenochtitlan had begun two years ago, when he had promised himself he would return to Luisa with a fortune. And although Luisa's news had changed everything, it had also changed nothing. The gold remained somewhere in Tenochtitlan and Luisa still waited for him to find it. *I wait for you still,* she had said. *I love you still.*

Lost in thoughts of Luisa, Benicio was surprised to catch sight of Tula as he exited the armoury. She walked with several of the other Totonac maidens down the beach, a spear in her hand and her basket brimming with fish. She had changed out of her white skirt and shawl and wore a simple dark blue undershirt and matching skirt, which lay heavy and damp upon her shapely legs. She had obviously been fishing.

She walked with confidence, almost arrogance, and he could not help but smile seeing her swish her round hips across the beach. Though she clearly had fallen victim to the sin of pride, her diminutive size made her swagger seem quite charming. And he had to admit that she had caught herself quite a haul. A delicious flat-nosed *dorado* poked its green head out of her basket. He was almost jealous. His stomach already churned at the thought of drinking down yet another bowlful of Totonac turkey soup.

She turned to gaze at the crowd of men exiting the armoury. Was she looking for him? He turned his head away so that she could not see that he had spotted her. When finally he turned back, he was startled to find that she had been watching him all the while. Their eyes met. Or did they? She turned away from him so quickly that he began to think he might have dreamed it.

Bah. Let her think she was faster and cleverer than him. Let her continue to believe that she studied him from the shadows, waiting for her next opportunity to pick his pockets. He had already won. She was his—legally and contractually. She was now part of an official alliance, one that had been signed and recorded on both Spanish paper and Totonac agave-bark scrolls. To abandon him now would be akin to treason. She would not only have to answer to her people, but also to her gods, which seemed far angrier and more punishing than his.

Thus she would accompany him to Tenochtitlan, compliant and biddable. She had no choice but to do so. Whether she would support him in his mission once they arrived was another matter. He could only hope to slowly earn her trust. He would therefore not go near her, or touch her, no matter how fiercely beautiful she appeared in the sunlight, with the sea behind her and the wind tousling her long black braids.

He would become her friend and find a way to explain to her that Luisa, the love of his life, waited for him still. Then he would beg her to help him find the treasure indicated on the map, so that he might return to his lady with honour.

Surely the woman—Tula, as she called herself—would wish to aid him, for it would mean that she could eventually be free of him.

Benicio ducked his head beneath the dining canopy and smelled the rich, toasted aroma of tortillas. A Maya woman who had been gifted to the Spaniards after their first battle smiled and handed him a bowl of turkey soup. 'Tortillas?' Benicio asked, holding up all ten of his fingers.

Five for me, five for Tula, Benicio thought, quickly draining his bowl of soup. The woman pulled ten tortillas from the cooking stone and handed him the stack. He thanked the woman and exited the dining area, anxious to return to his hut. He found himself looking forward to seeing his little thief and presenting her with this small gift. But when he walked into the hut he found that she was already asleep. She had curled herself up in her blanket and lay down upon her mat with her back to him.

She was deceiving him, of course. She could not possibly be asleep. It was not even completely dark outside yet, and she had got more than enough sleep the night before.

He sat down on his sleeping mat and took off his boots. He noticed a flank of cooked *dorado* lying on the brazier near him. It was the last of her fine fish and it smelled of oil and herbs and good dreams. He lay there for many long moments, trying to resist its savoury aroma. As if to entice him further, the silver fork had been placed beside it.

What trickery was she about now? No, he would not fall for this culinary seduction. It smelled…fishy. Besides, if she did not have the courtesy to greet him, if she chose to deceive him in such a small thing as sleep, then he would certainly not deign to eat her fish, no matter how delicious it appeared. But after many long moments, thoughts of rich, buttery meat ran rampant in his brain and he could not help himself. He picked up the silver fork and ate the *dorado* in half-a-dozen bites.

She had bested him once again. Not only had she obtained the better meal, she had lured him to consume it, the temptress.

He stretched himself out on his sleeping mat. He knew that he should give thanks. He was a gentleman, after all, and he could tell by the cadence of her breaths that she remained awake. 'Thank you,' he said, hoping that she sensed his genuine gratitude. But she made no stir in response. He lay back on his mat and studied the palm leaf roof until it was too dark to see.

'Goodnight, Tula,' he said finally. At least that was a phrase she knew.

He waited patiently for her response, looking forward to the sweet, tentative way she said his name, breaking it into a dozen syllables as if it were some long, difficult sentence.

'Goodnight, Benicio,' she said at last, and he smiled to himself in the darkness.

Chapter Seventeen

She would never look at him again. She kept her eyes fixed on the ground, even as he hurried toward her in anger, commanding her to come. She would not come. She would not look at him or wait for him or do his bidding—not after what had happened that morning in Cempoala's central plaza. What his countrymen had done had gone beyond the simple disdain with which they often treated the Totonacs. The Spanish men had shown themselves to be monsters.

That morning, Chief Cortés had marched fifty men into the central plaza of Cempoala in full armour. Their swords drawn, the men had stopped at the base of the Great Temple, awaiting Cortés's orders.

To Tula's eyes, the Spaniards had appeared almost farcical—fifty men holding their swords out at a structure so tall and majestic that it might have been a mountain. The Temple was not a mountain, though; it was the most sacred place in Cempoala, a place where priests laboured, praying to the gods and keeping the people of Cempoala safe and well.

'Citizens of Cempoala,' pronounced Cortés, 'I have come to save you from the Devil.' Aguilar and Malinali were there by his side and they had translated the Captain's words so that the Totonacs would understand the reason for the destruction about to occur.

Tula had understood nothing. What was this spirit called the Devil and why did the citizens of Cempoala require salvation from him? The Cempoalans were reverent, learned people. They kept the Long Count calendar, traced the paths of the stars and stored their history in thousands of ancient codices. Yet it was as if the Spaniards looked upon the Cempoalans as ignorant, naughty children.

The Totonac Chief appeared from behind the Great Temple, stretched on his litter. 'I cannot allow you to destroy our gods,' he'd said as fifty Totonac archers emerged from behind him. Their bows drawn, they took their positions standing face to face with Cortés's fifty swordsmen.

But Cortés would not be moved. 'Honour your agreement. Renounce human sacrifice and free your people from idolatry.'

'We have accepted your god,' the Chief had answered. 'Why cannot you accept ours?'

It was a fair question, but Cortés was not interested in fairness. He unsheathed his hand blade and held his sword to the Chief's throat. 'Honour your agreement or die.'

The terrified Chief had raised his hand and ordered his archers to lower their bows.

Cortés's soldiers had rushed to the high platform at the top of the temple and pushed the gods over the edge one by one. The ancient stone statues had come smashing down the steps in a thousand pieces. Her gods were being destroyed. The Totonac Chief had wailed as the eye of a winged serpent rolled to his feet and stopped there, like a child's broken toy. Tula had felt each crash like a blow to her own body. Her gods were being destroyed before her eyes.

Screams of terror had split the air. Many of the onlookers had sought shelter, as if at any moment the sky might come tumbling down beneath the wrath of their forsaken gods. Other Totonacs collapsed where they stood, howling and moaning as the bearded strangers washed their sacred temple with lime.

Tula willed herself not to weep. She had watched from amongst the Spanish company as the horror unfolded, letting the injustice strengthen her resolve.

The Spaniards did not respect the Totonacs or view them as equals—it was suddenly so clear.

The Totonacs were not part of an alliance with the Spanish, Tula realised. They were their vassals.

The destruction took half the morning. Soon the sacred, blood-stained steps had been whitewashed. The ancient statues were replaced with a shrine to some benevolent virgin goddess whom Tula doubted could protect anyone from anything.

The Totonac priests wept. They tore at their own flesh, as if their self-inflicted wounds might compensate for the crime that had just been committed. Cortés had not merely destroyed their stone effigies. He had destroyed a part of the Totonacs themselves.

It was the worst possible way to begin a journey between allies. But of course, that was the point. The Spanish soldiers were simply putting the Totonacs in their place. After their destruction was concluded, Cortés announced that they were now ready to begin their journey to rescue the Totonac captives. And, bound by necessity as well as the terms of the alliance, the Totonacs could do nothing but join the Spanish.

Thus they had begun their march to Tenochtitlan—already beaten. Tula had marched in the women's entourage during the day, grateful to be as far away from the Spanish soldiers as possible. The road wound its way through the lowland jungle and into the foothills, and with each step Tula's anger and resentment grew. When the army stopped at the small Totonac outpost of Xalapa, she tried to lose herself in the chaos of the dispersing men. But her attempt failed. Benicio had spied her amongst the women, and was now marching towards Tula with his lips pursed in anger. She had angered him by avoiding him—that much was clear. She knew she could not escape him at a run. Nor could she sneak away under cover of darkness, for she knew that she would only be returned to him. She belonged to him now, legally and contractually, and everyone knew it.

Still, she kicked and fought as he hoisted her on to his shoulder and carried her into the forest. She was glad now that she had lied to him about the location depicted on the secret map he carried. He could carry her across the land like a sack of maize, but she had already beaten him, for she had made sure that he would never find his treasure.

When he finally placed her upon the ground beside a large kapok tree, she lunged to its base, trying to hide herself in the shelter of the tree's tall roots. She pulled up her knees and hugged them to her chest, refusing to look at him.

She did not wish to see him, for she would see a man whose Chief had desecrated everything she held true. She would not see a man; she would see a monster.

Chapter Eighteen

No wonder Tula cowered before him now. Everything she had ever been taught to believe had been destroyed today by men like him.

Benicio unbuttoned his doublet and draped it over her shoulders, but she pushed it off of her as if it might harm her. 'I am sorry,' he said, though he might as well have been consoling himself.

He did not agree with what Cortés had done. The practice of human sacrifice was horrific, but so was hanging, beheading and burning—things that happened regularly in Spain, though Benicio had long ago learned to keep such ideas to himself.

Still, it made no sense that Cortés would do such a thing to his only allies. Then again, many of Cortés's actions made little sense. When Benicio had awoken that morning, for example, he had made his way down the hill to behold sinking masts amidst an empty harbour. In the night, Cortés had sunk all the Spanish ships.

Now his conscripts had no choice but to follow Cortés on his mission, for there was no longer any easy way home. What was worse, Cortés had placed a bounty on the head of any mutineer. Any man found to be leaving Cortés's 'holy company', as he called it, had been ordered captured or killed, with a guaranteed reward.

Benicio unbuckled his sword belt and lay down his scabbard on the hard earth. In a sense, he was as trapped as Tula was now. Benicio pulled two rations of dried fish from his bag. He held out a piece before Tula's folded arms, but she did not move to accept it. Instead she kept her eyes fixed upon the ground.

'You must eat,' he said, putting a piece into his own mouth, though in truth he had little appetite himself. Benicio saw a tear bulge, then break upon her cheek. She refused to look at him.

It occurred to Benicio that Tula probably could not stand the sight of him.

Benicio pulled his dagger from its hilt and studied it. He had an idea, and quickly jumped to his feet. In moments he was squatting by a nearby stream, dipping the well-honed blade in the water and dragging it over his chin. He was amazed at how quickly a decade's worth of beard growth could go falling to the ground. The other men would surely chide him tomorrow when they saw his clean cheeks. They would call him pretty and muse about the effects of too many hours in the sun.

Benicio did not care. He could endure far worse chiding if it meant winning back this woman's trust. He needed her on his side and he needed her to know that he was on hers.

He scraped the last of his long whiskers from his cheeks and splashed his face with water. When she saw him now, she would see a man very different from those who had desecrated her temple. She would see a man who was not a killer, or a warrior, or a thief. God willing, she would see a good man, a man she could trust.

He pictured her peering up at him with that shy, curious smile—the one she had flashed him that night in his hut. He hoped she would laugh at his new appearance, or even tease him about it. She seemed possessed of such a large spirit and he wished that she would share it with him again.

He touched his bare cheeks. He wondered briefly if it was really her trust that he so craved, or something else.

He marched back to the kapok tree and greeted her, but he might just as well have painted his body blue, because she kept her eyes fixed upon the ground. He sat down between the tree roots and faced her, hoping to force her gaze to meet his own. He needed her to see that he was no longer one of the men who had ruined her temple and destroyed her gods. He was Benicio, her partner.

Benicio, her friend.

He stayed facing her as the light of day waned. She was as obstinate as the roots themselves and seemed to bury herself in her own misery. Finally, Benicio stood. He needed to prepare their beds while there was still light. He hailed the nearest porter and retrieved two bed mats from the man. Then he set about creating two separate beds between the adjacent roots of the tree.

When he returned to where she sat, he saw the stains of tears upon her cheeks. She continued to stare at the ground. He placed himself before her once again, trying to think of how he might reach her.

He had another idea. He unclasped the small metal crucifix he wore around his neck and held it in his hand. He looked at it for a long while. It was a simple cross, fashioned in copper. When the authorities of the Inquisition would come to the university in search of Muslims and Jews, Benicio would always demonstrate his cross to them, careful to conceal the letters from Copernicus that he studied.

He stared hard at the tiny cross. It seemed odd that such a simple symbol could provide such magical protection, especially in light of all the killing that took place in its name.

He thrust the shiny object into her view, then crushed it in his hand. He might have been condemning himself to eternal damnation, though he doubted that his God would protest an attempt to win the trust of a brave, worthy woman.

Finally, she lifted her gaze and stared at the bent cross in his palm.

'You lost your gods today, so I shall lose mine,' he said, though he knew she did not understand his words. He threw the cross out into the jungle.

She shook her head in protest and stood to retrieve the object, but he grabbed her by the arm and pulled her back down. *Look at me*, he thought. *See me.*

Finally, her eyes met his and Benicio froze. It was the first time she had looked at him directly in many days and he found himself fighting to slow his breaths. Her fierce loveliness seemed to bubble up from some deep well within her, inviting him to drink. And drink, he did, for he had never beheld a woman so magnificently beautiful.

Finally, she released him, peering uncertainly at the small patch of sky above them, as if any moment it might come crashing down.

'No,' he said, recovering his wits. He took her face in his hands. 'Do not rely on the gods.' He stared into her eyes. 'Rely on me.'

And in that moment he realised that it was not her trust he sought, but her affection. He wanted her to want him, to need him, even. It was entirely improper, but he wanted to wrap his large body around hers and protect her from everything that could do her harm.

He released her face. 'It is all right,' he whispered lamely. 'Everything is going to be all right.'

To his surprise, she did not turn away. Instead, she blinked at him and offered him a half-smile.

He smiled back at her, hearing a nearby woodpecker beat a trunk like a lonely drum.

Benicio watched her place her hands atop the wide fig leaf that stretched across the roots in the adjacent root well. She traced her fingers across the leaf's deep veins, then nodded in approval. Whatever crime Captain Cortés had committed against the Totonacs on this terrible day, it appeared she would not hold it against Benicio.

On impulse, Benicio picked a purple flower he had spied growing on the ground. He stood and held it out to her and she accepted it graciously, taking a lusty whiff into her nose. She peered at him with those bottomless eyes, then let her gaze slide down to his chin.

'No more beard,' Benicio said. 'Do you like it?'

She reached out her hand and swept it across his cheek.

It seemed that she did.

A chill shivered down his neck and travelled to his limbs. He wished to catch her hand and keep it there where it rested upon his cheek, but he knew that her touch did dangerous things to his gentlemanly restraint. She brushed her fingers across his other cheek, this time a little slower, and Benicio felt his desire rising quickly. What in Hell was she doing to him now?

He closed his eyes. *Think, Benicio. Use your wits.*

He needed a distraction—something that would divert her from her dangerous path. A puzzle! He unwrapped his cotton armour and pulled his book from beneath his chemise. He unfolded the map before them, pointing to its middle. Tula sighed, then nodded. 'Tenochtitlan,' she intoned.

She had taken her hand off his cheek, thank God.

'*Taak'in,*' he said. 'Gold.' He pointed to the circle at the top of the diamond and she nodded again. But did she really understand? He needed her to know that he was not like Cortés. He did not wish to steal her gods. He only wished to steal her enemy's gold.

Tula tilted her head suddenly, seeming to strike upon an idea. She pointed to him. 'Gold,' she repeated. She pointed to herself. 'Sister.'

Benicio could hardly believe his ears. She had learned a Spanish word, but how?

'Malinali,' Tula said, seeming to read his mind. Cortés's translator had marched with the Totonac maidens for much of the day. Benicio had guessed that she had been trying to console the Totonac women over the loss of their gods. Apparently instead she had been giving them lessons in the Castilian tongue.

'Sister,' Tula repeated, then pointed west. 'Tenochtitlan.'

Was she trying to tell him that her sister was in the Mexica capital of Tenochtitlan? She crossed her arms at the wrists and raised them in the air. 'Sister,' she said. 'Tenochtitlan.'

'Your sister was taken to Tenochtitlan?' Benicio asked. He knew of the mass abduction at the Totonac *tlachtli* court. It had occurred the same evening that he and Tula had fallen into the cenote. 'Your sister was abducted?' he asked. She could not possibly understand him.

Or perhaps she could. The eyes that only moments ago were in tears now shone with an inner light. She pointed at him again. 'Tenochtitlan. Gold.'

'Yes, yes,' he said. 'I wish to find gold in Tenoch-titlan.'

Instead of pointing at herself, however, she continued to point at Benicio. 'Tenochtitlan. Sister,' she said, then she pointed at herself. 'Tenochtitlan. Gold.'

Slowly he absorbed her meaning. She repeated the command. 'Benicio. Tenochtitlan. Sister.' She pointed again at herself. 'Tula. Tenochtitlan. Gold.'

He nodded, studying the fierce, radiant woman with whom he had apparently just struck a deal: If he would help her save her sister, she would help him find his gold. He held out his hand. In response, she held her finger in the air.

One last thing, she seemed to say, and she pointed at his nose.

His *nose*? He touched it curiously, then winced. It was still tender from the break and still very much bent.

She nodded her head hypnotically and he found himself nodding his head in return. But what exactly was he was agreeing to?

She took a deep breath. Then she placed both hands on the side of his face and quickly and violently snapped the broken bones back into their places.

'Ah!' Benicio hollered, and an unbearable pain radiated through his body. *'Bruja!'*

But she would not indulge his cries. Coolly, soberly, she held out her hand and spoke. 'Benicio. Tenochtitlan. Sister. Tula. Tenochtitlan. Gold.' Their agreement was still valid. She had merely put him in his place.

Reeling in pain and a strange kind of awe, Benicio took her hand in his.

And he shook it.

Chapter Nineteen

The road out of Xalapa rose sharply and for the first time in her life, Tula felt the unfamiliar sting of frost upon her cheeks. Benicio had warned her to keep her hands covered over the mountain pass. He had demonstrated how to blow hot air into his own hands and had urged her to try.

When she hesitated, he had taken her hands in his and blown into them for her, making her laugh at the strange action. He had stared at her gravely, a mixture of worry and frustration knitting his brow: Clearly staying warm was not a game to him.

She blew into her hands now, as she had been instructed. The simple action helped slow the chill, as did his doublet, which he had insisted she wear, though there was still the problem of her sandal-clad feet.

Tula could not ask him for further advice now. As a foot soldier, he was required to walk with the other soldiers well ahead of the women and porters. Still, she knew that if he could walk with her, he would. He had done quite a lot for her already, including shaving his beard, renouncing his own god and, incredibly, promising to save her sister.

Tula was strangely pleased. All her life, she had worked to keep her family safe and comfortable. Now this man seemed to be trying to do the same for her. Although she knew that he was only using her for her knowledge of Tenochtitlan, he had shown her kindness and treated her like an equal, and for that she was grateful.

Indeed, he seemed to hold some strange reverence for her—something beyond simple friendship. When she had finally looked into his eyes yesterday evening, she thought that she had seen something resembling desire. She cautioned herself not to imagine ghosts. Still, it was the memory of that gaze that was helping her stay warm now, as the cold winds swirled all around.

The landscape became sparse. Tall, woody trees gave way to low bushes and soon the square outcropping of rock that defined the top of the Nauhcampatepetl Mountain was the only thing in view. The road became a trail. It wove back and forth in a hundred miserable switchbacks that seemed designed to break a person's will. Tula paused often, trying to catch her breath. She was not alone. As she looked above her, she could see the entire grave procession, fighting to keep the pace.

At the front were the Spanish war dogs—a dozen ferocious beasts that barked and growled at the passing mists. Next came the flag bearer atop his giant deer, which the Spanish called a *horse*. He waved the banner of the red cross, though he did not need to, for the Wind God played with it like a toy.

More men riding on *horses* marched behind him—Chief Cortés among them, his floppy red hat with its single long feather distinguishing him from the others. The horsemen were followed by the rest of the bearded soldiers—three hundred warriors carrying swords and bows and hollow sticks that threw fire.

Tula searched that solemn procession, trying to catch sight of Benicio. He and many other Spaniards had chosen to wear the traditional cotton armour of the Totonacs, for it was effective against the blades of their enemies and much cooler in the lowland heat.

Other bearded ones had remained inside their heavy iron shells—a choice that had seemed foolish as they trekked through the sweltering jungle. Now, however, as the mountain cold gripped them, Tula noticed that the iron ones were the only members who did not jump to create warmth, or cower against the bitter wind.

She searched among the men in white cotton for Benicio's tall figure and shorn face, and she thought she caught sight of him—the tall, broad-chested soldier with the graceful gait. Her heart leapt—probably from the increasing cold—and she quickly lost him in the parade of men.

Behind the Spanish soldiers marched their Totonac allies—an endless line of fierce, feathered warriors wrapped in thick cotton armour, some carrying spears and atlatls, others wielding the thick, club-like obsidian blades for which they were known.

The Totonac warriors were led by a lesser chief and his drummer, whose unwavering rhythms kept everyone on pace. They were followed by half as many porters—both Totonac and Taino men who had come with the bearded ones from Cuba. They trudged up the slopes under the weight of heavy baskets and hauling large ovens that cooked metal balls instead of food.

The women, of course, were last. They fell into a shivering line behind the porters—eight Totonac concubines and several dozen Maya women who had been gifted to the Spaniards at Potonchan. Leading them all was Malinali—or Marina, as she was now known—Cortés's beautiful, brilliant interpreter. In the morning, Malinali had ridden with Chief Cortés himself, then had dropped back to spend the afternoon 'among her own kind', as she put it.

She spoke with ease to all the women, keeping the mood light as snowflakes began to fall and the trail narrowed. Tula fell in behind her, hoping she might catch some of Malinali's special warmth.

'It will not be long before we are over the pass,' Malinali observed in perfect Nahuatl, keeping her eye upon her path. 'Then the journey really becomes difficult.'

Tula gave a nervous laugh. 'I cannot wait. The walk so far has been far too easy.'

'All that rises must descend,' Malinali mused. She gathered her long, colourful cloak around her. 'Tenochtitlan lies in a temperate valley, thank the gods.'

'Have you ever visited the great floating city?' Tula asked.

'I travelled there once a girl, yes,' said Malinali. 'My early life was one of privilege and luxury.'

'Perhaps you will live in luxury once again,' said Tula, blowing on her hands.

'I will indeed, for I march on the side of the victors.'

Tula raised a brow, surprised by Malinali's statement. On the trail above them, one of the bearded men collapsed in a fit of cramps. 'I know what you are thinking,' Malinali continued. 'How do I know that the bearded ones will prevail?'

Tula said nothing, though it was in fact exactly what she was thinking.

'It is because of you.'

'What?' Tula asked.

Surely Tula had misunderstood. Or perhaps Malinali was speaking in jest. Malinali turned around to face Tula and stopped. She pushed her hand out from between the folds of her cloak. There on her finger was the large jade-and-diamond ring that Benicio had traded for Tula that night at the banquet. Cortés must have given the ring to Malinali as a gift.

'It was your ring that gave me the idea for how Emperor Montezuma will be defeated,' Malinali said. Malinali returned her bejewelled hand beneath her cloak and resumed her swift, tireless gait.

'Cortes intends to defeat Montezuma?' Tula asked softly.

'Of course he does.'

'But how?'

Malinali kept her voice low. 'Let us see if you can guess how. What year is it in our Xihuitl calendar?'

'This year? It is One-Reed.'

'And what god presides over One-Reed?'

'The Feathered Serpent, Quetzalcoatl, of course,' said Tula. *The god carved on to the ring.*

'Tell me about Quetzalcoatl.'

'He is the God of Wind and of Learning; of Culture and Civilisation.'

'What legends are there of him?'

'There is the legend that he created the people of the Fifth World—the world that we live in—by going to the Underworld and pouring his blood upon the bones of our ancestors.'

'What else?'

'There is the legend that he was a rich and cultured king who never practised sacrifice, for he had nothing to fear from the gods. He was dethroned by the God of Earth and Death, Tezcatlipoca, and sent to the east where he became the brightest star in the sky. The morning star.' Tula paused, slowly recognising Malinali's plan.

'And?'

'And it is said that he will return one day to the most civilised city in the world—to Tenochtitlan—to reclaim it.'

'And what does Quetzalcoatl usually wear on his face?'

'A beard.'

'What colour is associated with the Feathered Serpent?'

Tula scanned the slope above her and found Cortés's large red hat, its single feather blowing with the wind. 'Red,' Tula said. She lowered her voice to a whisper. 'Do you really believe that Cortés is the Feathered Serpent?'

'Of course not. But I am just a woman. I know very little.' Malinali slid Tula a fiendish grin. 'Captain Cortés treats me well and he is very clever,' Malinali continued, 'but I do not trust him. Sometimes I despise his actions.'

'But you despise the Mexica more?'

Malinali did not answer. 'It is more than that. I have seen the reach of Mexica greed. They have created a mighty empire, but they take too much. Their debt to the gods grows too high. All of the blood in the world cannot repay it.'

Tula shivered. Malinali spoke truth. The Mexica took too much. Far too much.

'You have suffered beneath the Mexica as I have,' said Malinali, as if she had read Tula's mind.

'My two nephews and their father were taken,' said Tula. 'Since then, my eldest sister does not speak. It is as if she died with them. Now my youngest sister has been taken. Only seven days ago.'

'And you intend to save her from the flowery death?'

'I *will* save her.'

'I will help you if I can.'

'You would help me?'

'My debt to you must be repaid,' Malinali said, holding up her ringed finger once again. 'Without the ring that was given for you, we would not be on this journey now. I owe you. It is the law of the world.'

'My new master has said that he, too, will help me in my mission to save my sister,' Tula said, searching again for Benicio's tall figure on the hillside. 'We have an agreement. An alliance.'

'Do not place too much trust in him. Remember that he values treasure more than he values you.'

'The sickness of the heart?'

'It consumes them all,' said Malinali. 'And one day their civilisation, too, will fall.'

Tula nodded. 'The Spanish will fall just like the Mexica will fall, just like the Toltecs fell, and the Teotihuacanos before them, and the Maya before them and the Old Ones before them.'

'You know your history,' remarked Malinali.

'My father taught me. He said that kingdoms rise and fall just like worlds,' Tula mused. In the ancient story, it was not cities, but worlds that collapsed, one after the other.

'That is how it will always be,' Malinali said.

'When it happens, it is better to be on the side of the victors,' she said.

Cortés had stopped at the top of the pass and was signalling with his red hat. 'Speak of the future,' Malinali said, plastering a smile across her face and waving back at Cortés. 'I must rejoin my master now. It has been very nice to speak with you...er...'

'Tula.'

Malinali stepped off the path. 'I am humble, Tula,' she said. 'Some call me Marina now, but you and I know that I will always be Malinali.'

'And I will always be Tula.'

'Take care that it is so.' Malinali flashed Tula a look full of fire and mischief, then turned and walked without effort up the steep, rocky slope.

Chapter Twenty

The storm would not relent. It only worsened as the army made its way down the other side of the mountain to a forest of twisted, low-growing trees. When they finally halted, the Sun God was all but dead. Snow continued to fall and the wind blew like a monster's breath as they scrambled to make camp.

Tula was searching the forest for a sheltered place to sleep when Benicio finally found her. She gasped when she saw him, for she had given up hope that he would seek her out in the storm. She could no longer feel her feet and was so cold that her lips quivered uncontrollably, as if in fright.

She *was* frightened. She had never felt so cold. It was as if her whole body was turning to stone. She did not protest when Benicio lifted her from the ground and carried her to a cluster of boulders. There, he placed her on a rock and motioned for her to wait while he did battle with several nearby trees, slicing their branches with his long sword.

Tula could do little but sit and watch him. Her feet had become too frozen to stand upon and it was as if that deadly ice was now creeping up her legs. She blew furiously into her hands, trying to keep the ice inside her from growing while the soft white flakes of ice rained down. The moments stretched out long and desolate, and she felt a strange, intimate cold, like the breath of death whispering into her ear.

'Aaaooh!' yelled Benicio, heralding a small porter who seemed to materialise amidst the snow. 'Big Tree!' Benicio cried, followed by a string of salutations Tula could not understand. The trembling man carried a large bundle, which he dropped at Benicio's feet. Benicio studied the man, then sat him down beside Tula. He dug in the bundle and produced a thick blanket, which he wrapped around both of them.

Tula and the stranger huddled together as Benicio busied himself gathering firewood, which he piled in a great heap beneath their feet. He made sparks fly by cracking steel upon flint and soon a blaze was warming their toes.

Tula bent as close to the flames as she dared, feeling their magnificent heat restore movement to her cheeks. The man, too, seemed to return to life.

He held out his hands to the flames and muttered prayers of thanks to his gods. He was even able to stand—something Tula still could not accomplish.

But survival was different for women. They were of the moon, not the sun. They did not keep the warmth inside their bodies like men did. Why had she not thought to bring a feather cloak?

Benicio worked with urgency in the firelight, glancing at Tula with concern. He swept together all of his branches, dividing them into two piles, then began leaning them against the boulders. Soon, two small, lean-to shelters appeared, reinforced with piled rocks and mounded dirt. Benicio placed Tula's sleeping mat inside one shelter and his own sleeping mat in the other. It was only after many moments of staring into the dying flames that Tula realised there were three people who needed shelter, not two.

As the fire went to embers, she wondered how he planned to divide their shivering group. The snow was coming thick. Benicio kicked the cinders around the outside of both shelters. Then he urged the man to his feet and handed him a second blanket. The man appeared confused. He refused to take the blanket, pointing at Tula in alarm. He held up two fingers and shook his head.

But Benicio insisted and before long the man surrendered, bowing deeply to Benicio and embracing him like a brother. Then he disappeared with his blanket beneath the branches of the first shelter.

Tula had begun to shiver once again. She missed the fire. It had run out of fuel so quickly and all the warmth that had bloomed from it seemed to have emptied out into the dark forest, as if it had never been. She had never feared the night before, but she feared it now. It seemed as if it might swallow her.

She could not let herself die. If she perished, then Xanca would, too, and then Puhlko, and then surely her father, bereft and utterly alone. But she could not feel her feet. Nor could she feel her cheeks any more, or her lips. She blew into her hands, but the cold pressed down all around her and she knew not how to fight it.

Benicio lifted Tula from the rock and laid her gently upon the sleeping mat beneath the second shelter, covering her with the second blanket. He did not lie down at her side, however. Instead, he kneeled at her feet.

He bent low, keeping his head beneath the roof of their shelter, and appeared to be removing her sandals. He worked furiously, in huffs of breaths, as if attempting to win some unseen contest with the cold. Then he turned his attention to his own clothing.

Tula watched his shadowy movements in confusion, for he appeared to be removing every piece of clothing that he wore. He unwrapped the thick cotton armour that he had wound about his middle and tossed it beside Tula. Then he unbuttoned his animal-hide vest, pulled off his undershirt and peeled off some other garment until she was certain he wore nothing around his chest. Was he planning to give her all his clothing? To sacrifice his own life for hers?

She would not allow it. Trembling, she sat up and gathered all of the garments in her arms. She pushed them back at him, trying to communicate her wishes. But he grasped her by the wrists and the clothes fell out of her hands.

'I don't understand,' she yelped in Totonac. She tried to pull her wrists free, but he held them fast. The blanket had fallen into her lap and she felt the pitiless cold all around her. He said something in his language, then he pressed her hands flat against his naked, heaving chest.

Her heart skipped and she was unable to collect her thoughts. He was so strong and so...warm. It was as if the small fire that he had built upon the ground now burned inside him. She did not wish to remove her hands, but to keep them there, warming them against his hidden flames. Soon, however, he tucked her hands beneath the blanket and eased her back to her prone position on the mat.

He returned to his position at her feet. He quickly lifted her leg and placed one of her feet in the small space under his arm. He did the same with her other foot, wedging it securely in the space beneath his other arm so that her legs now stretched outward, motionless and tucked beneath his arms.

His hurried frenzy ceased. He breathed slowly and she felt him watching her across the rift of darkness. Waiting. She still had no sensation in her feet, but she could feel the slight movement in her legs with the rise and fall of his breaths.

She felt helpless beneath him, yet strangely alert. In another life, he might have been a priest come to bless her on her deathbed, or a healer come to say a spell over her lifeless feet. Or, she thought wryly, he might have been her husband, staring down at her on their wedding night, preparing to take her for the first time on their joining mat.

Slowly, she began to feel it—the heat. He was sending it to her through the force of his invisible gaze and she drank it greedily, letting it fill her up.

In her cold-addled mind, she imagined him lifting her skirts and running his burning hands up and down her thighs. Then he thrust her legs apart and moved in closer, tongues of flame dancing off his body. He was her flaming god, her demon lover, and he hovered over her in the nightmare snowstorm as if trying to decide how he would consume her. *You owe me a debt,* he told her, *for saving your life.*

Her body burned and ached with the desire to pay for the gift of warmth he gave. *Take it,* she thought recklessly. *Take what you are owed.* In her fantasy, she arched her hips up as if to dare him.

'Oooww,' she howled suddenly.

Her fantasy burst into cinders, replaced by a powerful stinging sensation beginning in her big toes and emanating outward in a thousand needling waves. It was as if her feet were covered with feasting fire ants, or a thousand tiny cactus spines. She dug her fingernails into the blanket, trying to breathe through the agony, but found herself screaming instead.

He placed a corner of the blanket into her mouth, then gripped her feet more tightly to his chest. She tensed and thrashed as the searing pain in her feet transformed into a sharp, throbbing ache. She heard him say something quiet and sweet, something meant to soothe, though it only seemed to make the pain worse. She spit out the blanket and let out a long, low howl.

'Shhh,' he whispered, gently kneading her heels.

Her feet continued to throb, but she realised that she could now feel the heat of his skin against which they were pressed. Tentatively, she wiggled her toes, amazed that they were still there. An incredible warmth radiated from his body and she wondered how he had conjured it. Had he been dreaming such dreams as she had, perhaps? Or was he really a god, after all?

She could not think about it now. She could only feel the returned sensation in her feet, brought back from the dead, and a heavy exhaustion, as if she had just run a great distance. She was still cold, but not as cold as she had been, and she became aware that he had probably just saved her life.

Moving quickly, he bound her feet with his undershirt. She heard the sound of moving cloth and could only guess that he was continuing to disrobe. What madness was he about now?

He wrapped his arm around her back and lifted her up, arranging the blanket beneath them and then wrapping it around them both. He unwrapped his thick cotton leggings and placed them around her head like a hat, tucking the rest of his clothes behind her against the rock.

Naked but for a small loincloth, he stretched out beside her under the blanket and began to fumble with the ties of her skirts. She moved to stop him, but she could feel the heat coming off his bare skin like a blaze. She began to fumble with the ties herself.

She felt a wave of gratitude towards him—this man who was trying so hard to help warm her. She wanted to show him that she trusted him now, so she wiggled out of her undershirt as he had his, baring her breasts in the darkness.

He could not see her, of course, just as she could not see him. But she heard him draw a breath, as if surprised by her action. He seemed to stiffen as she placed her own undershirt beneath his head. She fussed with the cloth, wrapping it around his head as he had done for her, and was rewarded when she heard him laugh.

Soon they were lying on their sides and facing each other inside the cocoon he had forged, with nothing but their loincloths and a pocket of air to separate them.

Incredibly, she began to feel warmer. She could not believe it, but the air between them was not cold. It was warm and balmy with their breaths and it seemed to seep beneath her skin and into her bones.

He squeezed her hands reassuringly and she felt a tiny bolt of lightning pierce through her stomach. Instead of letting go of her hands, he squeezed them a little more tightly, as if trying to communicate something to her. They lay in that position for many moments, his hands squeezing hers, and she felt once again that strange sensation of being pulled towards him.

Then she did something she had been wanting to do since the day before. She placed her hand on his cheek. She sensed him shiver as she drew it down across his shaved jaw. She placed her other hand upon his other cheek so that she had his face in her hands. His terribly handsome face.

Amazingly, it was also radiant with heat and her hands warmed quickly. He edged closer to her and rubbed her arm and she felt it become warmer still. She placed her hand atop his arm and rubbed up and down, just as he had done, and he laughed again. Encouraged, she placed her hands flat upon his chest one more time. *'Chi'chi,'* she said in Totonac. *Hot.*

She did not immediately move her hands, but left them there atop the thick cakes of his upper chest muscles, enjoying the feeling more than she should, until she began to hear the sound of her own heart-beats in her ears.

Labouring beneath the excuse of warming him as he had her, she moved her hands downwards to his stomach. Like all the bearded ones, Benicio kept himself concealed beneath layers of cloth, no matter what the temperature, and several times that day she had found herself wondering what lay beneath it. She brushed her hands lightly across his taut stomach, startled to discover rows of thick undulating muscle. His strength, it seemed, was in proportion to his size.

He let out a low growl. She wrenched her hands away, fearful that she had done wrong. But he edged closer to her and she could feel his fiery breaths on her skin. He held out his blazing hand and placed a molten finger atop her breast.

She gasped.

His finger was so hot, but she did not think he was trying to warm her any more. She felt the tip of her breast tighten almost painfully beneath its thick pad and she moaned.

'Diós,' he said and traced a slow circle around her nipple until she felt something like relief. Had her fantasy just become real?

She was no longer merely warm, she was burning up inside their little cocoon, yet she could not suppress the strange yearning she felt to get nearer to him.

She forced herself to remain perfectly still as his finger made its way to her other nipple. Yes, yes, he surely was a god, for no man had ever made her feel pain that was also pleasure, or coaxed the strange dampness that she felt growing between her legs.

He concentrated as he traced the bud of her second nipple, staring across the darkness with the same powerful intent that he had used to warm her feet. But his touch was so gentle and so maddeningly purposeful. It was if he were tracing a picture of the sun in the soft sand of her flesh.

He moved his finger to her lips. He traced his finger along her top lip, then her bottom lip, as if reminding her of her own boldness the day she had pressed her lips against his…twice. She did not feel bold now. She felt unusually helpless, as though her icy will had finally melted into nothing but a puddle.

He pulled his finger off her lip and paused. He curled a strand of her hair around his finger and tugged it lightly. He unfurled the strand, then tapped her nose playfully. He seemed to be holding a question there, right at the tip of his finger, awaiting her answer.

Did she wish for a third kiss?

He traced his finger along her arm as lightly as a feather and a chill ran across her skin that had nothing to do with the cold. Then he placed his finger at the top of her woman's mound.

Fear hovered at the edge of her mind as she realised that even though she had got warm, she was still not thinking clearly. Moments ago, cold and ice had numbed her limbs. Now she felt as if she were drowning in sensation. The situation had grown beyond her control and she laboured to remind herself of all the reasons why the answer to his question had to be no.

This was an accident, after all. Not planned. They could not have anticipated the storm or the need to disrobe and huddle close in order to stay warm. Any man and woman in their place would experience the same yearning with their naked bodies together in such a confined space. The desire to join with another was a natural one.

But Tula could not allow herself to indulge that desire. They were partners, not lovers. He had made that reality very clear. He loved the woman in the picture. Luisa, he had called her, and had stared at her with eyes full of longing.

He did not look at Tula with such eyes. He did not look at Tula at all, as far as she could tell, unless it was across the darkness, probably imagining that Tula was his Luisa.

He does not value you. Malinali had warned. It was a statement quite easy to forget in the fog of lust that had invaded her mind.

Still, it was as true as the wind and the snow. She was not his wife. She was not his kin. She was nothing to him. She was his means to an end. If she allowed their relationship to become more than an agreement between thieves, she knew that the only outcome would be her own end.

It was different for women.

She remembered her mother's wailing moans that day, in the hottest month of the year. Tula had glimpsed inside their house for half a second before being pulled back out on to the porch by her father's patient hand.

'Your mother is in danger,' her father had explained. 'We must leave her alone with your sister and the midwives.' He had placed his face in his hands as Tula's mother let out a long, painful wail.

'Father, I am afraid.'

'Tell me,' her father choked, 'what are the four greatest cities in history?'

Her mother let out another terrifying scream. 'Father—'

'Tell me now, Tula. What are the four greatest cities in the history of the world?'

'Ah...um... Teotihuacan, the birthplace of the Totonacs, is first,' Tula began.

'That is a clever girl. Go on.'

'Tollan, city of art and wisdom is next, then Chichen Itza, the city between the cenotes, then Tenochtitlan, the floating city.'

'I have taught you well, my curious one,' he had said. Then her mother let out a sound so full of pain that Tula had pressed her legs to her chest, as if to protect herself from it. Her father had jumped up and rushed into the house.

In moments he had returned wearing the face of sorrow. 'You have another sister now, my dear Tula, but your mama has passed. She now resides in the best level of heaven.'

When a woman joined with a man, she risked getting with child. When she allowed him into the deepest part of her, she put her life in danger. Even if she did not get with child, she risked giving away her heart. In time, the man would leave her. Whether through death or simple disinterest, loved ones always left. They were like rays of sun. They shone on your face and lulled you with joy, then disappeared with the night. Love was dangerous and fleeting, so it was better not to love at all.

She took his finger and gently removed it from her woman's mound, placing it and the hand it belonged to securely on his own hip. *I am sorry*, she wished to say. She belonged to him—that was true. But if he was giving her a choice, then she chose solitude.

It was different for women, and especially for Tula.

She rolled over, showing him her back. He traced his finger along the curve of her hip, still questioning her. She gave him no response. He pushed his body against hers, nuzzling his face in her tangle of hair. 'Please,' he whispered, sounding as if he were enduring some terrible pain. She could feel the extent of his desire against her backside. It was thick and long and as hard as a tree limb.

Long ago, not long after Pulhko had married, she had described the act of love between a man and a woman. Tula and Xanca had listened, fascinated, and had laughed in disbelief when Pulhko had described the 'cenote's edge'. That is what she called the point during the cycle of a man's desire from which it was almost impossible for him to turn back. Now Tula feared that Benicio hovered dangerously close to that edge.

She needed to stop him—to put an end to this terrible yearning that had taken hold of the both of them and left them without their good judgment. She wondered what movement she could make to pull him away from the edge. Then she realised—it was not what she could do, but what she could say.

'Luisa,' she said simply. 'Luisa.'

Chapter Twenty-One

They had slept apart since the night of the snow-storm. Days passed slowly as the high mountains gave way to a dry, sun-scorched plain. As the company proceeded ever onwards, their quest for warmth had gradually been replaced by a quest for water.

And certainly that was for the best. Benicio had lost his head that night in the cold. He had not anticipated the potency of Tula's nearness, nor the havoc that her disrobing would wreak upon his mind. Like some lovestruck lad, he had allowed his body's urges to overmaster him and he was confounded by it.

Even now, as he cleared two separate spaces for their sleeping mats, the thought of Tula's soft nipple beneath his finger was making his body come awake against his will.

He appalled himself. He knew that she had disrobed in total innocence, only following his lead. Women's nudity was more acceptable in the West

Indies than it was in Spain. Besides, he had not actually seen her breasts at all. He had not even been certain of their nakedness until he had made bold to touch one.

Now he could scarcely think of anything other than that moment. He had never been a pious man, but for the first time in his life he wished there were a church somewhere close. Then he could give his confession and absolve himself of this wretched desire that seemed to flow beneath the solid ground of his plans, threatening to erode them.

She was his partner, not his lover. She was the only person besides Rogelio who had seen the map. He needed to keep himself in her good graces. Stealing her honour beneath a pine-bow shelter was no way to do that—to say nothing of the fealty that he owed Luisa.

At least someone had been able to keep her wits in that moment beneath the blanket. Indeed, Tula deserved much credit for her cleverness, for there was only one thing that could have snapped him out of the fog of his lust: the name of his beloved. *Luisa*, she had repeated several times, each invocation like a hammer into his gut.

But it had worked. Thank God, it had worked. He remained a gentleman in at least some respects and true to the woman he loved. Tula had made sure of it.

He watched her now, wandering amongst the agaves in the waning light. She appeared to be searching for something, but what? She was well concealed in her dark skirt and matching shawl, though he knew that she had layered her white costume beneath it for warmth. He imagined what it might be like to remove those heavy garments one layer at a time, as if unwrapping some beautiful, forbidden gift.

As if unwrapping treasure.

Diós Santo. What was wrong with him? He was not some dishonourable rogue who went about ravishing island women as the mood struck him. He had read Plato and Aristotle and Cicero, for goodness' sake. He had pondered history and philosophy and the role of virtue in human affairs. He lived by a code—one of honour and restraint. Or, at least, he had done so once.

And he would again, if he could only find enough gold to buy his way home.

The sun sank below the horizon and there was hurried movement across the plain as the soldiers scrambled to make camp. Nearby, a Maya woman shrieked with joy as she reunited with one of the Spanish crossbowmen. Benicio watched as they shared a long, deep kiss. Even in the driest, most desolate place in the world, love bloomed.

Scanning the slope, Benicio spied Big Tree amongst the soldiers nearby. The stout-hearted porter was unloading bedding for one of the soldiers he served. He spotted Benicio and waved enthusiastically. He was now the grateful owner of Benicio's doublet, though each time they met he insisted that Benicio take it back.

Benicio would not hear of it. The night of the snowstorm, many of the porters had died from the cold, and Benicio was resolute that this man, at least, would survive. Still, he wished that Big Tree's burden was not so great. And now, with their water and food stores depleted, he and the other Totonac and Taino porters would suffer more than the Spaniards, even as they worked harder. Cortés asked too much of the strong, tireless men.

Benicio returned his gaze to the area where Tula had been wandering. He searched in vain for her figure amongst the pointy agave cactus limbs and feathery branches of scrub. Far below him, a large blue lake spread out like a mirror. But it was a mirror of deception, for the scouts had discovered the lake's water to be briny and undrinkable.

The small lagoons they had passed during that afternoon were equally salty and unfit for consumption, though some of the soldiers drank from them anyway. Those men had quickly fallen ill, retching and heaving on the side of the trail. It was a grave situation, for as far as Benicio could tell there was no end to the desiccated wasteland.

One thing was for certain: this was no island. Benicio had read enough about the geography of the world to recognise that snow-capped volcanoes, interminable jungles and saline seas were not the closed, compacted features of some isolated isle. They trod upon a mass of land whose scale could not be comprehended—not the land described by Marco Polo, but something altogether different.

It was, quite simply, a new world.

Benicio felt the chill of night prickle his skin. A porter arrived to distribute Benicio's two sets of blankets and sleeping mats. 'Do you have a bit of water?' asked Benicio, making the motion to drink. The man laughed bitterly and shook his head, and Benicio coughed in an attempt to rid himself of the dryness that plagued his throat.

There was still no sign of Tula, so he busied himself arranging their separate sleeping places, stacking rocks around them as a makeshift windbreak. He found himself hoping for a frost, so that he might have a reason to take Tula in his arms once again. He laughed aloud at the outlandish wish, trying to dismiss it from his mind.

But where was Tula? Daylight was fading, and

Benicio could hear the distant yelping of coyotes heralding the night. He had resolved to begin his search for her when he heard a familiar voice over his shoulder.

'Cold comes quickly to the high desert, does it not?'

Without turning, Benicio let the blanket fall from his shoulders. He unsheathed his dagger and held it pointing at the ground. 'Come no closer,' Benicio growled, 'or I shall not hesitate to use this.'

'Peace, Brother. I come in peace. And with a proposition for you.'

'I do not wish to hear it, Rogelio,' said Benicio. 'Be gone.'

'I suppose I can just ask your woman directly, in that case.'

Benicio turned around and beheld the red-headed demon himself. 'If you even look at her ever again, I will kill you.'

'Calm yourself, Brother,' said Rogelio, favouring his left leg as he shuffled closer. 'Have we not known each other long enough to dispense with such idle threats?'

'Get out of my camp.'

'When you departed Spain, did you also depart with your manners?'

'I owe no manners to the man who tried to take my treasure…and my life.'

Benicio surveyed Rogelio's defences: two steel vambraces on either arm, a single broadsword and a chest and back plate. Benicio was both better armed than Rogelio and, in his new cotton armour, could easily outrun him. He glanced quickly at Rogelio's injured leg. It wept blood through his thick hose.

'You will not take anything of mine,' stated Benicio. 'You are overmatched.'

'I shall take everything, for I have seen the map.'

'The map of the West Indies?' Benicio feigned, looking around him. 'Believe me, it is incomplete.'

'Don't play the idiot,' barked Rogelio. 'I am talking about the map the Maya priest gave you at the battle of Potonchan. The diamond with its four circled points. The map to the gold.'

'A piece of rubbish. I care not that you have seen it.'

'You care not? Then it is nothing to you that I know what it depicts.'

Benicio was careful not to react. Chances were that Rogelio had been given the same information that Benicio had—that the map showed the ceremonial centre of Tenochtitlan.

Rogelio propped his foot on a rock as if he were

Cristobal Colón himself. 'I will tell you what the map depicts and we can seek the treasure together.'

Benicio laughed. 'Seek treasure with you? The Devil incarnate?'

Rogelio pretended not to hear. 'And as a symbol of our partnership, we shall exchange women.'

Benicio's laughter increased. *¡Que bueno!* Trading women as we might trade horses. Shall I have mine reshod before the exchange?'

Rogelio growled. 'She tried to kill me that day, you know.'

'What?'

'Your Totonac woman tried to kill me that day on the beach.'

'I believe it was you who tried to kill me on the beach.'

'I was not trying to kill you, Brother, only to wound you.' Rogelio laughed. 'I knew the blade would not penetrate deeply.'

'Ah! So *you* did not try to kill *me*, but *she* tried to kill *you*?'

'She did, the little witch.' Rogelio's eyes scanned the surroundings, searching for her. 'She stuck me hard in the thigh with one of her arrows.'

And that is why you limp, Benicio realised.

In truth, Benicio remembered very little about that day on the beach. All he knew was that he'd been too exhausted from carrying his valuable armour to outrun Rogelio any more.

He remembered collapsing beneath Rogelio's weight and sustaining a sharp blow to his chest. The next thing he knew he had awakened to find a beautiful woman in the act of stealing the golden ring right out of his mouth. 'She may be a thief, but she is not a killer,' Benicio stated.

'It is understandable that you should think so. You want to believe that you are safe.'

'Convince me that I am not.'

'I spied her in the forest at the edge of the beach that day. She was soaked with water and appeared to be in distress. But when I approached to aid her, she sent arrows flying, followed by a barrage of stones. The final arrow stuck right here.' He pointed to the middle of his thigh.

'But you were wrestling with me. How did you know she was there in the forest?'

'She shrieked.'

'Shrieked?'

'After I stabbed you, she shrieked. That's how I knew she was there.'

'And then she impaled you with her arrow?'

'She did not throw with her hand, but with a throwing tool. She could have killed me.'

'If she is such a killer, then why do you wish her for yourself?'

'I seek justice, Brother. The wound she made has festered and does not heal. I have lost my ability to run. I fear that soon I will not walk. She must be punished for what she has done.' Rogelio glanced down at the bed mats. 'She must be put in her rightful place. She must be…conquered.'

Benicio gripped his daggers so tightly that his knuckles ached. He wanted to kill Rogelio right then. He wanted to stick his blades into Rogelio's neck and watch his evil blood bubble out on to the hardpan. But if he did that, then he was no better than Rogelio, whose lust for gold and power had twisted him into something that no longer resembled a man.

Benicio took a long, steadying breath. 'If you have seen the map, then why do you march with this tired company? Why not simply retrieve the gold and return to Vera Cruz where you can wait for some seaworthy brig to take you back to Spain?'

'It is my intention to do just that,' said Rogelio. 'Though you and I both know the punishment for mutineers.' He shifted on to his right leg and cringed in pain.

It was as Benicio suspected, then. Rogelio was bound for Tenochtitlan just as Benicio was. He would seek his treasure inside the Templo Mayor, the double temple at the head of Tenochtitlan's sacred square, which Benicio had learned was the tallest and most important temple in all Tenochtitlan. But Rogelio could not extract the treasure alone. His injured leg prevented it. That was why he needed Benicio.

There was a sudden rustling in the bushes behind Rogelio and Benicio's heart leapt. He hoped it was Tula and prayed it was not all at once. But it was merely one of Cortés's mastiff hounds foraging for game. The giant dog sniffed the air, then bared his teeth at Rogelio.

'Leave us, stupid dog,' said Rogelio, but the creature growled menacingly.

'*¡Fuera!*' shouted Benicio. *Get out of here!* Startled, the dog yelped and dashed off into the brush.

Rogelio gave Benicio a disingenuous bow. 'Can you see now? I need you and you need me.'

'I don't need you for anything,' snarled Benicio, 'for I too, know where the treasure is hidden.'

'Do you know *exactly* where it is hidden?' asked Rogelio. 'I did not think so. Besides, there is another reason you need me: I have something of yours.'

'What could you possibly have of mine?'

'You skipped away so quickly the morning Captain Saucedo arrived that you neglected to retrieve your second letter.' Rogelio reached beneath his breastplate and produced a small envelope. 'What was her name? The woman you spoke of so incessantly on our voyage to Hispañola? It was Luisa, was it not?'

Rogelio flashed the envelope before Benicio's eyes and the long, elegant 'f' of Villafuerte told Benicio all that he needed to know. He felt a lump in his throat.

'Ah, now I see that I have your attention.'

Benicio leapt forward to take the envelope, but Rogelio snatched it away, and grabbed the nape of his water bag. 'I can destroy this letter in two seconds and you will never know what it contains.'

'That letter is worth more than a thousand pounds of gold.'

'Then we are agreed. We shall join forces to pursue the treasure of Tenochtitlan. I shall give you your second letter and we shall swap our Totonac women, to solidify the pact.'

Benicio stepped backwards. 'I would never join forces with a man who would seek to…conquer my woman.'

'*Your* woman?' spat Rogelio. 'What about this woman?' He waved the letter in the air. 'I met her once, don't you recall? She loved my papayas.'

'Go to Hell.'

Rogelio scowled. 'If you will not give your Totonac woman to me, then I will take her myself.'

'Over my dead body.'

'Let us hope it does not come to that.'

'I am not afraid of you.'

'You should be, for I have nothing on this cursed earth to lose. You, on the other hand...' Rogelio fanned himself with the letter. 'Think about my proposition, Brother. Why not let my Totonac woman caress your pretty face for a while? Then you can get your treasure and return to your dear Luisa. Let us not squander this opportunity to make our fortunes.'

'I do not need your help to make my fortune.'

'We'll see,' said Rogelio, flashing a devilish grin. 'Tomorrow we shall reach the rebel city of Tlaxcala. Let us seal our own alliance there, Brother, and after we succeed, I will give you this fine little missive—on my honour.'

Benicio spat in the dirt. 'You have no honour.' Rogelio did not respond, for he had already begun to walk away. 'Rogelio?' asked Benicio, feeling the bile of hate bubble up into his throat.

'Yes?'

'Do not ever call me Brother again.'

'But brothers we are,' said Rogelio. 'The world has fated it.' Then Rogelio disappeared into the twilight.

Benicio stood unmoving. There was another letter.

When had she written it? If she had penned it before the first letter—before Armando's proposal—then it was likely some sweet outpouring of her fealty. But if it had been sent after the first letter, it was surely some important news. Either her engagement to Armando had ended, or the wedding had taken place.

Which was it? An outpouring of love, or a quiet severing of their unwritten pact?

He was so lost in his contemplations that he did not notice Tula lumber into camp, the mastiff following cheerfully behind her. She was carrying a stalk as long as a tree trunk, but green and pliable, its layered tip bending as she hauled it across the ground. In her face he read exhaustion and something else. A kind of pride, perhaps—like the dignity of a huntress lugging her hard-won bounty into camp.

She bent and tilted the stalk to the dog's lips and a clear liquid trickled out into her cupped hand.

Tula patted the dog on the head, then held the stalk out to Benicio, who could still not quite believe what he had just seen. The stalk was as large as his arm and many times as long. It had scars near its tip—a memory of trimmed branches—and a middle composed of loosely woven fibres. Benicio could not imagine where she had discovered such a verdant, succulent thing in this grey place.

She held out the limb beseechingly now and he felt much like the panting mastiff. He took the stalk and held it to his lips.

The taste of the liquid that poured forth was earthy and slightly sweet, like tea flavoured with honey, and Benicio could feel his body's almost instant revival. He drank greedily, seizing upon the liquid relief. His limbs grew lighter. His thoughts, clearer. Even his eyes seemed to see better in the waning light. Forcing himself to cease, he motioned for Tula to take his place beneath the heavenly trickle.

She shook her head. *I have already drunk*, she appeared trying to say. Still he insisted, and finally she capitulated, kneeling down beside him while he tilted the remaining liquid into her mouth.

He should not have looked down at her in that moment. Her cheeks were too flushed, her lips too red and bright with her exertion. His mind rollicked with forbidden thoughts of her and he had to turn away.

Luisa, Luisa, Luisa, he thought.

Thankfully, the stream of liquid finished. She took the stalk into her hands and stood, smiling up at Benicio triumphantly. God save him, he wanted nothing more than to take those rosy cheeks in his hands and kiss her hard.

She sighed, then pulled the stalk towards her. Benicio felt his arms being yanked, and he realised that he had not let go of the stalk himself. He looked down. There were his hands, right next to hers, almost touching them. And there, just above her hands was her taut stomach, and above that, her breasts. He felt himself growing hard with lust. He knew he should release the stalk. Instead, he pulled it towards him.

She stumbled forward, keeping her hands firmly in place. Now she was only a hand's length away from him. With a single pull, he knew he could have her body pressing against his. She peered up at him, lifting a single brow in curiosity. She was not going to let go of the stalk.

His heart pounded in his ears until it was the only thing he could hear. His lust for her tore through his body and he squeezed the plant until he felt it collapsing inside his grip.

'Benicio?' she asked. She looked down at the broken stalk and he saw her notice the evidence of his desire stretching beneath it. He stepped backwards and turned his body in shame.

'I'm sorry,' he said, trying to compose himself. He stood looking out at the grey plateau for many long moments. Finally, he cleared his throat and turned to face her. 'Thank you,' he said, glancing at the broken stalk. 'I did not mean to do that.'

She shook her head as if to tell him not to worry. *'Octli,'* she said, dropping the stalk upon the ground.

'Ah!' Benicio exclaimed, understanding that the liquid they had drunk was the source of the intoxicating drink that the Totonacs poured for the Spaniards so generously. Thank God that it had not yet begun to ferment, Benicio thought wryly, for then he would have certainly pulled her atop him and ravished her in the sand.

She patted the mastiff once more on the head. Their thirsts sated, there seemed to be nothing more to say. She settled herself on the mat that Benicio had placed for her many paces away. She rolled herself up in her blanket and turned her back to him.

'Goodnight, Benicio,' she said.

'Goodnight, Tula.'

He felt like he had been spun around a hundred times, then told to walk straight. Where was he? And what was he doing?

Ah, yes, Luisa.

He pulled his book from beneath his cotton armour and stretched out on to his own mat. He shook his head, trying to eradicate the vision of Tula that had invaded his mind. Mechanically, he opened Luisa's second letter—the one he had received in Vera Cruz—then realised there was no longer enough light to read it by. When had it become so dark?

He returned the letter to its place and sat up, unable to sleep. He noticed the small, shadowy figure of the mastiff curled up at the base of Tula's feet. The dog had begun to snore rhythmically.

Benicio smiled at the peaceful scene, glad that the fearsome animal had made himself her friend. With Rogelio's intentions now apparent, Tula would need all the protection she could get.

Benicio placed his dagger beneath his mat. He pulled his blanket over him and turned towards her. For many long moments, he watched her back rising and falling with her breaths.

How clever she was, he thought, to have conjured water from this parched land.

Rogelio said that she had shrieked that day at the beach, right after he had thrust his blade into Benicio's chest. Rogelio claimed that it was why he had abandoned Benicio—the sound of Tula's voice.

Benicio stretched out on his back and stared up at the stars, but it might as well have been daytime, for he was not seeing them. Nor did he take out Luisa's sketch and stare at it in the dim starlight, as was his custom. Instead, his mind churned with visions of Tula shrieking in the jungle.

By attempting to condemn Tula, Rogelio had unknowingly given Benicio another reason to stand in awe of her. Tula, this small, beautiful enchantress who coaxed fish from the sea and water from the desert, had also saved Benicio's life.

Chapter Twenty-Two

The wall protecting the border of Tlaxcala Territory was nine feet high and twenty paces wide. It stretched across the mouth of the river valley in three leagues of fitted stone. The Spanish–Totonac army had finally reached the home of the fierce Tlaxcalans, whom Cortés planned to rally to his cause.

Cortés guided his men through an open gate, then up an empty road that paralleled the river, increasing the speed of their march. Benicio began to wonder why not a single Tlaxcalan had yet come out to greet them. It was widely known that the Tlaxcalans refused to submit to Montezuma. Surely they would embrace the idea of joining with the Spanish and the Totonacs to invade the Mexica capital?

Benicio studied the quiet forest. Something was amiss.

He stepped out of formation, pretending to relieve himself on the side of the road. As the other men passed, he wrestled with the wraps of his cotton armour, pretending to be busy as the women's company approached.

He spotted Tula immediately. She walked next to Marina at the head of the entourage, her hair tied in two smart braids, her heavy skirts flouncing. There was a flower tucked behind her ear—a flower, by God!—and she appeared to be laughing, as if sharing some private joke with Marina.

Benicio bristled. This was no time to be laughing and wearing flowers. Marina of all people should know that this land of Tlaxcala was not safe. Cortés should not have taken their company a step beyond the gate without assurances of peace from the Tlaxcalan rulers. This valley was nothing but a trap.

Benicio jumped out from the side of the road and pulled Tula aside. 'You must stay here,' he commanded. 'Until I know that it is safe.' There was a wave of scandalous chatter as the other women passed and Malinali motioned to Tula to rejoin them.

But Benicio would not allow Tula to continue onwards. He might not have served in any army, but something inside him knew that there was danger up ahead. It was as if he could smell it.

Tula shook her head. She shrugged off his hold in frustration and made to rejoin the women, who were practically trotting now to keep up with the increased speed of the men's march.

'No,' Benicio commanded. He pulled her by the arm back to his side and pointed down the bank towards the river. 'You stay here, where it is safe. Stay near the river.' How could he explain to her that he was trying to protect her, that the women were wrong and that he was right?

He could not even begin to try, for once again she had slid her slender arm right out of his grasp. She hurried to catch up with the other women, who had disappeared around a sharp curve. Benicio sighed. He was not proud of what he was about to do.

He jumped to his feet and broke into his fastest run, reaching her well before she was able to disappear around the bend and rejoin the others. He grabbed her by the waist and pulled her to the ground.

He straddled her body with his and held her wrists together above her head. 'It's not safe,' he explained pointlessly and as he spoke he noticed that she was studying his lips.

A pang of lust vaulted through him. The enchantress was doing it again. *No, no, no.* He was shaking his head at her. *Your trickery will not work on me any more.*

But she caught his eye and he saw a sweetness in

her expression that could not have been feigned. His heart pounded as she studied his nose, his cheeks, his chin, returning finally to his lips. It was as if she were observing the territory that she had conquered, or would soon conquer. Then she did something unexpected. She ceased her resistance, sighed and closed her eyes.

What fresh deception was this? Had she given up her fight for freedom so easily? He doubted that very much. Perhaps she had resolved to feign rest until he relaxed his hold on her. Or perhaps she simply abhorred the sight of him.

Demonios, this was not going as he had hoped it would. His objective was to protect her and to win her friendship, not to allow himself to dangle like a fish at the end of one of her spears. Slowly, he removed his hands from her wrists. She did nothing, just continued to lie upon the ground, feigning sleep.

He jumped up and ran up the road. 'Malinali,' he called, motioning to the woman in the feathered cloak. He arrived huffing at her side. 'I need your help,' he explained.

'What do you mean?'

'I need you to translate. Please, come.'

Reluctantly, Malinali took her leave of the other women and accompanied Benicio back down the road where Tula still lay stubbornly still, her eyes sealed shut. They squatted beside her.

'She will not obey you, if that is what you want,' said Malinali.

'I only wish to keep her safe.'

'She does not wish to abandon the other women. She cares for them.'

'She will wish to run from this place once she understands the danger. So will you.'

Malinali shook her head and sighed. 'What do you want me to tell her?'

Benicio paused, realising that he did not know. She was as defiant as a child and he knew that any explanation or command he might give her would just be met with more silence.

'Tell her that her lips are like soft cotton pillows and that her lashes remind me of the feathers of the majestic nighthawk.'

Malinali gave Benicio a look of confusion, but quickly translated his words into Totonac.

Benicio studied Tula's face and thought he saw her blink.

'Tell her that she is cleverer than a priest, faster than a hummingbird and lovelier than the forest at dusk. Tell her that when she walks across the earth all of nature takes notice.'

Malinali rolled her eyes, but did his bidding.

Benicio watched as the beginning of a grin played at the edges of Tula's lips.

'Tell her that I would fight a jaguar with my bare hands to keep her safe.'

Malinali laughed, choking out the translation. Finally, Tula opened her eyes. She frowned at Benicio and shook her head, but he could tell that he had made her heart smile.

Benicio delighted at the small triumph. He spotted the iris behind her ear. Without thinking, he bent to smell it.

He was rewarded with a sweet, earthy scent. He took in another noseful and realised that he had in fact arrived quite close to her lips. His heart hammering inside his chest, he bent his head down closer.

He wanted so badly to kiss her. His lips hovered over hers like a theory that had yet to be proved. 'Malinali, tell Tula that I think about her all the time, that I cannot get her out of my mind. Tell her that I—'

At that moment, there was a loud boom.

He stood up in alarm. In the distance, he heard the shrieks of the women—beyond them, the sounds of gunfire. 'To the river!' Benicio commanded, motioning down the steep riverbank beside the road. He helped Tula to her feet.

'Follow the river upstream until you are outside the gates,' he told Malinali, pointing in the direction that they had come. Meanwhile, the rest of the women came running back around the curve. 'I will tell the men where you are hiding. We will come for you when it is safe.'

Malinali nodded in understanding. She shouted instructions to the frightened women and soon the large troupe had disappeared down the riverbank. Only Tula and Malinali remained on the road.

There was more gunfire in the distance and a crescendo of haunting, high-pitched screams.

Malinali motioned for Tula to follow her down the slope, but Tula hesitated. She took both of Benicio's hands in hers and said something urgent to him in her language. Her eyes flickered with emotion and she squeezed his hands tightly. Then she closed her eyes, lifted the back of his right hand and pressed her lips to it. An instant later she had disappeared with Malinali down the riverbank.

Benicio was stunned. Had she just bade him farewell? Had she told him to take care? He ran down the road to rejoin his compatriots, but he felt as if he were floating.

When he rejoined the rest of the company, he quickly tumbled back to earth. They stood, open-mouthed, as a legion of painted warriors approached.

The fearsome feathered men marched in ordered regiments of fifty men each—just like the Spaniards. Unlike the Spaniards, however, there were thousands of them. Tens of thousands.

'Crossbowmen and musketeers, support the flanks,' Cortés shouted. 'Infantrymen, fight to kill. Do not break ranks! For God and Spain!'

The men whooped and cheered, though Benicio suspected that many of them only did so to keep from crying. He saw several of the men making emergency confessions to Father Olmedo and Father Diaz. The Tlaxcalan drums beat out their ominous rhythms as waves and waves of the warriors approached. Then the two armies met and the sounds of violence rent the air.

Benicio had no choice but to fight. He unsheathed his sword and let it clang against the Tlaxcalans' obsidian blades. The men who fought next to him killed with abandon, slashing the shrieking warriors in single strokes. Benicio's own blows were slow and reluctant. Still, they hit their marks. In defending his life, he took the lives of dozens of strong, healthy men.

Slowly, the air filled with the stench of blood and the moans of the dying, and Benicio imagined how many wives had lost their husbands on this day, and how many fathers had lost their sons.

* * *

By the end of the day, and by some miracle, the Spanish and Totonacs had triumphed. For the second time since their arrival in the New World, the Spanish had managed to hold off the native people—thousands upon thousands of them—without a single casualty of their own.

Something was not right. Simple mathematics told Benicio that the Indians, who were well armed and physically stronger than the Spaniards, should not be dying in such great numbers. Their numbers alone should have decimated the Spanish army.

Yet hundreds of Tlaxcalan warriors lay dead on the ground, many placed there by Benicio's sword. More useless fighting. More unnecessary death. The other conquistadors praised him and slapped him upon the back, as if he were some kind of hero.

But he did not feel like a hero. His arms ached and his soul stank. As he slunk back to the river, he thought of Luisa. She was the reason he had done it—but why? To keep her in fine skirts? To pay for the servants she required to attend her? To own the lands that she wished to rule?

He had not been hurt, but Benicio felt strangely wounded. A familiar laceration had opened up inside his soul and bled there now, and every time he tried to imagine Luisa's spirit, he lost connection with his own.

He was so very tired and confused, and when he arrived at the river he collapsed upon its low bank, sending up a cloud of dry dirt all around him. He lay there for many moments, desiccated like the earth. At length he scooted forward like the lowly creature he was. He hung his head and drank, hating how good its sweet water tasted upon his tongue.

When he finally sat up, he was shocked to behold Tula's sandaled feet. She had sneaked up beside him without a sound. He squinted up at her and could see that she carried something in her overskirt. She bent to her knees and held it out to him. At its bottom was a cluster of tiny, urn-shaped fruits. They appeared to be figs.

'*Tuna,*' she whispered, nodding down at the bounty.

'No,' said Benicio, rolling away. He could not even think of eating. He never wanted to eat again.

She moved closer. 'Benicio?' *Are you all right?* she seemed to ask.

'I am fine,' Benicio mumbled. *They are clearing a place for me in Hell.*

He wished she would go away. He did not want her to see him now, fresh from battle, stained with blood and reeking of death. He was not the man she believed him to be. He was not some omnipotent god, come to earth to help save her sister from the wicked Mexica.

She was still holding out her skirt. He watched the river in silence, pretending she was not there. She reached out her hand to touch the wound above his eye and he flinched. 'Benicio?' she whispered.

Fuming, he tilted his head to look at her.

Christ, she was beautiful. Not in the sweet, round, comely way that Luisa was beautiful, but in the way of a star—sharp and restless and ablaze with light. Where did it come from, all that smouldering radiance? The Mexica had taken her sister—that was really all he knew about her. Surely it was anger that danced behind those dark, luminous eyes. Perhaps she had buried her wrath so deeply inside herself that it was part of her now, like his guilt had become a part of him.

Though in moments like this, with her pride and cunning stripped away, with her compassion wrapping around him like a cloak, she was only kind, only loving, and his heart seemed to reach towards her, catching inside his throat.

He buried his head in the dust. He wished she would go away. He did not deserve her kind of tenderness.

'Go!' he snarled. He swatted her hand away from

his eye and watched her recoil. Many moments passed as she sat there regarding him, as if considering what to do. He held himself frozen, certain she would soon give up her efforts to rouse him.

Instead, she redoubled them. She lifted a fig from the pile she had gathered and held it close to his lips. *'Tuna,'* she said. 'Benicio.'

Her voice was like a soft caress and he hated it. He was a killer, did she not realise that? He had slain over two dozen men today alone. He was not one of Plato's men of virtue and civilisation. He was no more than a beast, come to kill and plunder.

He shook his head. He closed his eyes and pressed his face against the cold ground. No, he did not deserve a woman like Tula. He did not deserve any woman. 'Leave me alone,' he pleaded, grinding his forehead into the dirt.

If she stayed any longer, he feared he would explode into a thousand broken pieces of himself. But there she remained, unmoving. 'Get out of here!' he yelled at last. He swatted at her again, carelessly swiping up an armful of dirt.

It mushroomed into a cloud—a dry, angry cloud of dust that was thick enough to blot out the sun. It settled on her face, on her blouse, on her fine skirt and on all of the figs she carried within it. She coughed as she shuffled backwards, blinking to recover her sight. The figs tumbled to the ground all around him.

He could not look at her now. He could not witness the state of disgrace that he had placed her in. Indeed, it made him hate himself even more. It meant that he was not just a soulless killer, he was also a brute. He was the kind of man that kicked dirt into a good woman's face. And not just any woman. *His* woman. His clever, beautiful, kind woman.

The woman he loved.

He stared blankly at the ground, stunned. She was the only thing real in his life—the only person in the world who made him want to be a better man.

His heart twisted in his chest, and he rolled over in shame. 'I am so sorry, Tula,' he muttered at last. 'I did not mean to treat you that way.'

But she was already gone.

Chapter Twenty-Three

He lay alone that night, shivering by the river. There was no sleep for his weary body, no rest for his wicked soul—only visions of wild animals and enemy tribes and dishonourable Spaniards prowling the forest.

Was she sheltered? Was she warm? Perhaps she had taken refuge amongst the agave plantations on the dry plains below. He pictured her there, exposed among the thorny plants and without Benicio to protect her from the cold mountain winds.

He could not even bear to think of the other possibility: that Rogelio had found her.

Benicio knew that Rogelio had many friends among the ranks—evil men who would not hesitate to seize Tula and collect on some promised reward. Benicio buried his head in his hands. He had shunned his most important ally, had humiliated the woman who had likely saved his life. What kind of man did that?

* * *

The next morning, she was nowhere to be found. He wandered up and down the river in the pale hours before dawn, watching his own breath.

After sunrise, Benicio and the other soldiers marched down the narrow valley to meet their enemy once again. 'Santiago y Cierra España!' cried Cortés and the men cheered and rallied at the invocation of their fathers' campaigns against the Moors.

But Benicio would not be moved. 'For fame and treasure!' he shouted bitterly and the men of his regiment looked at him in alarm. 'That's what we are really here for, is it not? That is why we kill? We wish to return to Seville and have our choice of well-born ladies.' Several of his proud compatriots started towards him in anger. Benicio spat on the ground and readied himself for a fight.

He would not get his wish, however, because in that moment the sound of a hundred trumpeting conch shells filled the air and thousands of Tlaxcalan warriors bore down upon their small company in a blur of feathers and war paint.

By the afternoon, the Tlaxcalan forces had been vanquished once again.

That evening, the conquistadors took refuge on a nearby hilltop, where an abandoned fort promised shelter against the mountain winds. They settled themselves inside the dark fort and tried to find rest.

For Benicio, there was only torment. Weary with fatigue, he stumbled around the camp. 'Tula,' he called. The other men watched him with a mixture of compassion and contempt. This was no time to be worrying oneself over a woman.

But Benicio did not care what the other men thought. He found himself at the riverside once again. There, upon the bank, was a single fig.

'Tula,' he whispered.

He sensed that she was near. If he was right, then he would find her. The two of them had an agreement to uphold, after all. An alliance. She would help him find his gold and he would help her find her sister. They needed each other.

There was also the small detail that he owed her his life.

He wandered into the women's camp. 'Tula?' he asked, then held his hand at his elbow to represent her height. The women merely shook their heads, returning their attention to their pots of bubbling beans.

The porters were even less helpful. The tired men emerged from their shelters and stared at Benicio with something like pity behind their eyes.

The rain began to fall, but still he wandered. There

had been so much killing that day, much of it accomplished by his own hand. He felt wretched and sullied and yearned for her forgiveness.

The sun sank below the horizon. Still standing, he pressed his tired body against the trunk of a tree and closed his eyes. When he opened them, a stout man was walking towards him through the grey rain.

'Greetings, Big Tree. A lovely evening for a stroll,' Benicio mocked, knowing the man could not understand him. Benicio noticed a wool blanket wrapped about the man's stocky frame.

'Where is your doublet?' asked Benicio, though he hardly cared.

Big Tree bowed low, then threw off his blanket. Benicio bent to retrieve it, but Big Tree stopped him and began to shiver. Benicio watched closely, realising that the porter was just pretending to shiver.

Clearly Big Tree was trying to tell Benicio that he had given away Benicio's doublet.

'It is nothing. I understand,' said Benicio. Since the beginning of the siege, the porters had been left to forage and survive on their own. Surely the man had traded Benicio's doublet in some nearby town and was now attempting to explain his actions.

Benicio pointed at the blanket. 'You traded it for the blanket, right? And perhaps some food? You did what you must.'

'No, no, no,' said Big Tree. He removed the imaginary doublet once again, then pretended to accept it from himself.

Benicio was growing tired of this. Big Tree did not need to explain to him why he had sold the doublet. Benicio motioned for Big Tree to go.

Big Tree refused. Instead, he placed his arms at the level of his thighs and swished them from side to side, as if he were holding a skirt.

A skirt?

Sensing Benicio's interest, Big Tree quickly repeated his movements, now in a different order: He removed his invisible doublet, swished his invisible skirts, then smiled and put on the doublet once again.

'Tula?' Benicio asked.

'Yes, yes,' Big Tree said. The porter had gifted his doublet to Tula.

Benicio gripped Big Tree by the shoulders. 'Where? Where did she go?'

The man shook his head and shrugged.

'When? Today? Yesterday?'

'Yest-a-dey,' Big Tree said and Benicio embraced him so hard that the poor man began to cough.

When Benicio released him, Big Tree bowed, whisking his blanket from the ground. He had finally repaid his debt to Benicio. He had somehow discovered Tula and given her the gift of warmth, possibly saving her life. It seemed that this humble Taino man from Cuba had more honour in his little finger than most of the Spaniards did in their entire bodies.

'Thank you,' Benicio said and gave the man the deepest, sincerest bow he had ever given anyone.

Big Tree bowed back, then turned and disappeared into the mist.

She could not be far, if only a day ago she had encountered Big Tree. And wherever she was going, she had not been captured. She was alive, she was well, and, thanks to Big Tree, she was warm.

Benicio smiled sadly. Of course she was alive, for she was a hunter and a survivor. He recalled her sweet, haughty walk across the beach of Vera Cruz and the pride she had shown when she found water inside the agave stalk. He was certain she had been equally proud to have found the figs that day by the river. Instead of showing gratitude, however, he had kicked dirt in her face. She deserved better than that from him. From anyone. No wonder she had left him.

The rain trickled through the bows of the tree like the tears of some foreign god. 'Goodnight, Tula,' he said, picturing her curled up in warmth. Finally, for the first time in two days, he let the oblivion of sleep take him.

* * *

The next morning, Benicio and the other Spanish soldiers looked down from their hilltop to behold a sea of Tlaxcalan warriors even larger than the day before. One terrified musketeer observed that there were at least twenty thousand of them. Benicio estimated their numbers closer to forty. Forty thousand Tlaxcalans against an army of three hundred Spaniards and five hundred Totonacs. Against those odds, any Spanish or Italian or French general would have waved the white flag.

But not Cortés. He ordered the cannons lit and told his men to shore up their hearts. The battle to conquer the New World had only just begun.

Benicio did his best not to kill. He fought alone, as far as possible from the front lines, smashing his steel sword against each man's obsidian club until exhaustion set in. But instead of delivering death, he delivered a command. 'Leave!' he would shout, pointing to the forest.

It was not always effective. Some men fought mindlessly, with the zeal of lifelong soldiers. Benicio had no choice but to defend himself against them, though he did it with loathing. He hated Cortés in those moments, but he also hated himself. He hardly cared about the treasure any more. All he wished was that he could find Tula and that the fighting would cease.

* * *

On the fifth morning, part of his wish came true. A party of Tlaxcalan nobles rode out to meet Cortés and concede defeat. Food arrived soon after, turkeys and berries and maize flour, along with dozens of slave women to prepare it. Benicio searched among them for Tula, but was disappointed. When a blushing Maya cook offered him a roasted turkey leg, he refused it.

After several days, the triumphant Spanish–Totonac army marched into the city of Tlaxcala. The tops of countless stone pyramids streamed white smoke as the army was ushered into a central plaza as big as a Spanish bull ring.

Before Cortés could even dismount, four venerable chiefs were bowing to their newest and greatest ally—the man whose army could not be defeated; the man who would help them finally overcome the Mexica.

The days passed like months in the dry mountain city of Tlaxcala as the Spanish–Totonac–Tlaxcalan army prepared for the final march on Tenochtitlan. Benicio spent many long hours in the marketplace, scanning every face he saw, hoping to find his only friend.

One day, he thought he spied a woman in a dirt-stained doublet dashing across Tlaxcala's central plaza. He ran after her, but lost sight of her among a group of beekeepers crowding the base of Tlaxcala's Great Temple.

Benicio stared up at the giant edifice, the familiar path of dried blood staining its steps. Just beneath it was a low building, open to the street, with large, colourful murals decorating its inner walls. Perhaps the woman had escaped into that strange, enchanting space?

Benicio wandered inside to behold scenes of battle and triumph, of gods and goddesses, of hunts and harvests and trade—all swirling in a riot of colour. The murals were as beautiful as any fresco or frieze adorning the walls of Spain's great cathedrals and Benicio lost himself inside the fascinating histories they told.

As he journeyed deeper into the space, the light diminished until all he could discern were shadowy movements at the back of a long hall. Suddenly, a flame illuminated the darkness. A man in a priest's robe held a torch into the air. He was followed by two poorly dressed young men who were obviously slaves. One of the young men was carrying an earthen pot.

The three stopped before a cluster of large wooden

cages. The first young man held out a small bowl while the other poured some of the contents of the pot into it. The first boy stretched the bowl through the bars of the cage. Benicio froze when he saw a hand emerge to receive it.

It was a human hand.

Benicio looked closer. A grown man crouched inside the cage like a beast, doubled over and unable to move. His face was tattooed with a soldier's emblem and the muscles of his arms bulged as he held the bowl to his mouth and drank. He returned the bowl to the boy and looked up, catching Benicio's eye.

Benicio shuffled backwards, his sudden movement echoing through the hall. Hearing the disturbance, the holy man looked up, quickly spying Benicio. The man's face twisted into an angry scowl and he whispered something to the two slaves. Benicio stumbled backwards in fear. He knew that if he were captured now, he would be placed inside one of the cages himself. He broke into a run.

He ran out of the great hall and back across the plaza, stumbling into the market and making his way to its busiest part. He hunched down, trying not to draw attention to himself, feigning interest in a tomato vendor's offerings while he struggled to regain his breath.

There was no doubt that he had just witnessed the feeding of a sacrifice victim. The caged soldier Benicio had seen would soon be splayed across some bloody sacrificial stone, an obsidian blade hovering over his heart. And the man was not alone. There had been dozens of such cages, perhaps hundreds, stretching deep into the shadowy hall.

It occurred to Benicio that the native people of this New World did not fight to destroy their enemies. They went to battle to find victims for sacrifice and slavery. They did not fight to kill, Benicio realised. They fought to collect.

Suddenly, Benicio saw the future. He saw a world in which relatively few Spaniards took this crowded continent and placed it beneath their steel boots— not through the advantage of gunpowder or horses, but due to the simple fact that the Spanish fought to kill and the native people did not.

Benicio stiffened as he considered the implications of this truth. Cortés was not going to Tenochtitlan to free prisoners or negotiate treaties. He meant to invade the capital city and seize it. That was why he walked with such arrogance, such certainty of triumph. If the Mexica soldiers did not fight to kill, then Cortés was sure to defeat them. He knew that he could not lose. In a sense, he had already won.

And Benicio and the rest of his men were just pawns, unaware of the bloody errand that lay ahead. They were no longer simple traders, nor were they explorers in search of treasure. They were warriors now, merciless, bloodstained invaders whose souls were quickly passing beyond salvation.

They were conquistadors.

'Greetings, Benicio.' Benicio jumped at the sound of his name. The small tomato that he had taken into his hand went flying and was captured in the air by a man with a scar so prominent and ugly that Benicio could have recognised him from a league away.

'Rogelio.'

'You look as though you have just seen a ghost.' said Rogelio, popping the tomato into his mouth.

'I have,' said Benicio. 'The ghost of the future.'

Benicio noticed that Rogelio leaned upon a cane. 'Ah, that ghost,' said Rogelio. 'He is ugly indeed.'

Benicio frowned. 'Speak plainly, or leave.'

'I have merely observed that you are without your lovely Totonac assassin these many days.'

Benicio gripped the hilt of his dagger, searching Rogelio's expression. 'If you know her whereabouts, tell me now, or I shall plunge this blade directly into that festering wound in your thigh.'

'Peace!' shouted Rogelio, dragging his lame leg

backwards. 'Do you think that if I knew her whereabouts I would be speaking with you?'

'Well, I have not seen her since we camped upon the hilltop,' Benicio admitted.

'It is as I feared,' said Rogelio. He reached beneath his jerkin to produce Luisa's letter. 'Here, take it.'

Benicio stared at the small, ragged envelope as if it might bite him.

'Take it, man,' repeated Rogelio.

Sheathing his dagger, Benicio reached for the letter and took it. He placed it quickly beneath his own jerkin and stared at Rogelio in suspicion. 'Why do you give it to me now, after withholding it for so long?'

'When you read it, you will understand.'

'You have read the letter yourself?'

'Of course I have.'

'You are the lowest worm on the ugliest rat in Hell.'

'Read the letter, Benicio, and you will see why I am certain that we shall yet be partners. I know exactly where the treasure of Tenochtitlan is hidden.' Rogelio stared down at his useless leg. 'If I return to Spain with enough gold, it will not matter that I am lame.'

'And what of your soul?' asked Benicio.

'My soul?' Rogelio asked, laughing. 'I left it upon the cobblestones of Plaza del Triunfo, a lifetime ago.'

'Indeed you did.'

'Benicio, do you not realise? So did you.'

Chapter Twenty-Four

Benicio could not bring himself to open the third letter. Not that morning, standing beside the tomato stall, nor that afternoon in the quiet pine forest outside of Tlaxcala. Nor even that evening, sitting by the small fire inside the house where he and several other Spanish soldiers had been quartered. He stared into the firelight, remembering Luisa's face, but unable to bring himself to read her script.

Even the next day, as Cortés's army, enlarged by six thousand Tlaxcalan warriors, set out for the Mexica tributary city of Cholula, Benicio couldn't bring himself to open it. It was as if, in all his worry over Tula, he had forgotten his responsibility and the promise he had made. Now God was reminding him of it again.

There was a distinct possibility that the letter contained news of Luisa's wedding. Perhaps even the birth of her first child.

The other possibility was that she had written him to announce that her engagement to Armando had been terminated and that she remained his doting maid, ever true.

If the second possibility, then Benicio's duty did not change, it only increased in urgency. He needed to get himself to Tenochtitlan and find the gold, though he admitted that without Tula, he had no idea where to look.

It was as if the second letter contained the power of Pandora's box. By opening it, Benicio would release that dreadful power into his life. No, he would wait until the right moment to read the story of his fate.

The next day, he marched with the Spanish-Totonac-Tlaxcalan army into the city of Cholula, the second holiest city in the Mexican Empire. Cortés had ordered the Spanish soldiers to appear unimpressed by the things they encountered. 'Do not reveal your wonder,' he urged the men. 'We must comport ourselves as though we already rule here.'

Benicio found indifference particularly difficult to project as he stared up at the limewashed stone temples, which rose around them like snowy volcanoes. There were hundreds of them, all glowing white in the blinding sunshine of the high country.

Atop them, Benicio watched the black-robed priests dance like shadows against the clouds of white incense smoke rising to touch the heavens.

If Tlaxcala had been a church, then Cholula was surely a cathedral. Its clean stone streets were lined with blossoming trees and urns of flowering plants decorated its many parks and gardens. Large stone aqueducts brought water to the city and channelled it through a series of beautiful fountains whose overflow fed an ingenious ditch system that flushed waste out.

In addition to the innumerable temples and holy halls, there were sprawling markets offering a greater variety of goods than Benicio had seen anywhere on the earth. Amaranth and sage vendors took their places next to the ubiquitous maize merchants, along with men selling every kind of flower and every type of fruit. Wood, flint, obsidian and copper vendors proudly spread their wares and sellers of amber, jade and salt smirked at their own prosperity. There were also schools, *tlachtli* courts, stores, hospitals and thousands upon thousands of stone houses, all with immaculately tended gardens.

As he marched through the mesmerising streets, Benicio thought of Gonzalo Guerrero, the Spaniard who had been stranded in this strange land and had chosen to stay. Surely he had beheld this elegant city, or cities like it, and had become enamoured of the rich civilisation that thrived herein. Benicio wondered briefly if, in a different life, he would have done the same.

Benicio and the other Spaniards had been quartered in a large gathering hall and provided with daily food rations. Many of the tired, wounded Totonac soldiers were allowed to return home, replaced by Tlaxcalan warriors ready to reap their revenge on their Mexica enemies. Meanwhile Cortés, Malinali and the other leaders spent long hours in negotiation with the Cholulan lords, presumably winning them to the Spanish cause.

But Benicio sensed a trap.

Each day, their rations grew sparser, though the conquistadors hardly noticed. They were too busy ravishing the women that the Tlaxcalans had given them to solidify their truce. Now every single Spanish soldier enjoyed the spoils of Cortés's ongoing conquest and they cheered him for it.

But Benicio did not cheer. He cringed as he watched the Spaniards fight over the Tlaxcalan women, grabbing their braids and pulling their fine skirts. It was not long before the men were stealing off with their prizes into dark hallways and hidden corridors, where they despoiled the young women before Cholula's sacred gods.

Their behaviour sickened Benicio. He bundled his sleeping mat and found a path that led to an uninhabited hill just outside the city. When he reached its top, a sublime view spread before him. The innumerable white temples that rose up around the city had not been placed haphazardly, as Benicio had thought. Instead, they were arranged in a configuration that perfectly mirrored the surrounding mountains.

There was only one mountain that did not appear to have a pyramid counterpart: the volcano Popocatepetl. It rose majestically in the distance, a plume of smoke bubbling from its mouth. The only local feature that came close to mirroring the great volcano was another mountain. It rose up from the heart of Cempoala in a remarkably symmetrical, stepped shape.

Then Benicio realised that he was not looking at a mountain. He was looking at an ancient pyramid—the largest he had ever seen.

What had seemed thoughtless and accidental at ground level was organised and beautiful from above—part of a much larger plan that the Spanish strangers did not see. Benicio sat down on a long flat rock, removed his book from beneath his jerkin and took a deep breath.

Dear Benicio,
I write with terrible news. Your brother Armando has died. He was dispatched to protect the chancellor, who was bringing news to Toledo of higher taxes on behalf of our new King. His regiment was met by an enraged mob. Armando's throat was slit by a man who likely helped shape the sword you carry.
I remain, as ever, unmarried.
Carlos pays me a visit every Sunday. He has grown rich as an official in Seville's Casa de Contratación, where he has already risen to the position of third in command.
Every day he receives ships from the Indies, but you are not upon them. Your father says that as his second son, you will remain the inheritor of your family's estate until official word is received of your passing. Meanwhile, he anxiously awaits your return.
God help me, I do, too.
Your Luisa
April 28th, 1519

Benicio let the letter drop. He felt the tears blurring his vision, but he could not bring himself to wipe them. Armando had died. His strong, righteous older brother had finally perished in his quest to bring glory to his family and to Spain.

Benicio felt sick. What madness had struck Armando that he would lay his life down so eagerly? He was a man who had been reared gently, who had been taught to think and to love, yet had been reduced to a life of violence, then died as a result.

Now Benicio followed in his brother's footsteps. The continents they laboured upon were far apart, but the end was the same: destruction, conquest, death. Armando killed to bring lands and wealth to the King of Spain and Benicio did the same. The paths of their lives had seemed haphazard, but, like the locations of the temples of Cholula, they were part of a much larger plan—one they had both failed to see.

He camped on the hilltop that night, lost in mourning.

He awoke to discover the sun high in the sky and his belly loud with hunger. He stood and gazed out over Cholula, imagining Luisa waiting for him across the distant sea.

The thought should have buoyed him. Instead, he felt nothing but confusion. How could she do this to him again? She had set him against his only remaining brother, in some contest over who could provide her the most comfortable life. It sickened him, yet he knew that a promise was a promise.

Though, as he thought about it, he had never actually promised Luisa anything. In his heart, he had resolved to return to her, but he had never actually said, 'I promise to return.' Nor had she promised she would wait for him, or said a word about how much treasure she expected him to produce. She had said only that she would wait as long as she could, however long that was. Indeed, they had made no promises to each other at all.

If he had promised anyone anything it was Tula. That promise was clear and specific: Benicio had promised to rescue Tula's sister. If there was any promise that needed fulfilling, it was that one.

He opened his eyes and looked around camp. It was as if he were seeing the world clearly for the very first time. He spied a pile of small packages on a nearby rock.

They were tamales—clearly placed there for his consumption. He had apparently had a visitor. He looked around him, but there was not a single movement in the quiet forest. Had some kindly stranger visited him in the night? The only person with any idea of Benicio's location was Rogelio. But why on earth would Rogelio bring Benicio tamales?

Benicio selected a tamale and opened its maize husk wrap. The corn cake inside was still warm and Benicio probed it for signs of poison. Instead he was greeted with a warm bean filling that, when he tasted it with his finger, seem perfectly healthful. He sat down and took a small bite. The tamale's flavour burst on to his tongue.

Tula. It was her—surely it was her. He could almost sense her near him. She was his guardian angel, his only friend. She had come and laid tamales by his side as he slept.

He imagined her sitting beside him, her legs pulled up to her chest, watching him with her eyes the colour of rich earth. It was not Rogelio, but Tula who would do something this kind. He wished he could be near her again, if only for a moment. He wished to see her beautiful face and beg her to forgive him. He stuffed Luisa's letter into his book and took his first bite.

Chapter Twenty-Five

She was close enough to feel his breath. It tickled the side of her arm, making it itch wildly. But she could not move to scratch it. She could not do anything but remain still and try to disappear behind the small boulder that separated her from the man she had somehow grown to care for.

He was not supposed to sit down in the dirt to eat the tamales. He was supposed to take them to the long flat rock where he had made camp during the past day and night. Instead, he had collapsed beside the boulder where she now crouched.

She closed her eyes, hoping to make herself invisible somehow. He was unwrapping the tamales with urgency and when she opened her eyes again she saw crumbs tumbling to the ground like snowflakes.

He had been so troubled over the past day and night that she suspected he had forgotten to eat. She wondered why he seemed so listless and broken. What demon had invaded his mind?

When she had followed him up the mountainside the day before, he had stumbled many times upon the trail, as if his mind were travelling somewhere else. After arriving at the summit, he had paced and mumbled for some time, unable to become settled.

When he finally sat down upon the flat rock, he had removed a piece of paper with something written upon it. He had stared at the piece of paper for a long while and tears had washed down his cheeks. He had let the paper drop, but did not move. It was as if he had been bitten by a deadly snake. His tears dried, he had remained motionless until long after the Sun God had descended to the Underworld.

She wanted to reach out to him now, for she knew he was hurting inside, just as he had been hurting that day by the river. *But he rejected you*, she reminded herself. *He does not wish for your company any more.*

Still, she had no choice but to continue the journey to Tenochtitlan. Even Malinali agreed that Tula had no choice but to rejoin him. Benicio was one of the largest, strongest men in the entire Spanish–Totonac–Tlaxcalan army and the only one willing to use that strength to free her sister and the other captives.

Besides, they had an agreement to uphold. An alliance.

Still she feared approaching him. He was not the kind of man who liked surprises. That was how it had seemed when he had scorned her that day by the river, over a moon ago now. Today he appeared even more troubled than he had been that day and Tula wondered if it was the right time to reveal herself to him.

He let two of the corn husks drop to the ground, then two more. Soon the maize casings of all six tamales came into Tula's view.

'*Gracias,*' he uttered, as if he knew she was there. Tula's heart leapt, then fell as she absorbed the meaning of the words, remembering Malinali's lesson.

'*Gracias* is how the Spanish say that they are humble,' Malinali had explained. It had been Tula's first lesson in the Spanish tongue. 'But it is more limited than "I am humble",' she noted. 'It does not evoke the world or the speaker's place in it. It is about acknowledging a debt only. It is…narrower.'

'Does that mean that the Spanish are…narrower than the people of this land?' Tula had asked.

Malinali had sat in silence for a long while before responding. 'They are only different.'

Tula was certain that Benicio had just acknowledged his debt to the one who left the tamales, though he did not know who that person was. Tula gave a tiny nod. *De nada*, she thought to herself.

She wished she had known the word *gracias* the night of the snowstorm, or the day he had stopped her from marching into danger, or the day that he had shaved his beard and relinquished his own god to help her feel safe. His actions alone showed her that he cared for her, whatever his reasons. And, despite everything, she cared for him, too. Very much.

She listened closely. He had finished eating the tamales, but he made no motion to rise. Had he detected her? She held her breath. Suddenly, he let out a sob.

What ghosts haunted him? She sensed that he was hurting not because he had been harmed, but because others had been harmed. His sadness was like a flood. It seemed to pour out of his heart and into hers.

'Lo siento,' Malinali had instructed. 'That is how you say that you are sorry in the Spanish tongue.'

'What does it mean?' Tula asked.

'It means, "I feel it",' said Malinali. 'The meaning is perhaps…wider than the Totonac meaning.'

Their studies had continued, week after week. By day Tula laboured among Malinali's servants, cleaning and preparing meals, keeping to the shadows so she would not be recognised by the Spanish men who lingered in Cortés's entourage. But every evening, after Malinali's translation duties were done, the two went to work. Soon they were communicating in Spanish alone.

Malinali had insisted that Tula stay with her in Tlaxcala, and now in Cholula, in the rich lodgings that were provided to Cortés and his closest advisors. She told Tula that she only regretted that she could not help Tula rescue her sister directly. But any action against Montezuma had been forbidden by Cortés unless he commanded it. Malinali gave Tula everything she had to give, as she laboured to repay the debt she owed Tula in the only way she knew how: language.

'*Gracias,*' Tula had repeated earlier that morning in Spanish, 'for helping me.'

'*De nada,*' Malinali had responded with a broad smile. 'Now go find him and get your sister back.'

Now Benicio gave one more sob, then sucked in a breath. She wished she could comfort him. She wished she could hold his hand and tell him about the short distance between joy and sorrow. He had become...her friend. He was her dear, tender-hearted friend and he needed her, just as she needed him. She took a deep breath and prepared to reveal herself.

Then she heard the screams.

Chapter Twenty-Six

At first, he thought the screams were an illusion—some trick of his grieving heart. But as he stood to determine their source, they only grew louder and more distinct. He opened his eyes and saw a funnel of smoke rising up out of the centre of Cholula.

He felt a new dread envelop him. What madness was breaking out in the city below? He had noticed that many of the Cholulan men were not happy with their strange visitors. They had wandered the city all week, whispering to each other and spoiling for a fight. The Tlaxcalans had warned of the Cholulans' loyalty to the Mexica, but Cortés would not listen.

Now Benicio determined that the screams he had heard were emanating from the enclosed courtyard adjacent to the Temple of Queztalcoatl. As Benicio approached the courtyard, he paused to observe dozens of Spanish and Tlaxcalan soldiers exiting, their swords and clubs in hand, their clothes stained with blood.

Benicio recognised some of the men. They were Cortés's front line soldiers—the most brutal and cruel of the Spanish regiment. He tried to speak to them, but they were not interested in talk. Their eyes were glazed over and they walked with the lurching, frenzied movements of recently accomplished violence.

Something terrible had happened inside the courtyard.

More bloodied Spaniards passed him as he made his way inside, including Cortés himself, surrounded by a dozen fearsome men. 'Nice of you to join us, Benicio,' he commented as he passed, flashing Benicio the evil eye. It was all Benicio could do not to smack the arrogant captain directly in the jaw.

Benicio stepped inside the courtyard to behold the most gruesome spectacle he had ever seen. A hundred Cholulan noblemen lay slain upon the ground. There were even some women, their fine gold-embossed skirts stained with blood. They appeared to have been dressed for some sort of celebration. Not a single one of them stirred.

Benicio spied Rogelio among several men overlooking the carnage. 'Did you take part in this?' he asked Rogelio, his voice trembling.

'I did not,' said Rogelio. 'As evil as you believe me to be, Benicio, I do not condone the slaughter of innocents.' He limped forward.

'Nor I,' whispered Benicio. He had witnessed many terrible things during his time in the Indies, but never such a slaughter.

'I know what you are thinking,' said Rogelio. 'You are thinking that you would leave this army now if you could. If it were not for...what was her name?'

'Luisa,' Benicio said, though in truth her name felt strange and bitter upon his tongue.

The two surveyed the hellish scene for many long moments. 'I cannot be a part of this army any more,' stated Benicio, 'for an army it is.'

'Nor I,' said Rogelio. 'Though the penalty for mutiny is death.'

'Death is better than this.'

'If we could escape on a horse, we might not be caught before reaching Vera Cruz.'

'With a bounty on our heads.'

'And without means to purchase safety, or passage back to Spain,' said Rogelio.

'I cannot flee now. I must reach Tenochtitlan,' said Benicio. 'I am bound to fulfil a promise I made.' *To save Tula's sister.*

'I must reach Tenochtitlan as well, for there is

treasure there, and I know exactly where it lies,' said Rogelio. 'Remember, I spoke with the Maya priest.'

'You tortured the Maya priest.'

'I regret it. I wish to make amends.'

'Ha! Was that the reason for the tamales?' Benicio asked without thinking.

'The what?'

'It is nothing,' said Benicio, trying to brush the comment aside. 'I know it was not you.'

Rogelio shook his head in confusion. 'Speak plainly, Benicio,' he said.

'This morning atop the hill,' Benicio clarified. 'Someone left me tamales.'

Rogelio paused. 'Ah, yes. It was I. You had been away from the Spanish quarters for so long. I knew that you required sustenance.'

'Gracias,' said Benicio joylessly.

So it had not been Tula, as he had hoped, but Rogelio, as he had feared. Benicio let the sad truth wash over him. His only friend had probably found another man to help her rescue her sister—someone far nobler and worthier than Benicio. He doubted he would ever see her again.

'It must be an equal partnership,' Benicio said at last. 'Whatever spoils we obtain we divide in half.'

'Of course.'

'And after we are safely out of Tenochtitlan, we shall part ways and never speak to each other again.'

'Agreed,' said Rogelio and held out his hand.

But Benicio did not take it. He only shook his head and nodded, hoping the small gesture was enough to solidify the pact that he had just made with the Devil.

Chapter Twenty-Seven

Tenochtitlan, Capital of the Empire of the Mexica— November 8th, 1519

It is so close, Benicio thought, feeling the itch of mutiny beneath his skin. He saw the twin platforms of the Templo Mayor looming in the distance, towering over the great floating city of Tenochtitlan. He had finally arrived. Somewhere inside that holy building, the treasure awaited him.

It had taken the Spanish–Totonac–Tlaxcalan company all morning to make its way down the long wooden bridge linking the capital of the Mexica Empire with the world beyond. Now they stood at the gates of the city they knew Cortés secretly meant to conquer, wondering whether they would be welcomed or slaughtered.

Montezuma II, the Emperor of the Mexica, stepped from his bejewelled litter in sandals stitched with gold. A giant man wearing the head of a black jaguar came forward and draped a massive feather head-dress about the monarch's broad shoulders.

With the splendid cloak in place, Montezuma seemed to rise above everyone in his company and when Cortés dismounted his horse and stepped forward, he was dwarfed by the strong, stoic priest–King.

Cortés moved to embrace Montezuma, but he was stopped by the emperor's attendants. Unfazed, Cortés held out his hand. The Emperor acknowledged the proffered hand, but did not take it. He whispered something to one of his advisors, who motioned to Cortés's ring, then gently took Cortés's hand and held it up for the monarch to study. Montezuma marvelled at the ring for several moments and Benicio had the profound sense that the fate of the world was being written, as well as something of his own.

He wished Tula were here, by his side, witnessing the culmination of their difficult journey. Surely she would be placing some enchantress's spell on Montezuma, the man who had ordered the sacrifice of so many Totonacs, and would be glaring at him with eyes full of scorn. Soon, however, her curiosity would take over and she would become fascinated with the history being written before her eyes.

Cortés made bold to present a necklace of pearls to Montezuma, who reciprocated with two necklaces of his own. Benicio saw a sly smile cross Cortés's lips as his new friend Montezuma made a welcome gesture. *Come, friend, and see my beautiful city*, he seemed to be saying to Cortés. And so it was that Montezuma invited the Spanish–Totonac–Tlaxcalan army into his great city, and the world would never be the same.

If Tlaxcala was a church and Cholula a cathedral, then Tenochtitlan was the Vatican itself. Benicio could scarcely believe his eyes as they travelled past garden islands bursting with vegetables and crops, permanently watered by the very lake that surrounded them. But the agricultural wonders were just a start. With its endless gathering halls, schools and *tlachtli* courts, its coddled gardens, pristine parks and even a menagerie featuring animals of every shape and colour, Tenochtitlan seemed to shout out its greatness to all who would listen.

Benicio was listening. Against his captain's commands, he smiled and waved at the jubilant children and the throngs of boatmen, who followed in canals that paralleled the roads, just as they did in Venice.

Soon, the holy precinct of Tenochtitlan rose up around them in a fluorescence of shapes and colours. At its heart was a large plaza that appeared to be perfectly aligned to the four directions, with sets of pyramids to mark each. At the plaza's head rose the tallest and most magnificent edifice of them all—the double pyramid that the Spanish called the Templo Mayor.

'There it is, Tula,' Benicio muttered to himself. 'Perhaps your sister is inside somewhere.'

The Spaniards were quartered in the grand palace of Montezuma's late father, which lay but a few hundred paces to the north of the Templo Mayor itself. The rooms were luxurious and comfortable, with lavish wooden furniture and bed mats stuffed with duck feathers.

Still, sleep eluded Benicio that night. He knew that Tula's sister and the other captives were being kept somewhere near, he just did not know where. Nor had Rogelio told Benicio where the treasure lay, saying only that he would tell him when the time was right. Benicio could not wait any longer. He did not want to be in Tenochtitlan when Cortés unleashed his cannons.

Benicio pulled on his boots and padded quietly down the tile hallway. When he pushed open the door, he gasped in surprise. Tenochtitlan's holy precinct spread before him, awash in moonlight. The full moon must have risen sometime after dark, for now it glowed at the top of the sky, illuminating everything.

Benicio wandered across the plaza, not surprised

to find himself standing at the foot of the Templo Mayor. There was not a trace of blood upon its steep steps and Benicio wondered if they had been washed in anticipation of the Spanish arrival. The glowing white structure did not seem ominous, as Benicio had feared, but beautiful and holy. It beckoned him and he began to climb.

For the first time since he had touched the shores of this new world, he was doing something he truly wished to do. He lunged up the stone steps, huffing his breaths. Was he mad, or did the moon seem closer already?

He wondered if Tula was looking up at it, too.

Benicio arrived upon the large platform at the top of the pyramid, panting and spent. He was rewarded with the most beautiful view he had ever beheld. Tenochtitlan, surely the greatest city in the world, slept beneath the moon. There was no movement in the streets or canals, and the limewashed buildings seemed to bask in the otherworldly light. Beyond the city, the inky waters of Lake Texcoco spread out like a dark skirt.

Like Tula's skirt, he thought. He wondered where Tula was right now. Did she still cringe at the memory of his cruelty to her? Or had it faded with time, as the blood upon the map Benicio carried?

Over the past several years, Benicio had filled

his heart with many regrets about the things he had done. Strangely, none stung so sharply as the wrong he had done to her that day by the river. And as hard as he had tried to forget Tula, she always sneaked into his thoughts. *Just like a thief.*

Benicio stared out at the moonstruck city for many long moments. He had known her for but a short time, but it was as if he had known her for much longer. And now, he missed her. God, how he missed her. His thief. His ally. His Tula.

Was he mad, or was the sky already beginning to change? He thought he could see the faint brush of light marking the beginning of the sunrise and it occurred to him that if he was facing east, it meant the Templo Mayor was the westernmost temple in Tenochtitlan.

That was strange. The Maya priest's map showed that the Templo Mayor lay in the north, not the west. Perhaps the old priest had not oriented the map to the true directions. Surely that was the case. If Benicio had been trying to draw a map on his own death-bed, he probably would have made the same error.

He peered behind him at the expansive platform that held the two sacred temples: on the left, the temple dedicated to the Rain God, Tlaloc; on the right, the temple dedicated to the Sun God, Huitzilo-pochtli. By day Benicio had observed the temples' distinguishing colours: for Tlaloc, dark blue, like the water; for Huitzilopochtli, yellow-red, like the rising sun.

He stood on Tlaloc's side of the platform and far from the terrifying rack of skulls on Huitzilo-pochtli's side. Between the two temples was a menacing empty table that stood at waist height and stretched the length of a person. Benicio shivered, imagining the doomed souls who awaited their deaths in this terrible place.

The air stirred somewhere close, tickling the hairs on his chest. Perhaps the Wind God Quetzalcoatl was telling him that it was time to go. He stepped close to the edge of the steep steps and took one last look at the moon.

'Goodnight, Tula,' he said.

A familiar voice rose up from below the pyramid's edge.

'Goodnight, Benicio.'

Chapter Twenty-Eight

He jumped forward as she reached the top and for a moment she was afraid he might go tumbling down the pyramid himself. She reached out to steady him, placing her face beneath the light of the moon so he would recognise her.

His expression froze and she feared she had unleashed his anger once again. She had not meant to startle him. She had only meant to speak with him alone.

'Benicio—' Tula whispered, but he would not let her finish. He wrapped his arms around her and lifted her into his embrace.

'You returned,' he whispered. 'My dearest Tula.' He stepped back on to the platform, then spun her around in a dizzying circle. 'You returned to me.'

She was too startled to speak. He seemed overjoyed to see her and, as he held her in his arms, she realised that she, too, was awash in joy. Her feet hovered far from the ground and she was aware that the true earth lay somewhere far beneath them. Yet feeling his arms around her, it was as if she were walking upon solid ground for the first time in many, many days.

Slowly, he placed her feet upon the blue tiles and stared down at her in wonderment. She could make out the chiselled features of his handsome face and could see the sheen of emotion in his large blue eyes.

'My heart is happy,' he said slowly, pointing to his heart. 'Do you understand?' Without waiting for her answer, he buried his head in her loose hair. He breathed in deeply of her scent, sending a chill across her skin. 'Can you forgive me?'

He collapsed to his knees and bowed his head. 'Please forgive me,' he repeated. He took her hands in his. 'You did not deserve to be treated the way I treated you. *Lo siento.* Will you forgive me?'

'Shh,' she said, though she felt like shouting her answer. *Yes, I forgive you!* Instead she placed two soft kisses on each of his hands and lifted him to his feet. They could talk more later, when they were safely off the temple and well out of sight. She glanced around nervously.

She had hoped to wake him in his chamber in the night, but when she had arrived there in the useless hours, he was gone. Disappointed, she had stepped out into the holy square and was alarmed to discover him traipsing up the most sacred structure in all the world.

'We are in danger here,' she whispered, adjusting the quiver of arrows across her back.

He stared at her in vexation, clearly shocked by her command of the Spanish tongue. There was no time for an explanation, however. She peered into Tlaloc's temple just beyond them. The sacred embers still burned inside the braziers, casting their delicate light against the walls. But the blood of the midnight priests no longer permeated the air, having long been consumed by the flames.

The priests who heralded the birth of the Sun God would arrive soon. If they discovered Tula and Benicio here, they would kill them on sight.

'We go now,' she whispered, hoping she had said the Spanish words as Malinali had taught her. 'Down.'

She moved to the edge of the pyramid and bent to take her first step. But he caught her by the sleeve of the doublet she wore—his doublet—and pulled her into his strong arms. His breath was pouring out of him and he pressed his face against the top of her head.

'Oh, Tula, I have missed you,' he whispered.

Part of her wanted to embrace him in return. Part

of her wanted to collapse into his strong arms and give herself to him, body and soul. She had missed him, too, and pressed against him like this made her heart seem to rest and a strange sense of peace suffused her body. She sighed. Part of her wanted to stay with him like this for ever.

But she could not do that, because he did not love her. He hugged her and cared for her, but he stared at another woman's picture, and whispered her name in the night. Luisa. He loved Luisa.

Perhaps he desired Tula, but it was only desire, not love. Surely it was desire that had made him touch her during the snowstorm, and desire that had stretched out his manhood beneath the agave stalk that evening on the high plain. And the sweet things he had said to her just before the battle? They were nothing but the expression of a man's lust. His body was drawn to hers, but only as any man's body might be drawn to any woman's.

None of it meant anything. Tula was merely Benicio's ally. Therefore, she could never let him be her love.

'The priests come now,' she said. 'We go.'

At any moment, the sunrise priests would begin their slow climb up the steps of the temple. They would emerge on the platform like soldiers, their golden masks upon their faces, their sacrificial knives inside their hands. They would find Benicio and Tula, and they would not hesitate to begin their work.

Tula squirmed to release herself from Benicio's embrace, but he would not let her free. She lunged backwards with all her weight, but he held her fast and stepped around her, placing himself closest to the edge. Then he began gently pushing her backwards towards the small set of stairs that led to Tlaloc's sprawling shrine.

They might have been dancing. She struggled to keep her feet beneath her as he pushed her further and further away from the pyramid's edge and closer to the earthly home of the God of Rain.

They arrived at the three sacred steps that led to the temple and he lifted her to the highest one. Paces away were the three arched entrances to the holy sanctuary where Tlaloc was served and adored. It was a structure meant only for religious men and women—priests who spent their lives studying the sacred codices, meditating and representing the needs of the people to the gods. Tula and Benicio did not belong here.

The world began to spin as he removed her quiver and eased her back on to the cold tile of the top step. He stared down at her, though his face was all in shadow.

She tried to sit up, but he pressed her shoulders to the ground and straddled her. Then she felt his lips upon hers.

She tried to pull away, but he would not let her. She struggled and squirmed, but he stretched atop her body and quieted it with his own. She was aware of the temple behind her, its flickering braziers, its faint smell of blood overlain by a thick, perfumed incense. It was an affront to the gods that they were even here. To be kissing on this hallowed ground was nothing short of sacrilege.

Still, something deep inside of her did not want him to stop. He kissed her urgently, as if he had saved up some important message that he couldn't wait to tell her, his restless mouth seeming to ply and knead and saturate her with its important news. How many times had she secretly yearned for this?

She began to move her lips with his. She kissed his cheek softly and breathed him in, and the fearsome, holy smell of the air was replaced with his familiar, musky scent.

'You returned,' he said, continuing to kiss her, tenderer now. 'You came back to me.' He pushed against her legs with his own, moving them apart so that his hips rested upon hers. A deep, throbbing yearning began to pulse inside her and she tried to remember who she was: a good woman, a loyal woman, a woman with a duty to her family and her people.

She could not let this dark desire be the master of her. They needed to get down from atop this giant stone gift to the gods, or they would become gifts themselves.

'Luisa,' Tula whispered, but it was as if he had not heard her. 'Luisa,' she said again, hating herself. 'Luisa.'

'Shhh,' he said. It was not working. He was ignoring the name of his true love.

Confused, Tula sat up. 'We go. Now,' she commanded.

And that is when she spotted them—a crowd of living shadows floating towards them like ghosts.

Chapter Twenty-Nine

'Benicio!' Tula shrieked. There must have been twenty of them, each displaying the same frozen expression, the same hollow, black eyes. They were not ghosts. They were priests—sun birth priests— wielding sacrificial blades and wearing ceremonial masks of pure gold.

'Stay behind me,' Benicio said, jumping in front of Tula, who gathered her quiver. The priests were surfacing upon the lower platform like a swarm. Ten, then twenty, then forty. Their daggers pointed at the sky, their long ropy locks moved and writhed like snakes against their black robes.

'Come now,' said Benicio, grabbing Tula's hand, and he pulled her towards Tlaloc's temple.

'No,' Tula said, unable to move. She could not enter that terrifying space. It was the Rain God's inner sanctum—not meant for human eyes. Besides, if they entered, they would surely be trapped by the priests. She stood unmoving upon the platform.

Then she realised that she was no longer standing at all. Benicio was carrying her. He rushed her across the high platform and they passed into the shadows of the Rain God's home.

The stink of blood inside the temple was overwhelming—a thick, putrid scent that mixed with the woody smell of incense in a sickening evocation of the flowery death. Tula could see very little, for the midnight braziers burned low. But she could hear the sound of flies buzzing in hidden corners and a slow, echoing drip that she knew was not water.

Benicio stumbled against a low object, catching Tula and placing her on the ground beside what appeared to be a cage. 'Please help!' shrieked a young voice in Totonac. Tula nearly fainted in surprise. She bent to discover a young Totonac girl with the thick cheeks and hollow eyes of one being fattened for sacrifice.

'We will help you,' Tula promised. Could it be true? Had they stumbled upon the Totonac captives? Tula stood and looked out over what appeared to be several dozen cages. 'Xanca, are you here?' she called out.

For a long while, there was no answer. Tula heard the menacing shuffle of the priests' footsteps nearing the temple's entrance. Then a small, familiar voice broke through the silence. 'Tula?'

Tula was too startled to speak. It was a voice she knew. A voice she loved. She shook her head, wondering if she was living inside some wishful dream. 'Xanca?' she repeated.

'Tula?' returned the voice.

Tula and Benicio ran towards the cage from which her sister's voice emanated. Tula reached her hand down through its wooden bars to discover the top of her sister's head. Xanca's fingers linked with hers. 'Is it you, Tula? Could it be you?'

'It is I,' Tula said and let out a desperate sob as the first priest stepped beneath the arching entrance. It was as if the Rain God were toying with her, dangling Tula's greatest hope before her just at the moment Tula was certain she would die.

'The cage requires a key,' her sister whimpered hopelessly.

The first of the priests was approaching them now. 'Benicio, I need time,' she whispered. 'Will you fight?' She knew that what she was really asking him is if he would die.

'I will fight for you until my end, dear lady,' he said. He grasped her by the arm and placed the cool metal of his hand blade into her palm. 'Use this to cut through the bars. Do not give up!' He found her lips and gave her one last, burning kiss.

Tula heard the clash of metal upon metal and saw Benicio's shadowy figure meeting a host of black-robed foes at the shrine's entrance. 'Xanca, move to the side,' she commanded. She took the blade and began to saw what she determined to be the thinnest of the wooden bars. She pressed with all her might, sawing frantically until she could feel a distinct groove forming.

She pulled her own hand blade from beneath her belt and handed it to her sister. 'Use it to cut upwards from below,' she commanded. Her sister did as instructed, and soon the thick wooden bar was weak enough to kick in two. Xanca pushed back the wood and squeezed out of the small opening.

The two sisters embraced. 'Are there others?' Tula asked.

'Yes,' said Xanca. 'All the Totonac women are here.'

'And the men?'

'Inside the Sun God's shrine.'

Tula heard the slice of a blade. In the low light, she watched Benicio slit a priest's throat. 'We must work quickly then,' she told Xanca.

They sawed furiously, struggling to free the captive women. Tula continued to hear the clang of blades at the mouth of the shrine. She knew that any minute Benicio could lose his life. Then the great crowd of priests would come running.

But Benicio held his ground, and soon all the women had been released. On silent feet, Xanca led the group under the archway of the southernmost exit while Tula kept watch. When the last of the women had exited, Tula turned to behold the fighting beneath the northernmost arch.

There he was, surrounded by at least twenty priests. Their fearsome golden masks seemed to float in the darkness all around him and their deadly obsidian blades glinted menacingly in the moonlight. Still, Benicio remained undaunted.

He thrust and swung his sword with impossible speed, holding off the throng and cutting anyone down who dared to come close. Many of the priests ran in terror, for Benicio was killing with a chilling precision. The priests' lifeless robes were spreading across the platform like black puddles.

Tula should have been aghast. Priests were holy. They whispered to the gods. Their lives were more valuable than other human lives, and when a priest fell, all creation mourned.

But Tula did not mourn. Instead, her heart beat with hope. Watching Benicio fight in the moonlight, so strong and fearless, seemed to stoke her own courage. There he was, risking his very life to save theirs. She felt overcome with gratitude. And something else, she realised: love.

'Ah,' she gasped. One of the priests had spotted her. He tapped another on the shoulder, and soon three of the masked fiends were headed towards the group of women. 'Run to the Sun God's temple!' Tula shouted to the women. 'We must free the men.'

But the women would not listen. 'They refuse to follow us,' shouted Xanca. 'They are afraid.' Tula watched in horror as the young women sprinted across the platform, heading towards the main set of stairs and their escape.

The three priests paused, watching the women go. They disappeared down the stairs one by one, impossible for the priests to reach. Their haunting black eyes returned to Tula and Xanca.

'They are going to come for us now,' whispered Xanca.

'But they will not have us,' said Tula and together they ran into the Sun God's temple.

It was even darker inside the enormous shrine than it had been in the Rain God's and the smell of blood was so thick it made Tula wretch. 'Call to the men and wait for them to call back,' she told Xanca, handing her dagger to her sister. 'I shall hold off the priests.'

With trembling hands, Tula fixed an arrow in the notch of her atlatl. The first of the three priests was already in range, his dagger glinting. She had only three arrows in her quiver: she needed to make each one count.

She thrust the arrow at the first priest, striking him in the chest. As he fell, the second priest paused, then turned and ran. The final priest paused to regard the second priest and, in that instant, Tula lunged into the temple.

She was many paces inside when the third priest finally caught her. He jumped forward and pushed her to the ground. She squirmed and flailed against him, his long, disgusting locks falling across her body.

He grabbed her by the throat and began to squeeze. His long, twisted fingernails dug into her neck, drawing blood. Tula could not pull his hands free. 'You will pay for offending the gods,' he hissed.

She wondered if it was to be the last word she ever heard, for tiny points of light swirled behind her eyes and as she choked for breath.

Benicio, she thought. *Benicio.* The priest's terrible golden mask hovered above her and she stared into the black holes of his eyes as she felt her body go limp...

For a moment she believed that she had died. Her

throat contracted in a great, painful heave. Then the tight fingers that had gripped her neck went slack. She coughed hard, sucking in air. The priest's body went limp and a warm liquid trickled on to her chest.

Two strong hands pulled the priest off her. She turned to discover that the priest's head had been severed from his body. It lay upon the floor, its golden mask staring hauntingly back at her.

And there he was, standing above her—the man she loved. He bent over and lifted her limp body into his arms. 'Tula?' For a moment she could not answer. She could only look into his eyes in wonder. 'Tula, by God! Are you all right? Can you breathe?'

'Yes,' she whispered.

He hugged her tightly to his chest.

'We must help my sister,' Tula said. 'Where are you, Xanca?' she called into the dark space.

'We must have light,' Benicio said. He ran to the entrance of the shrine, where a copper brazier smouldered beneath the last of its small coals.

Tula watched as Benicio retrieved the codex from beneath his jerkin. He began ripping the pages and balling them up, then placing them among the embers. Bright new flames began to lick the sides of the pan, then flared, roaring into a blaze that shone with enough light for them to see many paces away.

Soon they were at Xanca's side, observing a cluster of cages that stretched into the depths of the temple. Tula could not believe her eyes. So many young men. So many doomed lives.

Xanca had straddled a nearby cage and was working furiously to saw through its thick wood. But in the months since she had been taken, her muscles had withered and she could scarcely keep the knives within her grip.

Benicio placed the brazier on the floor and gently plucked both blades from Xanca's hands. In seconds, he had plunged through the wood and was peeling back and opening.

A young man jumped out of the cage and bounded into Xanca's arms. The two held each other for many long moments, rocking together in an embrace that went beyond simple gratitude. Finally, the young man released Xanca and stared at her in wonder, tears of joy streaming down his face. It occurred to Tula that the man was Xanca's beloved.

'This is Anan,' said Xanca, presenting the man to Tula.

'It is an honour to meet you,' Anan said and bowed low.

Benicio ripped two more pages from his codex and fed them into the flames. There was no time to contemplate the reunion taking place, or the love that seemed to shine in Xanca's eyes. Soon the sun would be risen and the citizens of Tenochtitlan would discover what they had done. 'We shall speak later,' Tula said, glancing at Xanca. 'Now we must free the other men and be gone.'

There were three times as many men as there had been women. Benicio continued to feed the flames of the brazier with his pages, lighting the way to where the young captives bent in their cramped cages, awaiting their flowery deaths.

Tula sawed at the wooden bars with all of her strength, but she sensed time ticking away. Xanca and Anan tried to help, but could do very little. For every one man that Tula, Xanca and Anan were able to free, Benicio freed five. He was a whirlwind of strength and determination, and Tula found herself lost in admiration of him.

The freed men greeted them with cries of joy and gratitude, then sprinted out of the shadowy space one by one.

'Stop,' Tula called in vain. Like the women, they could not endure a moment longer inside their dark prison.

The four ventured deeper into the space, working tirelessly to release the captives. Soon they had reached the far corner of the temple and the flames of the brazier sputtered. Benicio's book had run out of paper, but there were still seven men left to free.

'We work in darkness now,' said Tula.

'Not yet,' Benicio responded.

He revealed two paper envelopes and the sketch that he had shown Tula so long ago—the sketch of his Luisa. Benicio placed the first of the envelopes upon the copper pan of the brazier and they blazed long enough for Benicio quickly find the first two cages and saw the men free.

He placed the next envelope on to the fire. It gave him enough light to free the next two men while Tula, Xanca and Anan cut through the bar of the fifth cage. The flames sputtered and there were still two men left. Benicio placed Luisa's sketch into the fire.

'No!' Tula cried, but it was too late. The flames caressed her beautiful neck, then turned it to ash and in that final flash of light, Benicio released the last of the two men.

'I am humble,' she heard the man say, then listened to his soft footfalls as he escaped across the shrine.

They stood in darkness again and Tula realised the Benicio had just burned the only image he owned of Luisa. 'Benicio,' she whispered. She felt his hand reach for hers across the darkness and she took it.

'We must go,' Anan said and the group rushed across the empty expanse of the shrine, towards the night sky beyond.

'We must follow the others out of the city,' said Xanca.

'There are guards everywhere,' said Tula.

'Then how shall we escape?' asked Xanca.

Tula's mind raced. Tenochtitlan was a strictly governed city, with guards everywhere. In a few short hours the dead priests would be discovered atop the temple and the entire city would rise up in search of the missing Totonac captives. The men and women they had freed had a head start, but by the time their group reached the city gates, word would be out and their lives would be in danger once again.

Tula paused, observing the lifeless bodies of the two priests whom she and Benicio had battled. 'We shall become priests,' she said suddenly. 'That is how we shall escape the city.'

Xanca frowned. 'Become priests?'

'We shall cut their hair and wear it, along with their robes and masks.'

'The gods will strike us down!' exclaimed Xanca.

Tula looked up at the sky. 'They have not struck us down yet, have they? Perhaps they favour and protect us.' Tula stole a glance at Benicio.

Xanca looked from the fallen priests to the sky and then to Anan, who nodded. Xanca gave a resigned sigh. 'Tell me what to do, dear Sister. We shall follow you until the end.'

Tula held her knife to the blood-matted locks of the first priest. She told herself that cutting hair was no different than cutting the ropes of wrecked ships. Still she kept her eyes closed, praying that the gods would not strike her down where she knelt.

Benicio jumped to her side, removing the beheaded man's long locks in a few fast strokes. When he was done, he tied the ropes together into long strips that he arranged upon his head.

'No, no, Benicio,' Tula corrected in Spanish. 'You cannot be a priest. You must be...how do you say it?' She held her hands up as if they were bound.

'A captive?'

'Yes. I am sorry. You are our captive.'

Benicio grinned. 'I fear that I have been your captive for some time already, dear lady.'

Chapter Thirty

She cocked her head in that sweet, puzzled way of hers and he was glad she did not understand what he had said. If she knew how happy she had made him she would surely use it to her advantage somehow. The little enchantress.

Now, he simply nodded in assent. 'You are right. I shall be your captive.'

They slunk down the steps of the temple like thieves: three false priests covered in black robes and golden masks and Benicio, their Spanish captive, his dagger still wet with blood.

When the group finally reached the bottom of the pyramid, the stars had disappeared. A familiar, portly figure limped out of the pale shadows.

'What are you doing here?' hissed Benicio.

'I should say the same,' said Rogelio, looking past Benicio to his three gold-faced companions.

'We are leaving the city,' said Benicio. 'You cannot stop us.'

Rogelio limped forward, his face twisted in pain. 'What? Why?'

'We have freed the Totonac captives, but were witnessed by many priests. Soon the entire city will be looking for us.'

'But…what about the treasure?'

'It does not matter.'

'You are bound to honour our agreement,' sputtered Rogelio. 'You are bound to help me find it.'

'There *is* no treasure,' spat Benicio.

'You are lying.'

'I do not lie.' Benicio pulled the map from his boot and stretched it before Rogelio. 'Do you see there? Circles around each of the four single points. If those points are temples, they are single temples. Look around, Rogelio. There are only double temples here. And the Templo Mayor is in the west. According to the map, it should be in the north.'

Rogelio blinked in disbelief. 'If the treasure is not here, then where is it?'

'I do not know and I do not care,' said Benicio. 'There is no treasure. Therefore, there is no agreement.'

A single ray of sun touched the tip of the Templo Mayor. 'I am sorry, Rogelio, but we must go now.'

'You cannot leave me here alone. They will think I helped you.'

Benicio studied the wretched man who had tried to kill him that day on the beach. His face was pale, his body bent in pain and blood leaked through his hose. He was dying.

A strange pity invaded Benicio's heart. 'You may come with us, but you must obey my commands, whatever they are.'

Rogelio straightened and Benicio thought he saw the sheen of emotion traverse his countryman's eyes. 'I am glad you see fit to honour our agreement,' Rogelio said.

Benicio ripped open his leather jerkin and dropped it upon the ground. He sliced his knife across the garment with fierce precision, creating a dozen long strips. 'Bind him,' Benicio told Tula. 'I am going to find us a horse.'

In minutes Benicio was back at the foot of the Templo, towing a fine Spanish mare behind him. He boosted Rogelio to his place atop the horse and Rogelio moaned in pain. 'Lie on your stomach,' commanded Benicio.

Rogelio scowled, but did as he was told, stretching himself over the horse's back like a sack of cotton. Tula lifted her mask and Benicio held out the reins.

'This is called a horse,' said Benicio, trying to

speak simply. 'Do not fear.' Tula nodded warily, reluctant to take the reins.

'She will follow you,' said Benicio. 'Come, let us give her a name. What do you wish to call her?'

Tula thought for a moment. 'Big Deer,' she said, adjusting her golden mask.

Benicio lifted himself atop Big Deer and sprawled on his stomach beside Rogelio while Xanca and Anan bound his hands and feet. Then the unlikely companions began their journey down the large promenade leading out of Tenochtitlan.

The people came out of their houses to behold the priests and their strange prisoners. They gasped and whispered, studying the unusual beast with unrestrained wonder.

Meanwhile, Benicio was experiencing a wonder of his own. Once again, Tula had amazed him with her cleverness. Their disguise was working brilliantly and, while news travelled throughout the city of the escaped Totonac captives, their group clip-clopped down the central promenade, above suspicion.

The sun was high in the sky by the time they arrived at the main causeway bridge linking the island city to the lands beyond. A man in a long white toga stepped forward, then dropped to his knees before Tula in requisite obeisance. When he returned to standing, his eyes were full of suspicion. Behind him, four soldiers holding stone clubs stood at attention.

The man in the toga walked around Big Deer carefully. He lanced several questions at Tula and Benicio sensed her faltering. Benicio readied himself for a fight.

Chapter Thirty-One

Tula was glad for her golden mask, for it concealed the nervous sweat trickling down her face. 'The prisoners' blood is unclean,' she explained to the Keeper of the Bridge. 'We have been ordered to sacrifice them far from the city.'

'Why do you speak with an accent, holy one?' the Keeper asked her.

'I was recruited to the priesthood from far away,' Tula lied in her imperfect Nahuatl, wishing that she had paid more attention to her father's lessons.

'Why is your voice so high? It sounds like a woman's.'

'I need not explain that to you,' Tula said, feigning offence, 'though I am sure you are aware of the final step in a young priest's apprenticeship.'

'Please, remind me,' said the Keeper.

'The removal of the male burdens,' said Tula, trying to sound irritated. 'I am surprised you did not know that. May we cross now?'

The Keeper said nothing. Instead, he took an interest in Benicio, lifting and inspecting each of his legs as if he were a hunted beast. He walked around the horse and bent close to Benicio's face. 'And this one? I do not see any evidence of his corruption.'

'He suffers from a peculiar disease of the heart,' said Tula, fumbling for some credible explanation for Benicio's captivity. 'It cannot be seen, but it has invaded his body and twists his mind.'

The Keeper grabbed Benicio by the hair and lifted his head. He searched Benicio's eyes. 'Why does he not wear a beard like the others of his kind?'

Tula searched for the right answer. 'It is part of his disease. He wishes to be someone other than who he is.' The Keeper nodded, seeming to accept the explanation. 'We shall move on now, Keeper,' said Tula with as much authority as she could gather. 'Montezuma wishes these men bled by nightfall.'

'Of course you may go, holy one,' the Keeper said at last. 'And I shall give you two of my men to help you on your way.' He motioned to two of the guards.

Tula cringed beneath her mask, but managed a bow. 'Keeper of the Bridge, you are very generous. Montezuma and the gods thank you.'

The Keeper bowed low and the two guards took

their positions behind Big Deer as they started across the long bridge that would deliver them from Tenochtitlan.

As they walked, Tula touched the knife that lay concealed beneath her belt. She thought of severing Benicio's bonds, then realised that by the time she freed him, the guards would have Xanca and Anan at the tips of their spears. Tula imagined pushing one of the guards over the low wall and into the lake, though she was not sure she could accomplish it on her own. Both of the men were at least a head taller than her and twice as strong. There was no escape that did not result in someone's death.

Suddenly, Benicio howled. It was a long, desperate bay, like the bawling of a madman. Tula halted Big Deer. The first guard approached Benicio's head, while the second neared his legs. In a single motion, Benicio kicked the second guard in the stomach and slid off the horse.

The man went stumbling backwards and Tula knew this was her chance. She lifted her knife and quickly severed Benicio's bonds. Benicio ran towards the first guard, punching him deftly in the jaw. Meanwhile, the second guard had grabbed hold of Xanca and was pulling her down. Anan jumped atop him, unleashing a barrage of weak punches, and the three struggled upon the ground.

Benicio pried the second guard from Anan and sent a heavy blow deep into the man's gut. Then Benicio thrust him over the low wall and into the water. The first guard was staggering to standing when Benicio ploughed into his stomach and lifted him into the water to join the second.

'Can you swim?' Benicio asked Tula, removing her golden mask.

'Yes.'

'Fast?'

Tula nodded. Both guards had recovered themselves and were beginning to swim back to the low wall.

Benicio sliced Rogelio's arms and wrists free, then handed him Tula's mask. 'Go to the great salt lake beyond Tlaxcala,' he told Rogelio. 'We will meet you there. Can I trust you to keep them safe?'

Rogelio nodded gravely, then fixed the golden mask upon his own face.

Benicio turned back to Tula. 'We must separate now or perish.' The guards whom Benicio had tossed into the water were already over the wall. 'Your sister and Anan have no strength to run or swim. Nor does Rogelio. This is our only hope.'

'Let us swim then,' said Tula. 'I am sure that I will best you.'

A wicked grin stretched across Benicio's face. 'I fear you are mistaken, my little enchantress.'

Benicio hoisted Xanca and Anan on to Big Deer, then slapped the creature on its flank. 'Hiya!' he shouted and the horse burst into a gallop, whisking its three masked riders down the causeway and out of the fray.

The two wet, injured guards staggered after Benicio and Tula while a group of guards running down the causeway began to throw their spears. 'Now,' said Benicio, motioning to the water, and Tula jumped from the low wall and dived deep.

Spears and arrows ripped through the water around her and she imagined herself a dolphin fish swimming away from a school of sharks. She sensed Benicio somewhere near her, but she could not see him. She swam for her life, pushing the water out of her way as she made her way further and further from the causeway. She did not surface for a breath until she was far out of spear shot.

She looked back at the causeway. Several of the guards had entered the water and were swimming towards them. A guard who was still standing upon the causeway spotted her bobbing head and shouted. She glanced about for Benicio. He burst to the surface much closer to the bridge.

'I bested you!' she exclaimed. 'I am closer.'

Benicio looked around, spying their relentless pursuers. 'Yes, but who will reach the shore first?'

'I will!' she said and plunged back into the depths.

She could hardly catch her breath when she emerged from the lake. She lifted her head and there he was, his arms folded satisfactorily. 'You may be faster,' he said, 'but I will always be stronger.' He flexed the muscles in his arms and nodded proudly, and she could not help but laugh. He pointed back at the lake. Three men were swimming towards them, while several others travelled down the causeway, pursuing them by land. 'We must run now,' he said. 'Can you run?'

'Yes,' she answered.

'Fast?'

'What do you think?'

Chapter Thirty-Two

They crested the pass at daybreak. Benicio took Tula in his arms as they gazed out at the great salt lake spread out beneath them. They were hungry, thirsty and completely spent, but they had managed to evade their pursuers.

They headed for the rocky wasteland around the salt lake, where none would guess they had retreated. 'Look there,' Tula said pointing, 'the animal standing near that cluster of rocks.'

'Big Deer!' Benicio exclaimed, feeling an unusual flood of joy. Xanca, Anan and Rogelio had survived their journey.

Bubbling with excitement, Tula went bounding down the slope. He watched as she embraced her sister in a fit of sobs and a strange satisfaction stretched around his heart.

When Benicio finally sauntered into the small camp, he could hardly remember how thirsty and hungry he was. He embraced Xanca and Anan, and they decorated him with a garland of welcoming words in their lilting tongue. 'Where is Rogelio?' Benicio asked.

'This way,' said Xanca.

They followed Xanca down a path and around a large boulder and found Rogelio lying in the shade. Benicio stepped forward. 'I never thought I would say this, but *por Diós* am I glad to see you,' said Benicio.

Rogelio made no move to stand, but he cocked his head at Benicio and slid him a strained grin.

'You feared I would take the horse and the golden masks and be on my way.'

'The thought never entered my mind,' Benicio lied. He scanned the small camp, searching for the masks. Instead he noticed a thick reed sleeping mat near one of the rocks. There were several blankets lying upon it and dozens of jars of water nearby. Just beyond Rogelio's foot, a cluster of rocks supported a pot, which appeared to be full of stew. Beside them were many large sacks full of maize meal, chilli, dried beans and various fruits—enough food and supplies for many weeks.

'Where did you obtain so much food?'

'We traded one of the masks at a village nearby.

The people were more than happy to give us everything we needed.'

Benicio raised a brow. 'Clever.'

'And costly. I would guess that one of those masks
is worth the price of half a ship.'

'I would guess the same.' Benicio grinned, studying his compatriot in wonder. 'Rogelio, I fear you
are in danger of becoming an honourable man.'

Rogelio shook his head. 'I fear I am in danger of
becoming a dead man,' he said, glancing at his leg.
The wound encompassed Rogelio's entire thigh now
and had become blue at the edges. Rogelio swatted the flies that buzzed above it with a long cloth.
When they returned, he merely stared at them in
defeat.

Benicio shook his head.

'Do not pity me, Benicio. Surely I deserve this.
Ours is a just God, is he not?'

Benicio thought of all the good souls who had
lost their lives at the hands of the Spanish. 'I am
not sure.'

Tula squatted beside Rogelio and studied his
wound. *'Lo siento,'* she said. A single tear pulsed
down her cheek. She said something to Xanca in
their language and soon the three of them were lifting Rogelio to his feet.

Rogelio shot Tula a look of malice. 'Take your hands off me, witch. You did this. You hurt me.'

'I am help you now,' said Tula.

'No one can help me now,' said Rogelio, his face twisting in pain.

'Within everything, the opposite,' said Tula and she lifted Rogelio's leg in her arms and the three made their way slowly down to the lake.

They stayed by the salt lake for seven days, labouring to save Rogelio's life. Benicio wanted to join them. He craved Tula's nearness, and he wished to beg her forgiveness for his behavior that night atop the Templo Mayor. But he was unconvinced that their pursuers had given up their chase. Someone needed to keep watch, so Benicio made camp on the crest above the lake where he faithfully stood lookout.

Each day, Rogelio was sent to soak in the lake's salty water, while Tula and Xanca went gathering in the nearby forest. In the afternoon, they packed special herbs into Rogelio's wound and smothered it in medicinal pastes and tinctures.

Slowly, Rogelio's scowl faded. He was able to rest, and soon, to sleep. His wound ceased to weep and his eyes grew brighter. Every day, Benicio would visit him. On the third day, when Benicio joked that a bird wished to nest in Rogelio's beard, Rogelio let out a hearty laugh. By the fourth day, he was able to stand on his own. By the fifth, he could walk to the lake by himself.

On his visits to camp, Tula always welcomed Benicio and helped him to gather water and supplies, but she did not look him in the eye.

He could suspect why. His behaviour atop the Templo Mayor had been beyond disgraceful. He had forced her to the ground, ignoring her pleadings and hoisting his whole body upon hers until she could scarcely catch her own breath.

He had wanted her so badly in that moment—more than he had ever wanted any woman—though it was no excuse for his behaviour. He wanted to ask her if she could ever forgive him, or even begin to feel the same for him as he did for her.

Do you not want me as I want you? he wanted to ask her. On the sixth day, he got his answer. He had just finished his lunch and was returning up the slope when Tula rushed to his side. She held a golden mask in her hands—one of two that remained. 'One for you and one for Rogelio,' she said in Spanish, gleaming with that proud, adorable grin.

It took Benicio a moment to absorb the measure of her kindness. There were two golden masks. One had surely been spoken for by Rogelio. She wanted

Benicio to have the other? *'Gracias, Tula, muchas gracias,'* Benicio said, because he wanted to make her grin last as long as he could. 'But, no, I cannot accept it. It is for you and your family.' He bowed to her as he thought a Totonac man would.

But Tula shook her head. 'No, no, no,' she said. 'This is for you. Please, take it. It is your treasure.'

'I cannot take it. It is for your family. For tribute.'

She shook her head again. She pushed the mask into his hands. 'It is for your future, Benicio. It is *taak'in*. For you and your Luisa.'

If she had loaded her atlatl with her sharpest arrow and sent it hurling at his heart, she could not have hurt him more. Clearly, she wished for him to return to Luisa. That was why she kept saying Luisa's name, trying to remind him of the woman he wanted only to forget. Tula did not want Benicio, she wanted to be rid of him.

Benicio steeled himself against the flood of hurt that threatened to topple him. He painted a smile on to his face and shook his head. 'No, Tula. The mask is for you.' Then he turned and hiked back to his post.

The next morning, Benicio watched Tula lift her skirts and begin the long hike up the slope to Benicio's lookout. Her march was full of resolve and his nerves prickled as he tried to divine her purpose.

'Good morning, Tula,' he said, nodding formally. Thankfully she had not brought the golden mask. Still, he wondered what on earth she had come to tell him.

'Good morning, Benicio,' she said with a polite smile. She pointed down the slope to where Rogelio was gathering dead branches among the sage bushes.

'Rogelio walks,' she announced, breaking the heavy silence.

'Thanks to you,' said Benicio.

She frowned. 'I can sit?' she asked. He nodded and she took her seat on a low rock several paces away. She sat there for many long moments, as if trying to think of how to begin. 'We can leave soon,' she said. 'Go home.'

Benicio nodded, though a strange pain pricked inside his heart. Return to Cempoala? Already? But of course he had known that this day would come. Benicio imagined delivering Tula to her father and receiving the man's heartfelt thanks, along with his best wishes to Benicio for a safe passage back to his homeland.

The problem was that Benicio did not know where that home was any more. He searched for another topic. 'Your Spanish is very good. How did you learn?' he asked her.

'Malinali—ah—Marina teach me. Tongue of the future, she say.'

'You stayed with Marina?'

'Yes. I stay with her after…the river.' Tula looked at the ground 'She help me. Like a sister.'

'How many sisters do you have?' Benicio asked, feeling a pang of guilt. It should have been Benicio teaching Tula Spanish, not Marina.

She held up three fingers. 'Xanca, Pulhko and now Marina—spirit sister.' Tula smiled. She cocked her head at Benicio in a way that made his blood race. 'And you, Benicio? Sisters? Brothers?'

'Two bro—' Benicio said, stopping himself. He sucked in a breath. 'Ah, one brother. My other brother died.'

Tula stayed silent for some time. She shook her head. *'Lo siento,'* she whispered.

It must have been the way she said the words, as if whispering them to his soul, for a wave of grief encompassed his body and all he wanted to do was curl up with her upon the ground and press his nose into her hair.

'Thank you for your sentiment,' he said coolly. 'My brother was a soldier. He died fighting. In my homeland people have been fighting for many thousands of years. Many kingdoms, rising and falling. Much suffering and sadness.'

'Here it is the same,' Tula said, sitting up. 'I learn history and read the ancient codices. First the Old Ones, then the Maya, then the Teotihuacanos, then the Toltecs, now the Mexica.'

Benicio could not believe his ears. 'You studied history?'

'Yes—my father teach me the past.'

'I studied history, too.'

'You read the codices?' she asked, her eyes brightening. 'You also learn the past?'

'Yes,' said Benicio. 'I love to learn.'

'I also,' said Tula, nodding with enthusiasm. She flashed him dazzling grin. She was so beautiful. Not as a bird that is beautiful, but as the wind that lifts the bird—so full of soft energy and lightness. 'I learn the past so I can know the future,' she said.

'What do you know about the future?' asked Benicio, marvelling at his fellow scholar. 'Tell me.'

'I know that the Mexica grow fat. Too fat. Very soon they will be no more.'

'Why do you say that?'

'Quetzalcoatl, the Feathered Serpent, has returned.'

Benicio remembered Cortés's ring. 'Do you think Cortés is Quetzalcoatl?'

'No, but Montezuma think it and he will not fight Cortés. The Mexica will fall. Soon we have new rulers.'

'The Spanish?'

Tula nodded gravely.

'And when the Spanish rule, what will happen to the Totonacs?' Benicio asked.

'New masters. New lists of tribute.' Tula looked out over the salty flat, as if she could see her future in its empty whiteness.

'There must be another way,' Benicio said.

'Only one other way,' said Tula. 'Hide.'

'Where?'

'Go to the jungle. Live like the Maya.'

'How do the Maya live?'

'In quiet. In secret. Humbly,' she explained. Tula paused, and he saw a tear form in the corner of her eye. 'Benicio, I do a bad thing. I no tell you the truth.'

'What? I do not understand.' She had lied to him?

'You still seek gold for your Luisa, yes?' She did not wait for a response. 'Benicio, the treasure not in Tenochtitlan. I know where the treasure is. I always know, but I no tell you. Please forgive me. We go to get now.'

Chapter Thirty-Three

It was the golden mask that had finally changed her mind. He had insisted that she take it, despite the fact that it represented the only means he had to return to his home. She could not continue to lie to a man like that—a man who would put her needs above his own. Whatever treasure there was to be had in the place depicted on the map would be both of theirs. They could divide it equally. He had saved her life and the life of her sister, after all. The least she could do was help him reach his dream.

They rode for many days—down out of the mountains, through the lowland forests and finally to the coast, journeying ever southward as they weaved in and out of murky jungles on to beaches of white sands.

They kept several blankets between them in the saddle, and spoke to each other only when necessary. Benicio had distanced himself from Tula since the moment she had told him that he could return to Luisa as a wealthy man. It was as if in that instant he had ceased to see Tula standing before him and could only envision Luisa.

And what did Tula expect? He had never told her that he loved her, or gave any sign that his plans had changed. Just because he had fulfilled his part of their pact did not mean that he cared for her. She had been a fool to care for him, and she would not indulge herself in the waves of sadness that threatened to wash over her now. She should have known better. The gods always took loved ones away. It was the law of the world.

Day followed endless day, and it seemed that the nearer they got to the treasure, the farther they got from each other. Soon they turned inland towards the heart of Maya territory.

Tula kept her dagger at the ready. The Maya were fierce, secretive people, whose great civilisation had crumbled long ago. Still, they had never been conquered by the Mexica, or anyone else for that matter, and they did not hesitate to take prisoners. They lived in small cities and settlements almost impossible to reach, their once-great cities all but swallowed up by the jungle.

Tula felt as though she were being swallowed up herself. The days were getting shorter and it should have been much cooler, but the jungle did not seem to know it. Tula wiped her brow as the heat wrapped around her, her thoughts bubbling.

By now, Xanca, Anan and Rogelio were surely back in Cempoala, resting in the comfort of her father's cool stone house. Tula had been reluctant to part ways with them at the salt lake, but Xanca had assured her that it was the right thing to do.

'Treasure is treasure,' she had reasoned. 'It can be used in place of much tribute.'

Tula and Benicio had promised to return to Cempoala within twenty days, their empty maize sacks filled with the untold riches Tula was sure they would find.

'Yes, go!' Rogelio had urged, his eyes bright with greed, and Benicio had snapped Big Deer's reins, steering the mare southward.

And now here they were, in the land of the Maya, so close to their goal, yet so completely lost. Tula wandered beneath the trees and vines, praying that some Maya hunter might find them and point them to the ancient city where Tula knew they would find what they sought.

'Are you sure?' Benicio asked suddenly. They had stopped to let Big Deer dip its head into a small stream. 'About the circles, I mean. The ones on the map?'

'I am sure,' Tula said.

She stared down at the water trickling in its small channel. Streams such as this one were common in Maya territory, but large rivers were not. For the bulk of their water, the Maya relied on cenotes, natural round wells that pockmarked the jungle. 'It is the only answer. The circles on the map are cenotes.'

'And the dot in the middle of the map?'

'It is the temple of Kukulcan.'

The priest who had drawn the map had been wearing the sacred ring of the Wind God, Quetzalcoatl. To the Maya, Quetzalcoatl was known as Kukulcan. Long ago, Tula's father had taught her that Kukulcan's holiest temple was located in the abandoned Maya city of Chichen Itza. It had been constructed between four sacred cenotes.

'Are you certain?'

Clearly Benicio no longer trusted a word Tula said. She had lied to him, after all. For many long months she had deceived him, telling him that the treasure lay in Tenochtitlan. All the while she knew the truth: It did not lie in the greatest city of the Mexica, high in the mountains. It lay in the greatest city of the Maya, deep in the jungle.

'But why locate a temple in the middle of four cenotes?' asked Benicio.

Benicio had barely spoken to her since their departure and only to ask doubting questions such as these. By lying to him for so long, it seemed that she had destroyed all his confidence in her.

'I do not know the minds of the ancients,' Tula said, stroking the mare's long neck.

Benicio had not ridden with her atop Big Deer at all that day. Instead, he had chosen to walk—something he did as often as he could. He did not sleep near her in the night, even when it was cold. He had even grown back his beard, as if he wished to return to the man he was before he met Tula. And that was for the best. Despite their strange attraction, he had remained true to Luisa and she admired him for it. It was the least she could do to keep her distance from him and do her part to reinforce the wall that had grown between them since that moment atop the temple.

'Why not build four temples around a single cenote instead?' he puzzled now. 'Are temples not the most sacred sites in your world?'

Tula shook her head. How could she explain it in a way he could understand? To the Maya, cenotes were like temples beneath the earth. They were sources of power, portals to the world beyond. A Maya priest on his death bed would not draw a circle in his own blood unless he was depicting a cenote. He had probably been drawing some kind of map for his soul—a way for his holy essence to find its way home.

'The Maya culture is old, very old,' Tula explained once again. 'The Maya know that men can build great temples, but the earth will always…eat them. The Maya remember this. Other people forget.'

There was a sudden rustling in the jungle behind them and Tula turned to discover a large, colourful quetzal bird perched on the branch of a broad-leafed mahogany tree. She placed her finger upon her lips and pointed to the elegant bird, its long blue-and-green feathers nearly touching the ground.

'It is a quetzal,' whispered Tula. 'A sacred bird.' She remembered the day she had visited Benicio in the cenote near her home. A bird very much like this one had appeared and led her away, just as the priests were arriving. It had saved her life.

The bird hopped to a more distant branch. 'We must follow this bird,' said Tula. She tugged the Big Deer's reins.

'What are you doing?' Benicio bristled.

'Trust me,' she said. The bird hopped from limb to limb, seemingly unafraid, and they followed it through the jungle. Suddenly, they broke through the undergrowth to behold the sun-bleached stones of an ancient city.

'We are here,' Tula said, overcome with relief. 'We

have arrived in Chichen Itza.' She turned to look for the bird, but it had disappeared into the jungle. Tula called softly after it in Totonac. 'I am humble.'

'What did you say?' asked Benicio.

Tula dismounted Big Deer. 'I cannot say it in your language. The word does not exist.'

Benicio frowned, taking Big Deer's reins.

'It is like to say *gracias*, but it is bigger,' explained Tula, 'and also smaller.'

Tula stared out at Chichen Itza's stone ruins—a rabble of chalky, collapsing buildings covered in bushes and strangled by vines and tree roots. The Temple of Kukulcan rose up among them like a ghost, half-covered in a carpet of green plumage, the headdress of the jungle.

'There is the sacred temple.'

It appeared totally abandoned. Not a single holy soul traversed its high platform, not a speck of blood sullied its stones. Tula pointed at its steps. 'My father tell me there is one for each day of the year,' she explained to Benicio. 'Two times in the cycle of the sun, a serpent goes down.'

'The Feathered Serpent.'

'Yes. He goes from the Temple to the Sacred Cenote.' Tula pointed from the pyramid northward down a long, raised cement road. 'The Sacred Cenote is down that road,' Tula said. 'The Maya Rain God, Chaac, lives there.'

'Is that where the treasure lies?'

Tula scratched her head. She retrieved the map from beneath her belt and opened it. 'The Maya priest, he speak to you?' she asked Benicio, puzzling over the map.

'What?'

Tula looked up and studied Benicio closely. 'The Maya priest say something to you before he die?'

Benicio paused. 'He said the word for gold.'

'Taak'in.'

'Yes.'

'Any other word?'

Benicio seemed to be thinking. *'Ma tu'ub.* He also said *ma tu'ub.'*

'Ma tu'ub!' exclaimed Tula. 'Why you not tell me?'

'I...forgot,' said Benicio. 'What does it mean?'

'It means do not forget,' said Tula, her lips twisting into a mocking smile.

For the first time in many days, Benicio smiled back. 'Well, that does not help very much, does it?'

Tula shook her head. 'It changes everything!' She stuffed the map beneath her belt and began walking south, away from the Sacred Cenote. 'The treasure is not inside the Sacred Cenote.'

'But how do you know that?' Benicio asked, dragging Big Deer behind him.

'Because nobody can forget the Sacred Cenote. Just look at the road.'

Unlike the Temple of Kukulcan and the other buildings nearby, the road heading to the Sacred Cenote was clear, not a single bush or vine encroaching its stone cobbles. It was obviously kept that way, probably by Maya pilgrims and local priests.

Tula's southbound path took them through the rest of the ancient holy precinct of Chichen Itza. Tula did not try to conceal her wonder as they passed through the dense collection of temples and gathering halls, many of which her father had taught her about when she was a child.

Soon they came upon a strange, half-finished temple with a large, round tower protruding from its wide base. Tula knew this building, for her father had described it once: it was the place where the ancient Maya studied the heavens.

'What is this place?' asked Benicio.

'It is where the old Maya come to watch the gods at night.'

'You mean the stars?'

'Yes, the stars,' said Tula absently. 'The beautiful ones. Mixcoatl's sons and daughters.'

Benicio stared at the building in wonder. 'An observatory.' He tied Big Deer off on a nearby tree.

Meanwhile, Tula had spread the map upon the ground. 'What is this?' she asked. She pointed to a trickle of blood that made a kind of path down from the map's central dot.

'I do not know,' said Benicio, his attention consumed by the spectacular domed building.

'This is the last place he touch?' she asked.

'I think so, yes,' Benicio said absently, his gaze still fixed on the snail-shaped dome. 'Why does it matter?'

'Within everything lies its opposite,' said Tula and she continued southward, this time at a slow run.

'Where are you going?' Benicio called after her.

'South,' she cried, 'to find the treasure!'

Chapter Thirty-Four

Big Deer reared up, almost stumbling into the small round pool of water, which appeared without warning amidst the thick undergrowth. Benicio guided the horse backwards and dismounted, tying her off on a tree. He picked his way through the tangle of bushes and vines and peered over the edge.

The clear, clean water rippled outward in undulating waves—evidence of Tula's dive. She was down there already, propelling herself through the depths. Benicio had only spent a few moments inside the observatory, but when he had returned, he had quickly lost her path through the dense jungle. Then, just moments ago, he had heard the splash.

Thank God he had found her, for the cenote would have been easy to miss. Its waters were high, but tree limbs and vines criss-crossed the open space above it, shrouding it in shade. Peering over the edge, Benicio saw several rocks exposed just beneath its rim, creating natural resting places in the cool shade. Benicio removed his boots and stepped down on to one of the rocks.

She had chosen not to wait for him, just as she had chosen not to visit him all those days he had stood on lookout. And on their journey to Chichen Itza, she seemed glad that he had stayed well away from her. She had even helped him wedge the blanket between them in the saddle every day, as if she despised his touch as much as he feared hers.

And she had every right to despise him, he reminded himself, for he had forced himself upon her that night at the top of the Templo Mayor. She had every right to keep her distance and continually remind him of Luisa.

Clearly Tula did not want Benicio. She wanted him to return to Spain and reunite with his lost love. The sooner she could find the treasure, the sooner she could be rid of him and move on with her life.

Perhaps that was for the best. Clearly she could not stand to be with him. And he could not stand to be with her any more, either—at least, not when she wore her hair down like she had begun to do, in long dark ropes that looked like silk. And not when she kept mounting the horse on her own, as if it were nothing, her strong, shapely thighs flashing naked with the flare of her skirt. And not when she smiled at him in that way, when the sun was in her face, just as she had done that night beneath the glow of the moon.

It was unbearable. He had tried to purge her from his mind, but it was impossible, for there she was, alive and radiant. And when he tried to flood his mind with thoughts of the past, all he could remember was the moments they had shared together. They had burned into his limbs like a disease, making him weak, destroying his resolve, turning his goals to ash. He had become her servant that night on the steps of the Templo Mayor, her most devout apostle, and he knew that from that moment on, he would do anything for her.

So that day at the lookout, when she had told him that she had lied to him and reminded him once again of his duty to Luisa, well, he had to obey, even though she had quietly crushed his heart.

He stared down into the dark waters, wondering if she could see anything at all. His heart pounded. How could she still be holding her breath? He was twice her size and would certainly be choking for air by now. She was in danger, he could sense it. He dived in.

He tried to keep his sense of direction as darkness enveloped him. Down, down he dived, flailing his arms about in the hopes of touching her, but she was nowhere to be found. 'Tula!' he cried through the water, swallowing a mouthful.

He thrust out his arms and probed all around him until he came upon a wall, then felt his head bump against hard rock. 'Tula!' he called, his lungs beginning to convulse. His body wanted to rise, but there was some kind of ceiling above him. He did not know how to escape. He sucked in another lungful of water and realised that he was drowning.

Suddenly, he felt her hand upon his arm. She was dragging him towards her. She placed her arm about his waist and kicked upwards. Soon, the ceiling above him had disappeared and he saw that he was floating towards a dim light. Then everything went black.

When he awoke, a stream of water was shooting out of his lungs. He was lying on the ground on his stomach, sputtering back to life. He felt her hands upon his back as he coughed more water, then collapsed. He breathed in the air and felt her hands caressing his back.

He lay there for many long moments, aware that she was saying something in her language, some angry string of words that none the less caressed his ears. He rolled over.

There she was—his goddess. She was kneeling

before him, and the sun shone behind her in a halo of light. She had saved his life and now she hovered beside him like some heavenly vision.

'You almost die,' she said. 'Why do you go in the cenote?' The tears streaming down her face caught the light. He reached up and wiped them with his thumb.

'I was worried about you,' he said. 'You saved my life. Again.'

'You save my life many times,' she responded curtly. 'I am sorry I lie to you, Benicio. I owe you a debt.'

'You owe me no debt,' said Benicio, but she seemed not to hear.

She pointed at the cenote. 'I pay it now. I find treasure.'

He tried to pretend enthusiasm, but he could not think past her big, dazzling eyes, her abundant lips and her long, elegant neck, which he studied for a long while before noticing the large jade necklace hanging heavily around it.

She unclasped the necklace and placed it into his hands. 'You see? I find gold, Benicio! Much, much gold. And rings. And plates and masks. I touch with my hands!' She was shouting with excitement and no small measure of pride. 'I find it for you, Benicio. For you and Luisa. Treasure!'

Tula jumped to her feet, her eyes glittering with the certainty of success. 'I bring treasure now for us.' She stepped towards the cenote and prepared to dive.

'No!' shouted Benicio. 'Please, do not go.'

'I bring treasure. It is good, yes? You give to Luisa.'

Benicio frowned. Why must she always remind him of his return to Spain, when all he wanted to do was forget it? 'No, it is not good.'

'What? Why?'

'Because I do not wish for gold—not any more.'

She stared at him in stupefied silence. 'I do not understand.'

'I do not want to return to Spain.'

'But your Luis—'

'Shh!' he snapped. 'Please do not say her name.'

Tula cringed at his sharpness, then shook her head in confusion. 'I do not understand the words you say. We come to find gold for you. I bring it now.'

'You are not understanding me,' said Benicio, but it was too late. She stepped over the edge of the cenote and Benicio heard a splash. Without thinking, he lunged over the edge after her.

He kicked fiercely, hardly believing that he had willingly plunged himself into the very same pool in which he had almost drowned. But he did not care. He needed to make her understand the truth: that his heart did not wish for Luisa, or to find Luisa's gold—not any more. It wished for Tula. Tula was the woman he loved and he would fight for her until the end.

Chapter Thirty-Five

She dived into the depths, letting her confusion propel her. Surely he mocked her. Either that, or he had truly gone mad. She had seen it happen before. After the battles in Tlaxcala, several of the Spanish soldiers had simply stopped fighting. They had un-buckled their armour plates and staggered off into the forest.

And now, Benicio was in essence doing the same. He was abandoning his dream: to return to his land with a horde of treasure to present to his woman. He was forsaking everything he had set out to do.

But she would not let him succeed. She dived ever downwards, angling to a small alcove where the enormous concrete jars had been wedged. She plunged her hand into the wide mouth of the first jar.

There was so much treasure—plenty for the both of them. She could feel the smooth gemstones, the elaborately designed loops and clasps. She trod water as her fingers traced along the outlines of heavy metallic plates and bowls, and into the hollow eyes of dozens of sacred masks.

It was an incredible horde and she wondered for a moment why the Maya priest had told Benicio about this place at all.

It was said that holy men could see into people's souls. Perhaps the priest had seen the goodness in Benicio's. And Benicio was a good man, despite all his efforts to convince Tula otherwise. She knew that he loathed killing, and loved the people of the world. He could have abandoned Tula and the Totonac captives that night atop the pyramid, but instead he had risked his life saving them. She suspected he had risked his life trying to save the Maya priest, as well.

Do not forget, the priest had told Benicio, urging him to learn the words. It occurred to Tula that perhaps the priest had not wished for Benicio to steal the golden horde at all, only to remember it.

Tula placed as many necklaces as she could around her neck and as many rings as she could upon her fingers, imagining that such a horde could be used by Benicio to give his woman many beautiful things. She had lied to him and now she needed to redeem herself and fulfil her promise. Besides, she owed him her life, as well as her sister's. This time, instead of stealing his gold, she was going to gather it for him.

She grabbed the hem of her skirt with her fist, reaching with her free hand further and further downwards into what felt like densely packed metal labrets. It was a cache of kings—enough jewellery to adorn a small village of nobles.

Or many generations of them.

A lump came into her throat and she paused. Suddenly, it was so clear. She was not meant to gather this treasure—not any of it. Not a single necklace or ring or gem. *Do not forget*, said the priest, but he wasn't talking about the gold. He was talking about the glory and ruin of Chichen Itza itself.

And in that moment, she felt his hand upon her arm. He pulled her out of the alcove and caught her by the waist, and soon they were thrusting upwards like twin fish, the cool clear water caressing their skin, surrounded in bubbles of their exhaling breaths.

His arm remained firmly around her waist as they burst to the surface. He guided her towards a partially submerged rock just below the cenote's edge. He lifted her upon its flat surface, then hoisted himself next to her. 'Tula, I need to tell you something,' he said, struggling to catch his breath.

'Benicio, I need to tell you something,' she said.

But it was as if he had not heard her, for his words came in a flood. 'Tula, I must tell you that I have had a change of heart that will surely bring me dishonour, for I have made a promise to someone back in Spain that I am unable to keep.'

She stared at him in confusion, for he had spoken many difficult words, one after the other.

He shook his head, then began again. 'Tula, I am not a good man.'

Tula placed her finger upon Benicio's lips. 'Benicio, you are a very good man.'

'No, Tula, I am not. I have killed so many men. So very many—'

'It is not your fault. You follow Cortés.'

'And why? For gold, Tula! For evil, wretched gold. Gold for a woman who I hardly know, a woman who is not content unless she is covered in silks.'

Tula was completely confused. He was speaking so quickly, and she did not understand many of the words he was using. 'Benicio, I—'

'Tula, I do not want Luisa. And I do not want the treasure.'

Tula gasped. Had he somehow understood what she had finally understood just moments ago? She nodded in affirmation. 'And I do not want the treasure,' she said, though that was not why she had gasped. Could it be true? He did not want Luisa?

She could not think clearly, and she knew not what to say. On impulse, she unclasped one of her heavy necklaces and let it fall back into the water. Benicio appeared confused as he watched the golden necklace disappear into the depths. 'What about your family's tribute?' he asked in alarm. 'This treasure could help you, Tula. You must keep it all.'

Tula sighed and shook her head. 'What did the priest say to you?'

'Do not forget,' said Benicio.

'Do not forget,' repeated Tula. She held up her rings. 'He does not want you to forget this.'

'The treasure of Chichen Itza?'

'The…greatness of Chichen Itza.'

'But how can anybody forget the glory of Chichen Itza? Its temples and palaces still stand. Its past is here for all to see.'

'But what happened to Chichen Itza?' Tula urged. 'I tell you at the lake. Do you remember?'

'Chichen Itza fell, did it not?' said Benicio.

'Yes, but how?'

'Another kingdom rose to power in its place.'

'You are a good student,' said Tula. 'That is what we must never forget.'

'That kingdoms come and go?'

Tula nodded. 'If I take this gold for tribute, it will just make the new rulers more powerful.'

'But if you do not take it, your family will continue to suffer.'

'Even if I take it, we will continue to suffer,' Tula said. 'The priest was trying to tell you to be wise, Benicio. You and all the Spaniards. Do not become like the Mexica, or the Toltecs before them, or the Teotihuacanos before them, or the Maya before them. Do not take too much.' Tula switched to the Totonac tongue. 'Be humble.'

'My countrymen will never understand that phrase, I fear.'

Tula touched Benicio's hand. 'No, but you can.'

Chapter Thirty-Six

Benicio wished she had not touched his hand. He could feel the slight pulse of blood in her fingertips, distracting him from her words. Her eyes were bright and clear, and the drops of water in her eyelashes sparkled in the dappled light. 'You are so beautiful, Tula,' he said.

'You are speaking of these?' she asked, touching her ringed fingers to the heavy necklaces around her neck. 'They are indeed beautiful.'

'No, I am speaking of you.' He reached his arms around her neck and unclasped one of the necklaces. He held it over the water and released it. It disappeared into the depths and with it, a measure of his misery.

'You do not need adornment,' he said. 'You are more beautiful than any goddess.' He unclasped another necklace and let it drop. 'Can I say that and still be humble?'

She flushed red, then shook her head, but there was a smile at the edge of her lips. He unclasped another necklace. Then another. He could feel her warm breaths upon his cheek as he unclasped the final necklace. It was as if he were undressing her, though the rest of her body remained fully clothed. His desire stirred.

He let the necklace fall into the cenote and they sat in silence on the flat rock, their bare feet dangling in the cool water. Something had changed between them, though he could not say just what. He nudged her foot with his own.

She opened her mouth to speak and he noticed that a drop of water had settled itself in the groove above her upper lip.

Without thinking, he leaned over and tasted it.

And that was a mistake, because some invisible longing that had crouched inside him all these months leaped forward, and he realised that he would not return to the world above until he had made her his.

He moved to her lower lip and sucked it softly, trying to keep his desire submerged within him. Amazingly, she did not try to pull away. Instead, she sat still, though even she could not conceal her flood of breaths. In truth, he wanted to push her back on to the rock, pull up her skirts and take her right then.

'I want you, Tula,' he said, pulling himself away. Her hair hung in wet ropes about her cheeks and neck, framing the regal cheekbones that encased the dark, dangerous pools of her eyes. Her beauty made him feel weak. She was like a painting made real, or some perfectly sculpted bust miraculously imbued with life.

But it was more than that. It was the fire that smouldered within her that drew him, that intense ability she had to seize upon the things around her and transform them into something new. She was his witch. His enchantress. His secret queen. He wanted to bow down before her and pledge his undying fealty. He felt reverent of her. He felt...humble.

Her lips twisted into an impish grin and her dagger brows relaxed into playful half-moons above her eyes. She pulled off one of her rings and tossed it over her shoulder. It hit the water with a plop, then disappeared into the depths. She smiled at him. She lifted her hand before him and nodded encouragingly.

Following her lead, he pulled another golden ring from her finger and tossed it over his own shoulder. He made a funny face as it plopped into the water behind him, causing her to giggle. She pulled off another ring and tossed it aside, licking her fingers as if she had just cast away a half-eaten cob of maize.

He pulled another ring from her finger and placed it upon his head. Feigning sleepiness, he yawned and lay down upon the rock. The ring tumbled off his head and into the depths.

Delighted, she laughed, then appeared to strike upon some clever idea. She pulled the last ring from her finger and placed it in her mouth.

She lay back on the flat stone next to him, thrusting an invisible blade into her chest and feigning a dramatic death. Finally, she closed her eyes and lay there, unmoving.

Had she just mocked him? Of course she had, the brazen temptress. And she had also issued him a challenge. *Try to retrieve the ring inside my mouth,* she had told him. *Just try.*

He placed his leg across her prone body, then lifted himself astride her, straddling her round hips and becoming instantly aware of his desire. *Slow,* he told himself, forcing deep breaths. She was so much smaller than him, though her strength was indisputable. He braced his hands upon the flat stone beneath her, careful not to crush her. He bent over and touched his lips to hers.

She tasted earthy and sweet, just as he had remembered. He kissed her softly and coaxingly, trying to encourage her mouth open. But she would not be so easily won. She lay perfectly still, her body stiff, her mouth shut tight, relishing the game she had engineered.

Still, she had no appreciation of the opponent she faced. He lifted her shawl and placed his hand upon her breast, letting her feel his hot breath as he reached beneath her shawl to caress her nipple.

'Mmm...' she moaned through her teeth. He kissed her neck, watching with satisfaction as her back arched upwards in response. His kiss upon her neck became a suck and her breathing intensified. He sucked lower down her neck, struggling to keep rule over his desire. Then he took a soft bite.

'Ow!' she cried out, but quickly shut her mouth, giving him a wicked idea.

He kissed her lips again, then nuzzled against her ear, kissing and breathing in turn. He watched with satisfaction as the tiny hairs on her skin rose to attention.

As if in retaliation, she arched her back again, pushing her hips against him and feeling his arousal. She moved in a slow circle against him and his self-control seemed to melt with the heat. His desire had risen to its full girth. It poked outside his loincloth and all he wanted was to thrust himself inside of her and find his release.

Instead, he took the very tip of her nipple and squeezed. 'Ah!' she cried out and he was instantly kissing her again, his tongue successfully through the barrier of her teeth and probing inside her soft mouth.

He almost cried out in his triumph. But he was not done yet. Now he had to retrieve the ring with his tongue—something she was wickedly determined to deny him.

He decided upon a strategy of soft, probing kisses while he slowly lifted her skirt. He caressed her smooth, damp thighs, trying so very hard to keep his touch gentle and teasing, reminding himself to stay calm. But when he placed his hand atop her woman's mound and let his finger slide inside her, he found himself quite close to losing control.

He had never felt so much hot, slippery wetness. There was nothing to coax from her: she was ready for him like a flower moist with dew. He pressed his need against her stomach and she gasped, then moaned quietly. It did not matter what language she spoke. She was communicating quite clearly now. She wanted him.

Suddenly, he did not care about the ring or her silly game. His body was ablaze with desire for her, a desire so overwhelming he felt as if any moment he might burst into flames. He stopped probing for the ring and untied his loincloth. He placed her hand upon his engorged shaft.

But it was too soon. She stiffened in alarm, pulling her hand away and bracing it against the rock. She pushed upwards, trying to sit up, and her lips accidentally crashed into his. Soon she had braced herself on both her arms and was pushing him firmly backwards—with her lips. She pushed and pushed until he was lying on his back against the rock and she was straddling him. Then she sat up to observe her accomplishment.

Well done, he thought, lying powerless beneath her, though he was far from bested. Still, now that she was in command, he was powerless to do anything but obey. Her legs wrapped tightly around his waist, straddling him. The weight of her stomach pressed against his shaft and he breathed, trying not to explode. He feared that she intended to slowly drive him mad.

She bent over him and braced her hands on the flat rock behind him just as he had done to her. Then she placed her lips upon his. She did not have to kiss him long before his tongue had woven with hers and the ring slowly slipped into his own mouth.

'Ah!' she yelped, then snickered. He quickly slipped the ring around his tongue, letting her tongue writhe and struggle in an attempt to dislodge it. Slowly, he lifted her skirts and found her again.

Chapter Thirty-Seven

She felt his finger slip into the folds of her womanhood. It felt dangerous and forbidden, his finger in that place, yet she did not want him to withdraw it. Indeed, something inside her craved it. Her hips rocked unbidden and she felt waves of pleasure ripple beneath her skin.

He began to move his finger in rhythm with her own movements, sliding it back and forth across her shallow folds. Part of her feared what he might do. Another part of her prayed for it. She kissed him harder, as if her body had set out towards some important goal whose end she could not know.

Slowly, however, he withdrew his hand, and for a moment she feared he would sit up and take his leave. Instead, he grasped her by the hips with firmness and pulled her thighs over his naked shaft, so that she could feel his hardness.

'Tula, please, let me love you.'

Tula's heart caught in her throat. 'It is dangerous. For women it is different,' she said.

'I understand.'

'I cannot bring a child into this world.'

'I will not give you one.'

'But…how?'

'I know how to keep you from harm. That is all I ever want to do.'

She felt his hard shaft between her legs. It was so large: she had no idea how she could possibly contain him. 'I do not know. I have never—'

'Shh,' he whispered. He moved down the rock and positioned himself beneath her so the tip of him touched her naked folds. 'You are in control,' he told her. 'No harm will come. You can do what you wish.'

He peered up at her, and she saw a trace of sunlight dancing on his strong, angular face. He did not want the treasure or Luisa. Instead, he wanted Tula. She knew it now with certainty, and it was as if all that had been frozen within her were suddenly melting. As she looked into his eyes, she knew that he was her Sun God and his warmth would never cease.

Tentatively, she took him in her hand and gently moved his desire in and around her folds. He let out a moan and waves of unexpected warmth rippled through her body.

She had no idea of the pleasure she could derive from simply watching him experience pleasure and something inside her wanted to increase his pleasure even more.

Slowly, she pushed herself down upon him.

'Ah,' she heard herself gasp, for the sensation was like nothing she could have ever dreamed. He was so large, but he fit inside her perfectly, squeezing into her and filling her with a wondrous sense of pleasure and fullness. She kept him just inside her for many long moments, every part of her own body alert. She bent and kissed him again.

'Tula, *Diós Santo*, please,' he gasped helplessly and she felt his strong hands upon her waist. 'I am going to move you now, yes?' he asked, but it was not a question, for he pushed her down on to him in full.

She cried out in pain.

But there was not just pain. There was also bliss and fullness, and a dizzy satisfaction—as if she were drinking in the colours of the sunset. All those reds and pinks and oranges—they seemed to flood her mind with their perfect truths.

'Are you hurt?' he breathed.

'No,' she said, feeling as if she had drunk too much *octli*, or wandered for too many hours in the sun. He kissed her gently and softly now, running his fingers through her hair as he rocked his hips upwards, pushing into her rhythmically.

She gave into his soft rocking and her body began to move on its own. Up and down she went, sliding over him with a growing purpose, bending to place her mouth upon his.

He returned her soft kiss and moaned, and she wondered if he felt what she did—this pain that was also pleasure. This strange sense of merging. She moved and moved, feeling a wave building inside of her. 'Oh,' she gasped, her energy increasing.

All the thoughts went out of her mind, every single thing she ever knew, everything she had ever wanted or hoped for or dreamed was gone. All that remained was him and her and the invisible depths towards which they were swimming. Together.

Then—splash. She cried out in ecstasy, exploding into a thousand tiny droplets. Unknown muscles clenched and unclenched, throbbing and humming. She gasped in astonishment as her body shivered and flexed with the most profound pleasure she had ever known.

She collapsed in a wash of foam atop him, covered in sweat, trembling with sensation. Her body quivered with satisfaction as the deepest part of her caressed him. She lay there for many long moments, feeling his length still inside her, feeling the hard pounding of his heart against her own chest.

He placed one arm on her back and the other at the back of her head. In a single motion, he had her lying on her back once again. He touched his lips to hers and let the ring drop into her mouth. 'We are not done yet, my lovely enchantress.' Then he pushed into her once again.

He should have let her rest. He should have peppered her with kisses and sweet reminders of the love he felt for her. But he was too far gone. Her ecstasy was his and when he felt her come apart on him, it was all he could do to keep from exploding himself. Now he thrust into her with a need beyond thought.

'Yes,' she said, in her sweet voice, with her sweet accent, with her damn sweet scent wafting into his nose. He thrust into her again, a little harder, trying so very hard not to harm her, but feeling his need like a monster crossing the sea, threatening to destroy the lovely ship they had built.

He thrust again, and again, lost in a sensation so exquisite that he never wanted it to end. It was not that he was merely making love to a woman, but that he was making love to her, the woman he wanted, the woman he had always wanted, the woman whom he had been waiting for the whole of his life.

She raised her hips to meet his, cringing and sighing in turn, struggling to accommodate him. Her body was so warm and luscious. It whispered to his body of its yearning and closed around him like a swaddle. He thrust deeper inside of her, feeling his excitement increase.

'Do I cause you pain?' he gasped, as if he could possibly stop himself now. He bent to kiss her and found his answer in her lips. *Go on,* she told him. *Find your bliss.* He thrusted and thrusted while she continued to kiss him, her mouth moving in rhythm with her hips. So much hot wetness. He felt surrounded by it, bathed in it. His breaths came in fierce, desperate gulps, as if he was again choking for air.

There was only her, all around him, urging him to find his truth, his place in the universe. Then he felt it—the beginning of his extinction. He was running towards it, on strong legs, feeling that sweet but painful surge, of everything he was.

His release took him. He spilled himself on to her stomach, his body convulsing with more power and violence than he had ever known. He felt her soft hands upon his thighs, encouraging him, and he took them and placed them firmly on his pulsing shaft.

She held him tightly and he moved in an accelerating rhythm, propelled forward by the sight of her and the waves of pleasure that would not cease. Finally, he collapsed atop her, nuzzling his nose in her hair and breathing her scent, utterly conquered.

Then he rolled off her and lay on his back beside her, already missing her nearness, already wishing to return to her.

She reached over to hold him and nuzzled her face beneath his arm. He gazed up at the tangle of trees and vines that shaded their small sanctuary, protecting it from the world. He wished he could stay this way with her for ever.

A howler monkey croaked, a green parrot flew overhead and the moment passed. She was kissing his chest and breathing in his scent. Soon she had stretched her leg over his chest and was straddling him once again. She remained fully clothed, yet she appeared naked to him, and when he looked at her, he felt as though he could see into her soul. It shone so very bright.

She stared down at him with big eyes, a smile playing at the sides of her lips. She bent down to kiss him and quietly passed the ring back into his mouth, giggling softly at her triumph.

Chapter Thirty-Eight

They followed the coastal trade routes back to Cempoala, each night making their camp at a different beach. Tula would catch their dinner while Benicio found water and they would watch the moon rise up over the mystic waters.

Benicio made love to Tula every night beneath the stars. In the morning, when the spray of surf hit their skin and the cries of shore birds filled their ears, he made love to her again. He studied her, like the scholar he was, and learned what she liked and what she loved. He tasted every inch of her, from the tips of her fingers to the bottoms of her feet. He showed her what it meant to be loved and she melted into him and they became one.

On the last day of their journey, they came upon the beach where they had first met. The tide was out and the cove was clear and tranquil in the morning light. 'How long can you hold your breath?' Tula asked Benicio suddenly.

'Longer than you,' Benicio chided.

'Come and try to prove it!' Tula exclaimed, and dove into the water.

When the sunken ship rose up before him, he could scarcely believe it was real. It was a fine Spanish galleon, fully equipped, and Benicio wondered if this was the legendary ship that the explorer Córdoba had lost in a storm. Or perhaps it was one of Grijalva's famous vessels. Tula grabbed hold of its loose rigging and floated around its tall mast, and he could see her delighted smile as she danced beneath the waves.

They explored the galleon all morning, then collapsed on to the shore together and stared up at the cloudless sky. 'It is the greatest fish I ever find,' Tula explained. 'I share it with you so I can keep it as my own.'

'Thank you,' Benicio, still breathless from the swim. 'You are such a good swimmer.'

Tula sighed. 'To swim makes me happy,' said Tula. 'What makes you happy?'

You, thought Benicio. *You make me happy.* He wanted to say it and to tell her he loved her, but the words caught in his throat and the moment passed. 'The stars,' he said at last. 'The stars make me happy.'

'You mean the gods?'

'Stars are not gods. They are worlds. Some are made of rock, others of fire, and others of nothing but clouds. They do not go away. Even in the day-time, still they are there. The Maya of Chichen Itza studied them closely.'

'How do you know?'

'Do you remember the round building?'

'Yes.'

'You were right. It was made to study the stars.'

'You went inside it, yes?'

'I did. While you were diving into the cenote, I was discovering an observatory.'

'What did you do there?'

'I looked up at the sky and said what was in my heart.'

'Why?'

'Because I wish to keep it always there. So I had to give it away.'

'You are learning,' said Tula.

When they reached the outskirts of Cempoala the next morning, Tula was twittering like a bird. 'You will meet my father,' she explained excitedly. 'And my sister, Pulhko. She does not speak, but she listens. Do not be afraid. They will like you.' When they finally reached the central plaza, she jumped off the horse and broke into a run.

Soon she was standing on the doorstep of her house, taking long, deep breaths. 'Open the door and go in!' Benicio called, approaching at a gallop. 'What are you waiting for?'

But before she could enter, a woman appeared in the doorway. She was tall and dark, with long black hair that she wore in a single braid at her back. When she recognised Tula, she shrieked with delight and the two women fell into each other's arms.

They stayed that way for many long moments, hardly noticing Benicio dismount Big Deer. He took a breath and walked to the base of the porch, catching the dark-haired woman's eye.

'Hello, Benicio,' she said in perfect Spanish. 'I am Pulhko. I am Tula's elder sister.'

Tula stared at her sister in awe and Benicio wasn't sure if Tula was surprised to hear her sister speak Benicio's tongue or to hear her speak at all.

'It is an honour to meet you,' said Benicio, giving a low bow. When he rose, he saw a man's familiar round shape inside the doorway, though it was perhaps not quite as round as before.

'Rogelio?'

'Benicio, you devil,' Rogelio said. He walked

through the doorway with barely a limp. 'We were starting to worry.' He took Benicio in a warm embrace.

'You look well,' said Benicio, regarding Rogelio's slimmer frame and healed leg. 'But what are you doing here? Why are you not in Vera Cruz with the other men?'

'I was just…visiting,' Rogelio said, smiling curiously.

'You will not like the news I bring,' Benicio said. 'We return without a single bit of treasure.' Benicio gripped the hilt of his dagger, bracing himself for Rogelio's wrath, but Rogelio only nodded.

'Is that so?'

'Are you not enraged, Rogelio?'

'Not quite.'

'Are you not going to attempt to stab me?'

Rogelio rubbed the place upon his chin where his beard used to be and gave a playful smirk. 'It is not necessary.'

'But the Maya treasure—it is all you have been waiting for. *Por Diós*, Rogelio, it is all you have ever lived for.'

'It was,' admitted Rogelio. 'I have found something better to live for now.' He glanced behind him to Pulhko, who was talking excitedly to Tula.

Pulhko looked up momentarily and caught Rogelio's gaze, and there was a smile in her eyes.

'She has scars like me,' explained Rogelio, touching the gash across his face, 'but they are hidden from view.'

Benicio stood in stunned silence, trying to absorb the news.

'Ah! That reminds me,' said Rogelio, pulling an envelope from beneath his belt. 'This arrived on a galleon from Cuba not a week ago. The Overseer of Vera Cruz gave it to me to give to you. It seems that news of our mutiny has not yet arrived.'

Benicio stared at the small, beige missive as if it might bite him. He narrowed his eyes at Rogelio. 'I assume you have read it already?'

'No, man,' said Rogelio, his eyes shifting towards Pulhko again. 'I fear I may have developed a bit of a conscience since we last met.'

'I may have had a change of heart myself,' Benicio said. He plucked the envelope from Rogelio's hand and in exchange offered his own. 'Thank you for bringing Xanca and Anan safely to Cempoala.'

'It was nothing,' said Rogelio casually. 'I only had to fight off a few jaguars.'

Benicio laughed. 'Please, call me Brother.'

Rogelio's eyes took on a liquid sheen and he began to speak, but the door swung backwards and suddenly Xanca was bounding out of the house in a fit of excited shrieks. She was followed by Anan, who marched right up to Benicio, embraced him, then unleashed a tirade of angry words. 'He is asking why you took so long to return,' said Rogelio.

'You speak Totonac now?'

'Just a little,' said Rogelio. He turned to Anan and said some incomprehensible thing.

'Remind me, I need you to teach me how to say something in Totonac,' said Benicio.

'I will teach you whatever I can, Brother. I am at your service.'

'Then tell me why Anan stares at me with daggers in his eyes.'

'He says that he and Xanca have waited patiently for your return. Almost two cycles of the moon now.'

'But why is he so enraged?' asked Benicio.

'It is Totonac tradition for an engaged couple to sleep apart. Anan recently announced that he and Xanca have been engaged to be married for a little over a year now,' said Rogelio, winking.

Benicio burst into laughter, slapping Anan on the back. 'I am very sorry my friend,' he said. 'Your problem shall be remedied soon.'

Chapter Thirty-Nine

The wedding of Xanca and Anan was the talk of Cempoala, for it was said that the gods themselves had spared their lives. And they were not alone. Almost all the former captives had managed to return home since that fateful night atop the Templo Mayor. It was considered a great miracle and the citizens of Cempoala rejoiced.

Xanca and Anan held hands as they marched to the base of the Great Temple of Cempoala while the whole city looked on. 'Behold these radiant young souls,' the High Priest pronounced. 'Even as the Mexica falter, the gods favour the Totonacs still!' The people cheered and Benicio's valour was all but forgotten.

Tula, however, did not forget. As the High Priest tied Anan's robe to Xanca's skirt and pronounced their holy union, Tula reached for Benicio's hand, for she knew his selflessness and bravery against the swarm of priests was the real reason that any of them had survived.

That night at the wedding feast, Benicio, Pulhko, Rogelio, Tula and Tula's father took their seats next to Xanca and Anan before a great fire. Behind them, Cempoalans of all ages wandered about eating ears of maize and dancing to the team of drummers thrumming out their exultant beats.

Those who were not eating or dancing were speaking of the news: a messenger had just arrived from Tenochtitlan to announce that Cortés had taken Montezuma captive. 'Does it not seem like another sign from the gods?' Xanca commented, her eyes glinting. 'Soon the Spanish will rule and the Totonacs will finally be free.'

Anan sprang to his feet. 'Shall we dance, Wife?' he asked, holding his out his hand. 'To celebrate the liberation of the Totonacs?' The guests hollered and whooped until Xanca took Anan's hand and they joined the throng of undulating bodies.

Tula smiled, though her heart could not rest. That morning, she had spied a Spanish messenger crossing the central plaza. She watched in alarm as he halted his horse, overcome by a fit of coughs. A hundred small white balls had colonised his skin and he appeared too sick to ride, yet he composed himself and continued, bent on his mission to Tenochtitlan.

When Tula had described the scene to Benicio, all the colour had left his face. 'It is a grave sickness, Tula. It cannot be cured. You must stay far away from anyone who is sick.'

Tula studied the throng of dancers, relieved to find none with the terrible spots. Benicio had told her that it would not be long, however. 'I do not think the Totonacs are yet free,' she said now, trying not to sound too grim.

'I am with you, Daughter,' Tula's father affirmed as he stared into the bonfire. 'We must take care not to let this fleeting joy blind us.' A shadow flickered across his face.

'The bearded ones bring sickness,' Tula whispered.

She glanced at Benicio. He had grown back his beard and now he tugged at it solemnly. 'It is called the smallpox,' he said. 'It is more deadly than any gun or sword. It destroyed the people of Hispañola in only a year. It will destroy the Mexica. It will also destroy us.'

Tula's father threw the turkey bone into the fire. 'They have stolen our gods, now they wish to steal our lives,' he snarled.

'Not all of them,' said Tula. She nodded at Benicio, grateful he still could not understand most Totonac words.

Her father took a breath. 'No, not all,' he conceded. 'But there are many more bearded ones across the sea. Soon they will come like a swarm.'

'What is to be done?' whispered Pulhko.

'In the land of the Maya there is safety,' Tula said. 'There is refuge. The Maya will survive this...this new world.'

'And what is so special about the Maya?' asked Pulhko.

Tula shot her father a look and he nodded solemnly. 'The Maya do not forget.'

The next day, Tula rose from her bed mat, walked out into the garden and headed for the mango tree. The wedding had lasted late into the night and Tula's father had invited Benicio and Rogelio to sleep in the hammocks strung beneath the mango tree's ancient branches.

One of the hammocks was empty and Benicio was nowhere to be seen. 'He has gone to Vera Cruz,' said Rogelio, opening a single eye.

'Why?' asked Tula.

Rogelio gave a long, luxuriant stretch. 'Does Pulhko wake yet?'

'Why Benicio go to Vera Cruz?' Tula repeated, betraying too much emotion.

'To send a letter,' said Rogelio. 'But do not fear—he will soon return.'

'How do you know?'

Rogelio seemed to read the concern on Tula's face. He spoke in Totonac. 'Because I have seen how he looks at you, Tula.'

Tula turned away, a tear tickling the inside of her eye. 'It means nothing.'

'A clever woman once told me that within everything is its opposite,' said Rogelio gently. 'Perhaps he has gone so that he might return.'

Tula bowed to Rogelio, unable to speak. She ran from the garden and stumbled out into the central plaza, choking back her tears. She had witnessed Rogelio give Benicio a paper packet the day they had arrived. She knew that there was only one person in the world who would have sent it. *Luisa.*

Since then, she and Benicio had had little time together alone. Why had he not told her about the letter? And why had he left without telling her where he was going?

Tula wondered if Benicio had had a change of heart. Was there something on the small piece of paper he had stuffed so quickly beneath his jerkin that could pull him back to Spain? Some unexpected news, perhaps? She was sure that there was, or he would not have concealed it as he had.

Her stomach churned with a growing dread. Tula had seen how carelessly and falsely many of the bearded ones used words and Benicio was still a bearded one.

'You do not think he will return,' stated Tula's father. He was standing on the front porch, not six paces behind Tula.

'Father, I did not see you there,' Tula said, wiping her eyes and forcing her brightest smile.

'You do not have to hide your tears from me, Tula.'

'He goes to Vera Cruz,' she blurted. 'To write words on a page and send them away to the woman he loves.'

'That woman is right here, standing before me.'

'I fear it is not so, Father.'

'It is so.'

'He has not said the words of love.'

'Words mean little. It is deeds that show what is in a man's heart.'

'The people we come to love always leave us in the end. It is the way of the world,' said Tula.

Tula spied the tamale woman making her morning journey around the plaza, a scarf swaddling her head to protect from the morning cold. Tula searched her skirt pocket for cocoa beans, though she did not have an appetite. She only wished to share a tamale with her father and feel normal for a moment, to pretend that the world was as it had always been.

'The floating temples come and go from the Vera Cruz harbour like bees to a hive now,' her father remarked.

The comment stung like an arrow, but Tula swallowed her pain. 'More settlers arrive?'

'Settlers, seekers of gold, religious men, plunderers. Already the Overseer of the settlement asks the Totonac Council for more food. Soon, he will cease to ask and will simply take.'

'The Spaniards will become Takers?'

'My heart fears it.'

'What is to be done?' Tula asked. The tamale woman had stopped several houses away. She was accepting payment from a young man without looking him in the eye.

'You spoke with wisdom when you spoke of the land of the Maya,' said Tula's father.

'You would have us move south?'

'It is the only safe place.'

'But Anan's family is here. His mother and father. All his brothers.'

'Anan would follow Xanca to the ends of the earth.'

Her father spoke truth. He had always spoken truth

and had always taken care to express exactly what was in his heart. Tula wished she could say the same about the man she loved. 'It will be a difficult journey, Father. The jungle is dense. The path is long. We will not have the benefit of a horse.' Tula closed her eyes, letting the sadness pass over her like a wave. *Or the benefit of Benicio.*

Tula willed herself not to cry. There was no time for tears. *If only we had our own floating temple,* Tula thought. Then she realised—they did.

It was there in her small cove, resting beneath the waves, just waiting to be reborn. 'Father, I have an idea.'

Suddenly, the tamale woman collapsed in a fit of coughs. Her tray of tamales tumbled to the ground and her scarf fell backwards. Tula and her father ran towards her, then stopped as she lifted her head. Dozens of tiny dots marked her face.

Tula remembered Benicio's warning. 'Father, we must not go near her, or we shall become sick.'

'It is the smallpox, is it not?' her father asked. He did not wait for her to respond. 'Tula, tell your sisters to gather their things! We leave at daybreak.'

Chapter Forty

Benicio sat in the Overseer's office, his quill hovering over the page. It had taken him the entire day to gather the implements of communication and now he was at a loss for words. He ran his hand over the rough brown surface of the agave-bark paper, hoping it would accept the Spanish ink. The last ream of real paper available in Vera Cruz had been spoken for by the Spanish priests, who seemed to be arriving in droves now. They needed every leaf of it, apparently, for their hymn books.

Unwilling to give up on his endeavour, Benicio had found a Totonac paper-maker who agreed to give Benicio two clean agave-bark pages in exchange for the complete weeding of his tomatoes—a task that had taken Benicio half the afternoon. Thankfully, he had procured the ink more easily: The Overseer carried a great supply of it hidden behind his desk. In return, he requested only that he be spoken of favourably to Captain Cortés, should Benicio ever encounter the great man again.

Never, thought Benicio, with some satisfaction, though he was most grateful for the ink. He grasped Luisa's third letter and read it one last time.

Dear Benicio,

I do not know if you receive these letters. Some say that you are dead. Others say that you march with Cortés and that your mission shall result in great riches for Spain. If that is the case, Godspeed you.

Carlos and I have wed. His work in the Casa de Contratación has been more than fruitful. There is so much wealth coming out of the West Indies now—so much gold and treasure—and he collects a small bit of all of it in the form of tax. He has also granted my fondest wish. After all these years, I am to be made a marquesa.

I have given birth to two sons. They came in quick succession, as gifts of God often do. The second reminds me of you, for he spends his days paging through books and his nights pondering the stars. He is beautifully made and has a gentle soul, and I fear he is too good for this cruel world.

Wherever you are, I hope that you have found your peace.
Sincerely,
Luisa
November 8th 1519

Benicio placed the letter on the table and tugged at his beard. The setting sun was sending rosy beams of light through the small window of the room, lighting tiny pieces of dust that swayed in rhythm with Benicio's breaths. They were so beautiful lit up in that way—those tiny particles of dust. Like flickering stars in some distant part of the sky. Outside, Big Deer gave an encouraging whinny. Benicio put quill to paper and began.

Dear Luisa,
When you left me that day in the Plaza del Triunfo you held my heart in your hands. For years I toiled, trying to deserve you, to please you, to find the treasure you craved. I became a greedy, wretched man. A killer.
You are right that the world is cruel. You have no idea how cruel, Luisa. For a long time I believed that you were the only good thing in it. But I have discovered that there is other goodness. It lingers between tree roots, down deep wells and

wrapped up in blankets, invisible from sight. It is humble. It does not wish to be served. It only wishes to love and be loved. It is not vain, it does not crave glory or riches, it wishes to remain... small.

I have found my goodness, Luisa. I am glad that you have found yours. I shall not be returning to Spain, but I will keep my mother and father, you and Carlos and your two boys always inside my heart.
Sincerely,
Benicio
January 1st 1520

It was already dark when Benicio presented the letter to the Overseer—too late to return to the hammock that awaited him in the garden behind Tula's house. He guided Big Deer up the small path that led to his old hut. This would be the last night he would spend in the small dwelling. Soon news would arrive in Vera Cruz of his and Rogelio's desertion, along with the bounty upon their heads.

Benicio wondered if Tula would consider moving to another Totonac town, though he knew he had no right to ask her to make such a sacrifice. Still, it would be difficult to conceal himself for long. He tended to stand out in a crowd.

* * *

The next morning, Benicio galloped to Cempoala, anxious to see the face of his beloved. He guided Big Deer across the plaza to discover a Totonac man bent over in sickness, his face colonised by the terrible pox.

Benicio rushed to Tula's stone house to find its inhabitants gone. He stared around at the barren rooms, just yesterday bustling with life. They were safe, thank God. They had escaped.

Benicio mounted Big Deer and gave her a kick. There were only two directions in which they would have headed and Benicio made an educated guess as to which.

He road as fast as he could through the jungle, passing the cenote into which he had fallen that day with Tula, the maize field where he had bested her, and in and among the great kapok trees, keeping his eye out for a certain woman whose face was lovelier than moonlight upon the sea.

Surely Anan and Rogelio had gone with them, and Benicio smiled as he imagined Rogelio's shocking red hair and lumbering frame, marching through the jungle in nothing but his Spanish boots and hose.

Benicio imagined that he, too, appeared rather strange, having traded his golden mask for the Totonac loincloth and cape he now donned, and the two quetzal feathers that he had fastened to his floppy Spanish hat.

He had also secured a full set of arrows for Tula, along with a new atlatl and several weeks' supply of maize, which he carried along with his own weapons inside the reed basket he had fixed to Big Deer's new leather saddle. He had shaved his beard again that evening, as well, and though his face had already begun to itch with the new growth he did not scratch it, for his fingers were otherwise occupied with the ring he turned over and over in his hand. He had stolen it from her very mouth only weeks ago. Now he wished to give it back.

When he finally spotted the group of travellers, they were stopped at the edge of the jungle, overlooking the beach. Benicio instantly spied Tula's compact figure amidst the foliage. She was on her toes, pointing towards the waters of the cove.

Towards her ghost ship, thought Benicio.

Xanca, Anan and Tula's father looked on, nodding interestedly. Meanwhile, Pulhko and Rogelio stole a kiss beneath a magnolia tree, florid with new blooms.

There were the people he wished to defend; the people whose love he was determined to earn. And there she was among them—the woman without whom he was nothing.

When she finally spotted him, she let out a gasp, as if it were some great surprise for her to see him emerge from the forest. Had she believed he would not come? Had she any idea of the total and complete grip she had, would always have, upon his heart?

It was all he could do to dismount Big Deer in time for her to leap into his arms. 'I think you return to Spain,' she breathed between sobs. 'I think I not see you again.'

'Now why did you think that?' Benicio asked, spinning her around and around until they were both dizzy. He set Tula on the ground.

'You wear Totonac clothes!' Tula exclaimed, tears of joy leaking on to her cheeks.

'I am a Totonac now,' Benicio said with an exaggerated bow, 'if you will allow it.'

Tula glanced at Benicio's bare chest, then reached out and touched Benicio's freshly shaved cheeks. 'You are so…'

'Handsome?' Benicio offered.

'Naked,' said Tula, though the glint in her eyes showed him that she approved. Her father bowed to Benicio and everyone gathered round.

'Of course we will allow it,' Tula's father said.

'It took you long enough to find us,' said Rogelio,

clapping Benicio on the back. 'Did you write a letter or a novel?'

'It took me all of the day just to find a single page to write upon,' Benicio explained.

'How you know we are here?' asked Pulhko.

'The ship, of course,' Benicio said.

'What ship?' asked Xanca.

'The ship that is just there,' said Benicio, pointing to the cove.

'I try to tell them, but they do not understand,' said Tula.

'I have seen it for myself,' said Benicio to the group. 'It's planks can be dried and fashioned together again. They will make a sturdy boat.'

'It is well!' said Rogelio. 'We can float our way to the land of the Maya.'

'We shall escape the smallpox,' said Pulhko. 'We shall survive.'

'I think you go to Spain,' Tula repeated, shaking her head in happy disbelief. 'I think you take the golden mask. Your treasure.'

'No, no, no,' Benicio, said, wiping her cheeks. He gripped the ring between his fingers. 'Do you not see, Tula? *You* are my treasure.' Benicio glanced at Rogelio, who nodded encouragingly. *'Tula, quit pax hui'xin,'* Benicio pronounced, in broken Totonac. *Tula, I love you.*

And with that Benicio dropped to his knee in the verdant jungle, swept off his feathered hat and asked Tula of Cempoala, the most wonderful woman in all the world, if she would do him the honour of becoming his wife.

* * * * *

If you enjoyed this story, you won't want to miss this other great read from Greta Gilbert
ENSLAVED BY THE DESERT TRADER

And for something short and sexy make sure you pick up Greta Gilbert's UNDONE! *eBook*
MASTERED BY HER SLAVE

MILLS & BOON®
Hardback – August 2017

ROMANCE

An Heir Made in the Marriage Bed	Anne Mather
The Prince's Stolen Virgin	Maisey Yates
Protecting His Defiant Innocent	Michelle Smart
Pregnant at Acosta's Demand	Maya Blake
The Secret He Must Claim	Chantelle Shaw
Carrying the Spaniard's Child	Jennie Lucas
A Ring for the Greek's Baby	Melanie Milburne
Bought for the Billionaire's Revenge	Clare Connelly
The Runaway Bride and the Billionaire	Kate Hardy
The Boss's Fake Fiancée	Susan Meier
The Millionaire's Redemption	Therese Beharrie
Captivated by the Enigmatic Tycoon	Bella Bucannon
Tempted by the Bridesmaid	Annie O'Neil
Claiming His Pregnant Princess	Annie O'Neil
A Miracle for the Baby Doctor	Meredith Webber
Stolen Kisses with Her Boss	Susan Carlisle
Encounter with a Commanding Officer	Charlotte Hawkes
Rebel Doc on Her Doorstep	Lucy Ryder
The CEO's Nanny Affair	Joss Wood
Tempted by the Wrong Twin	Rachel Bailey

0717 GEN STD HB

MILLS & BOON®
Large Print – August 2017

ROMANCE

The Italian's One-Night Baby	Lynne Graham
The Desert King's Captive Bride	Annie West
Once a Moretti Wife	Michelle Smart
The Boss's Nine-Month Negotiation	Maya Blake
The Secret Heir of Alazar	Kate Hewitt
Crowned for the Drakon Legacy	Tara Pammi
His Mistress with Two Secrets	Dani Collins
Stranded with the Secret Billionaire	Marion Lennox
Reunited by a Baby Bombshell	Barbara Hannay
The Spanish Tycoon's Takeover	Michelle Douglas
Miss Prim and the Maverick Millionaire	Nina Singh

HISTORICAL

Claiming His Desert Princess	Marguerite Kaye
Bound by Their Secret Passion	Diane Gaston
The Wallflower Duchess	Liz Tyner
Captive of the Viking	Juliet Landon
The Spaniard's Innocent Maiden	Greta Gilbert

MEDICAL

Their Meant-to-Be Baby	Caroline Anderson
A Mummy for His Baby	Molly Evans
Rafael's One Night Bombshell	Tina Beckett
Dante's Shock Proposal	Amalie Berlin
A Forever Family for the Army Doc	Meredith Webber
The Nurse and the Single Dad	Dianne Drake

MILLS & BOON®
Hardback – September 2017

ROMANCE

The Tycoon's Outrageous Proposal	Miranda Lee
Cipriani's Innocent Captive	Cathy Williams
Claiming His One-Night Baby	Michelle Smart
At the Ruthless Billionaire's Command	Carole Mortimer
Engaged for Her Enemy's Heir	Kate Hewitt
His Drakon Runaway Bride	Tara Pammi
The Throne He Must Take	Chantelle Shaw
The Italian's Virgin Acquisition	Michelle Conder
A Proposal from the Crown Prince	Jessica Gilmore
Sarah and the Secret Sheikh	Michelle Douglas
Conveniently Engaged to the Boss	Ellie Darkins
Her New York Billionaire	Andrea Bolter
The Doctor's Forbidden Temptation	Tina Beckett
From Passion to Pregnancy	Tina Beckett
The Midwife's Longed-For Baby	Caroline Anderson
One Night That Changed Her Life	Emily Forbes
The Prince's Cinderella Bride	Amalie Berlin
Bride for the Single Dad	Jennifer Taylor
A Family for the Billionaire	Dani Wade
Taking Home the Tycoon	Catherine Mann

MILLS & BOON®
Large Print – September 2017

ROMANCE

The Sheikh's Bought Wife	Sharon Kendrick
The Innocent's Shameful Secret	Sara Craven
The Magnate's Tempestuous Marriage	Miranda Lee
The Forced Bride of Alazar	Kate Hewitt
Bound by the Sultan's Baby	Carol Marinelli
Blackmailed Down the Aisle	Louise Fuller
Di Marcello's Secret Son	Rachael Thomas
Conveniently Wed to the Greek	Kandy Shepherd
His Shy Cinderella	Kate Hardy
Falling for the Rebel Princess	Ellie Darkins
Claimed by the Wealthy Magnate	Nina Milne

HISTORICAL

The Secret Marriage Pact	Georgie Lee
A Warriner to Protect Her	Virginia Heath
Claiming His Defiant Miss	Bronwyn Scott
Rumours at Court (Rumors at Court)	Blythe Gifford
The Duke's Unexpected Bride	Lara Temple

MEDICAL

Their Secret Royal Baby	Carol Marinelli
Her Hot Highland Doc	Annie O'Neil
His Pregnant Royal Bride	Amy Ruttan
Baby Surprise for the Doctor Prince	Robin Gianna
Resisting Her Army Doc Rival	Sue MacKay
A Month to Marry the Midwife	Fiona McArthur

0817 GEN STD LP